Dark Money

DAVID MEDANSKY

First Edition 2017
MMXVII

Library of Congress
Control Number: 2016951281

WGA(W) Registration Number: 1848983

Medansky, David
I. Title 1. Las Vegas. 2. Mafia. 3. Law
4. Chicago Board of Trade

ISBN: 978-1-938015-59-5
Ebook ISBN: 978-1-938015-60-1

Printed in the United States of America

10 9 8 7 6 5 4 3 2 1

Hybrid Global Publishing
355 Lexington Avenue
New York, NY 10017

DEDICATIONS

*This book is dedicated to my beautiful wife, Debbie,
and to my parents Lloyd and Eileen.*

This book is also dedicated in loving memory to:

*Lawrence Allen Medansky
April 7, 1955—July 14, 1974*

*Line Editing/Proofreading by: Patrick Hodges
Front Cover by: Molly Phipps*

*Special thanks to Martin Seldin who inspired me to write this
novel and for introducing me to Big Julie of Las Vegas.*

You cannot worry about the past, what has been; you can only focus on the future, what will be. If you dwell on what has been, you will miss what can be. Sometimes good is found in the darkness of a soul.

—*David Medansky*

"Be who you are and say what you feel because those that mind don't matter and those that matter don't mind."

—*Dr. Seuss*

Prologue

Paul Bazzoli sat across from his boss, Anthony Sindler, in a booth at Chicago's Pizzeria Uno's on Ohio Street, a large deep-dish pizza positioned between the two men. Neither had touched the slice of pie the waiter dished out on the small plates in front of them. Bazzoli, although hungry, dared not touch his food until his boss finished his homily and ate first.

Sindler continued, "The money we take from the casino is our money. It's not stealing if we take cash from ourselves. We just don't show it on the books as revenue, so we don't pay taxes on it. Think of it as our piggy bank."

"Alright boss. I'm just nervous that the IRS might start breathing down on us." Bazzoli feigned worrying about skimming money from the casino; a ploy to keep his boss from learning the truth. He skimmed from the skim; a calculated risk given the nature of his employer.

"Fuck the Internal Revenue Service. Who gives a shit what they think? They can't prove a thing. Go ahead and eat. Your pizza's getting cold."

With that Bazzoli took a mouthful of the delectable mouthwatering pizza. He had a glass of Chianti to wash down his afternoon meal.

Bazzoli, a member of the Outfit, a Chicago crime syndicate, was a lieutenant for Sindler. He traveled to and from Las Vegas every other week to collect money from the various casinos owned and operated together by Midwest 'crime families' from Chicago, Kansas City, Cleveland, and Milwaukee. These Vegas casinos included the Dunes, the Sands, Hacienda and the Riviera. The position paid him handsomely. Despite the generous compensation, he wanted more. Gambling was a license to skim and everybody wanted a piece of the action. Bazzoli felt no different.

Sindler paid the check and spoke softly before parting ways. "See you in a few days my friend. Be safe."

Bazzoli took a taxi to O'Hare Airport to catch a United Airlines flight to Vegas. Happy to leave the Windy City in October for a warmer climate, he smiled as the cab arrived at the terminal.

The United flight landed at McCarran Airport in Las Vegas at approximately four p.m. The Vegas sky, clear with nary a hint of clouds, and an early evening temperature of seventy-two, greeted passengers flying the "Friendly Skies." The warm sun began to fade in the western horizon. Bazzoli slipped through the airport terminal and caught a taxi to the Dunes.

The Dunes opened in May, of 1955 along with three other casinos: The Royal Nevada, Hacienda, and Riviera. Basically a low-rise motel casino, topped by a sultan statue, it was located diagonally across from The Flamingo. He checked into his lavishly furnished suite before heading to the casino.

The one-armed bandits buzzed with an electrifying noise of loud bells and chimes as silver dollars dropped into the cash trays with clangs and clatters. The cards at the blackjack tables fluttered with a soft murmur as players anxiously waited for the next hand to be dealt. The roulette wheel spun in quite silence as the ball whirled around, banging and clacking, before settling into a pocket indicating the winning number. Beautiful cocktail waitresses wearing short leather skirts and black sequenced halter tops that extended their bosoms, called out,

"Cigars, cigarettes, cocktails," moved to and fro around the casino.

Bazzoli, after refreshing himself in his room, made his way through the casino. Oblivious to all of the excitement, he methodically made his way towards the craps table. Smoky air hung in the casino intoxicating patrons.

Standing six foot one, weighing one hundred ninety-five pounds, he towered over the other players. He had an average build with dark brown hair and eyes. His rugged face was clean-shaven. He'd been to Vegas too many times for any of the exterior exhilaration to be meaningful. Besides, this was business, not pleasure.

He asked for a ten-thousand-dollar marker. The marker acted as a promissory note, credit with the casino. The pit boss came over, and had him sign a document. The dealer pushed ten-thousand dollars in chips to Bazzoli. He ignored the gawks and stares from several other players. He could care less if anyone else wondered about him and his large buy-in. It was none of their business.

"How's the table tonight?" Bazzoli asked the dealer. He noted the dealer's slicked back hair and formal attire; a white shirt and black vest.

"The dice are cold tonight Mr. Bazzoli."

He took a deep calming breath and smiled. "Outstanding."

A new person prepared to roll the dice. The person rolling the dice was called a "shooter." Bazzoli put a purple five-hundred-dollar chip on the Don't Pass Line. The stick person dumped the dice bowl out on the green felt layout and passed five dice to the shooter. The shooter, a tall, thin man in his mid-thirties, selected two dice. If the shooter rolled a seven or an eleven on the Come-out roll, Bazzoli lost his Don't Pass Line bet. All of the other players who made a bet on the Pass Line won on a seven or eleven. If the roll was two, three, or twelve the Pass Line bettors lost their bets. Bazzoli won his Don't Pass Line wager on a two or three. A twelve meant a push for the Don't Pass bet. Any other number: four, five, six, eight, nine or ten would be marked as the shooter's point.

After the shooter established a point, in order for the Pass Line bettors to win, the shooter had to roll the point number before a seven. If a seven appeared before the point, the Pass Line bettors lost and Don't Pass Line bettors won. In its essence, craps was a simple game. Other "side" bets could be wagered after a point had been established.

The shooter turned to his lady friend standing beside him and said, "Sweetie, blow a little kiss on these bones for me for good luck." She gently pursed her lips together and blew a soft kiss on the dice. After the lovely lady finished, he tossed the two cubes toward the opposite end of the table. They danced and spun on the table before settling down. The stick person called out, "Nine, the point is nine, mark it!" The dealer turned the puck used to indicate the point from "Off" to "On" and placed it on the box marked "Nine."

Several rolls later the shooter rolled a six and one. The stick person called out, "Six and one, this shooter is done. Seven out, line away." A loud groan went up from all of the players at the table except for Bazzoli who won his wager. The seven came up before the point-number.

He played for several hours betting against the shooters. He was up more than fifteen thousand dollars when he asked to color-up his chips. The dealer counted the chips on the layout for the box person to verify. The dealer then passed twenty-five thousand dollars in large-denominated cheques to Bazzoli for him to take to the cashier's cage. He tossed a purple five-hundred-dollar chip to the stick person and said, "For the boys." It was a nice tip for the dealers who appreciated his generosity. He left the table without paying off his marker and headed to the cashier's cage. Neither the pit boss, box man, nor dealer said a word about the marker.

Bazzoli knew his marker would mysteriously disappear leaving no evidence it ever existed. He used this one method, among others, to skim money from the casino. The casino personnel, aware of the skim, did not ask any questions. Every employee knew he worked for those who owned and operated the casino.

The cashier counted out twenty-five thousand dollars in one hundred dollar bills in front of him. He quickly stashed the cash into a plain brown paper bag and brought it to the front desk. The clerk at the front desk handed him a private safe deposit box in which Bazzoli placed the bag. He kept the key and handed the box back to the clerk. The clerk placed the locked box in the casino's vault for safe keeping. Tired from a long day of traveling, he retired for the night.

$ $ $

The next afternoon, dressed in a black suit, white shirt and conservative tie, nonchalantly walked to the front desk and removed the brown paper bag from the safe deposit box. He took the funds and made three separate deposits of approximately eight thousand dollars each into his personal accounts at three local banks.

Later, he returned to the Dune's and strolled into the counting room. This was the most secured and sensitive area of the casino, where employees sorted and counted cash from the table games' drop boxes, and he had full access. He entered without being questioned, or even acknowledged, by the employees. They were told by management to purposely ignore Bazzoli. He carried a large black brief case and filled it with cash. The currency, never logged in, or recorded, had no official record of it. For all practical purposes, the money could not be traced.

Paul Bazzoli left the counting room as silently as he entered and made his way to the airport to return to the Windy City. Once back in Chicago, Bazzoli delivered the loot to James LaPierta. LaPierta kept a portion of the currency for the Outfit and split the balance to Anthony Chiavola, Sr., Carl DeLuna, and Milton Rockman for delivery to their respective families. Each family received more than forty-thousand dollars a month.

★ ★ ★

On a cold, dreary, windy day, typical of Chicago weather in April, Bazzoli met Sindler for lunch at the Club International, a members-only club for businessmen who could afford the hefty dues and wanted privacy. Club International, located in the Drake Hotel, was founded in 1920. It overlooked Lake Michigan. The Drake, designed in an Italian Renaissance style, rivaled the Palmer House.

"I want out," Bazzoli began the conversation before they had a chance to order.

Sindler eyed Bazzoli with a suspicious gaze and took a drag from his cigarette, the tip which had a red glow as the smoke swirled in the air above his head. "Out? Nobody gets out. The only way you get out is to die. Do you have a death wish? What's all of this nonsense?"

"I've invested my own money in a few legitimate businesses and want to retire to enjoy the fruits of my labor."

"Paul, you're putting me in a difficult spot. The other families, they're gonna wonder and ask a lot of questions."

"I know, but I have a plan to escape this racket and make myself scarce. All I ask if you ever think you see me just pretend it's not me. Can you do that for me? And one more thing, don't believe everything you read about me in the newspapers." Bazzoli winked.

Sindler shook his head without saying another word. The two finished their meal, said their goodbyes and departed the Drake going their separate ways.

★ ★ ★

The United red-eye flight from Chicago landed at McCarran Airport at approximately six a.m. The Vegas sky clear, with a beautiful orange and red hue, as the sun rose over the eastern horizon. The early morning sixty-five degrees eased Bazzoli as he exited the airport terminal and caught a taxi to the Dunes. Before he could check into his suite, two men grabbed him and forced him into the back of a black sedan in front of the lobby.

Witness to the abduction stated that Bazzoli resisted, but the car sped off heading toward the desert.

The Las Vegas police did a cursory investigation based on an anonymous tip. They found a charred body buried in a shallow grave just off the Highway 15 running between Los Angeles and Vegas. Along with the body were Paul Bazzoli's wallet and other personal items. A few weeks later, his disappearance and alleged demise appeared in the *Chicago Sun Times* obituary.

CHAPTER ONE

EVANSTON, ILLINOIS-MAY, 1974

Edwin R. Goldberg sat in his seat in the back of the Economics classroom at Northwestern University pondering his future. A gorgeous spring day, the air outside was crisp, with nary a hint of fish stench, as it came off Lake Michigan. The bright sun distracted most of the students. Edwin was no exception. Except, the light that distracted him came from a different bright star. It shined from his girlfriend of six months, Valerie Taylor, a beautiful vixen with shoulder-length auburn hair, sparkling blues eyes, and a slender build. She gave Edwin a seductive wink causing his face to blush.

Goldberg, a soon to be MBA graduate from Northwestern University, uncontrollably bounced his foot, nervous about his situation. His thoughts turned to his inability to land a job. The anemic economy and the war in Vietnam appeared to be winding down. It meant the frail job market for his skills would last longer. This recession had high unemployment that coincided with high inflation. 'Stagflation' became the buzz-word used by economists to describe business and the financial world.

Edwin, good looking, and tall, with dark brown wavy hair, wore glasses. His observant green eyes dazzled most women. Not very athletic, Edwin was geeky and shy. Valerie's obsession for him to find a suitable job made Edwin's stomach twist and churn. She came from a middle class family but wanted a more affluent life style. He also came from a middle class family, but had no assets or wealth of his own.

Her efforts to marry a wealthy student failed during her time at school. Desperate to become affluent, she chose Edwin as a last resort. She saw he had potential to find a lucrative position in the corporate world.

After class, Edwin escorted Valerie to his studio apartment just off Howard Street. As they walked, Edwin asked, "Any luck with your job applications?"

"No!" Valerie responded emphatically. Put off by the question. "How about you?" Her eyes searched his face.

He detected a hint of anger in her voice. "I've sent out several resumés and contacted a headhunter, but no interviews yet," he countered.

"I thought for sure you would've had several offers by now? What seems to be the problem?" she said, her nostrils flaring slightly. This was not how she pictured her life.

"Hell if I know. Only one of my classmates got an offer. It was for a large firm in New York. The market seems to be saturated with MBAs."

"What is your plan B, so to speak?"

Edwin hesitated before answering. Deep down he understood that Valerie wanted him to have a high-paying secure job. They'd discussed their future despite having been together for less than six months. "I can always open my own business as a consultant."

Valerie gave him a wide-eyed look, "Very funny. And what makes you think you can earn any money in this bearish economy?"

"Well, I could work with your father at the Exchange. What does he do exactly?"

"I'm not sure how to describe what he does. All I know is that he works for a floor trader as his assistant."

Valerie, early on in their relationship, had told Edwin about her father, Aaron Taylor. Taylor worked for William Beckwith, a floor trader at the Chicago Board of Trade. Prior to being Beckwith's assistant, Aaron held his own seat on the Board of Trade trading soybeans and sugar. Unfortunately, Taylor made several poor decisions that resulted with him losing just about everything.

Taylor made substantial money, but recklessly managed it. The cliché that "one day you're up and your kids are going to an Ivy League school and the next day you're mortgaging the home and cars" was a truism for Aaron.

"Please don't beg my father for a position. It would embarrass me."

Edwin chuckled out loud—"Did you really think I was serious about asking your father for a job? Come on, Val, you know I'll find something soon."

Valerie didn't say another word. Her mind raced with the thought of being married to Edwin, and what it would be like if he didn't have a high paying job. She didn't like the unpleasantness of it at all, and grimaced.

Meanwhile, Edwin, dead serious about working at the Exchange, gave it a lot of thought. Deep down he knew Valerie was right. He should not ask her father for a job. He planned to do some research about trading in the futures market immediately after finals if a job opportunity did not present itself. Each day he scoured the newspaper's employment section and sent out his resume and cover letters. Even the headhunter he hired hadn't had any luck getting him an interview.

After they arrived at Edwin's residence, Valerie said, "Can we order Chinese food from Golden Dragon? I have a craving for Lemon Grass Chicken."

Edwin's stomach churned. It grumbled hungry for food. "Fine, call it in. I'll have the Curry Beef."

After their meal, Valerie plopped down on the sofa to study. Edwin remained at the small dining table. The table sat covered with his open books and a newspaper. Staring out the window, and unable to concentrate, he was jolted back to reality by a passing ambulance's piercing siren.

Startled, Edwin knocked the newspaper on to the floor. It landed open, to a page with a small one inch-by-one-inch ad that caught his attention. The ad simply read, "Earn $100,000 a year with a new company in the travel industry. Call 312-555-1212 for more information." Edwin clipped the ad and put it between the pages of his book. He thought it might be interesting to pursue if nothing else worked out.

Later in the night, Valerie said, "I should get going. We both have early exams tomorrow."

"I thought you were staying tonight."

"No, not tonight, I have a headache and really need to get some sleep." Valerie aromatically put a hand to her head. She often used the headache excuse to avoid sleeping with Edwin.

Again, another headache? he thought as Valerie, not wanting to engage in further conversation, hurriedly kissed him goodnight and departed.

Edwin watched Valerie walked down the street from his window. At ten, the street still crawled with people. Turning away from the window, he contemplated the ad he had stuck between the pages of his book once more before retiring.

CHAPTER TWO

The sun rose slightly above the eastern horizon as the Boeing 747 landed safely at McCarran Airport. A loud cheer rang out from the passengers as they woke up from the red-eye flight out of New York. Standing six-foot-six, weighing two hundred and sixty pounds, Julie Weintraub, affectionately called "Big Julie," stood at the front of the plane barking out instructions to his guests.

Big Julie, had so much personification that he could easily be mistaken as a Damon Runyon character, spinning humorous tales of gamblers, hustlers, actors, and gangsters. Big Julie, a self-confessed "degenerate craps player," popularized the all-expenses paid gambling junket from New York to Las Vegas that built the Dunes Hotel into the most prevalent casino in the country. He had a heart of gold and his junketeers loved him.

To qualify for a junket, Big Julie required a person to have a minimum of two thousand dollars they were willing to gamble with. A junketeer could not just bring the cash and keep it in their wallet. No sir. They were required to play. In return for their action, the junketeer would get free airfare, free meals, free shows, and just about anything else they wanted in exchange for a commitment to gamble five hours each day with a minimum bet size. Big Julie brought in both low and high rollers. He made taking care of people his number one priority.

The casinos rewarded Big Julie with a handsome commission; a percentage of the gamblers expected losses. Big Julie often boasted, "The man who invented gambling was bright; the man who invented the chip was a genius." He knew people bet more when they played with chips instead of actual cash. It never meant as much for someone to lose colored chips. But cash, that elicited another emotion.

The tour bus delivered the guest to the front door of the Dunes. As they all got off, Big Julie called out to the Bell Captain at the Dunes, Salvador Gambino, "Hey Sal, is Joseph here yet?"

"Yes sir, he's waiting for you at the bar."

"Thanks."

Before Julie made his way to meet with Joseph, he attended to his guests and made certain they were checked-in and all their needs were taken care of.

Joseph Carter, Big Julie's partner from Chicago, was in charge of bringing junketeers from the mid-west. The two met while traveling through Europe and had become close friends. With Carter's knowledge of Las Vegas and how casinos operated, Big Julie considered it a match made in heaven. He never inquired how Joseph gained so much knowledge of the industry. It wasn't important. All that matter was that Big Julie had a partner who could bring-in more business to the Vegas Strip.

The bartender just finished pouring Carter another drink when Big Julie approached him. "Joseph, my old friend, how the heck are you?"

With a gruff voice, Joseph said, "Excellent."

"What about your people? Have they been taken care of?" Big Julie asked.

"They're probably at the tables already. Why do you cater to them so much?"

"Because I know when they return back home, they'll tell all their friends what a great time they had. Most of them will embellish how much they won and how they made a killing. Those who lost won't admit it, or if they do, they won't tell them how much they really lost. And then their friends will travel to Vegas with me, or at least be on my list."

"How many junketeers do you have on your list?"

"Maybe two thousand. And you my friend, how many people have you got?"

Carter took a sip of his drink followed by a drag from his cigarette, "About fifty for now. I'm thinking about hiring a few assistants to help me build up my clientele and coordinate all of this. Contrary to popular belief, I'm tired of this town."

Big Julie couldn't fathom anyone getting tired of Vegas. This was only Carter's third trip. Of course, Big Julie had no idea how much time Carter spent in Vegas almost twelve years earlier. Even though Vegas had grown exponentially during that time, Carter disconnected from the excitement. He'd become jaded and calloused to all the exhilaration that enticed so many others to Vegas. "What's all of this gibberish?"

Carter took another puff from his cigarette and watched the smoke swirl above his head. "I've got my other business interests to attend to in Chicago. Besides, if I had your money, I'd burn mine."

Before Big Julie could respond, Gus Bernstein interrupted the conversation. "Big Julie, we've got a problem with Al Feldman. You need to get this resolved."

Big Julie excused himself. When they got clear of ear shot, he asked Gus what the problem was. Gus explained that Al Feldman got a room without a refrigerator. Al Feldman, one of the few orthodox Jews that traveled to Vegas with Big Julie's group, presented unique problems. Orthodox Jews didn't eat the food in Las Vegas—it wasn't kosher. The airplane flights were a simple fix. Big Julie just had to inform the airlines of his passengers' special dietary requests. When they arrived at the hotel, Big Julie put them up in a suite, whether their play entitled them to one or not. The Orthodox junketeers brought their own food and their suites had to have refrigerators.

Al Friedman stood at the registration desk, tapping his fingers impatiently, as Big Julie approached. Al whined, "Why doesn't my room have a refrigerator? You know I have my own food."

"Hang on, Al I'll get this straightened out in a few minutes. The tables aren't going anywhere." He patted the man on the shoulder and gave him a reassuring smile.

Big Julie spoke to the registration clerk and within five minutes Al had another room—one with a refrigerator.

★ ★ ★

Later that evening, Big Julie had dinner with Carter, Neil Cohen and Neil's wife, Susan. Susan, an attractive, slender, young-woman, with a beautiful smile, could capture any man's heart. Neil and Susan helped Big Julie run the junkets from New York to Las Vegas. Carter listened intently as the three reminisced about their clients. Fascinated with the stories they told about some of the experiences they had, Carter became engrossed in the amount of money Big Julie's clients lost at the table. The more they lost, the more he received from the Dunes.

Carter had other ideas about how to make his money. Knowing Big Julie's reputation for integrity and being a stand-up guy, Carter kept his ideas to himself.

CHAPTER THREE

Graduation had come and gone and Edwin still had not found work. The morning sky turned a hazy shade of gray and orange as the sun began its ascent. Edwin laid in bed, half-awake in a stupor. A raucous buzzing of the city outside his studio apartment had woken him.

He went into the bathroom and splashed cold water on his face. He hoped the events of last night were a dream—no more of a nightmare—than reality. Unfortunately, Valerie's break-up with him was very real.

True to her word, Valerie left Edwin because he did not have a high-paying position by the time he graduated. Valerie also hid from Edwin that she met someone else, a flamboyant gentleman who liked to flash his money and had a very brash demeanor.

Edwin opened the morning newspaper, hoping an opportunity would present itself. He was not disappointed. Again, the same ad that intrigued him a few weeks earlier appeared. "Earn $100,000 a year with a new company in the travel industry. Call 312–555–1212 for more information." Edwin found the previous ad he had put away and compared the two. They were identical. This time he immediately called the number. A voice on the other end of the phone line answered, "Global Enterprises, Joseph speaking. How may I help you?"

"My name is Edwin Goldberg, and I'm calling about your ad in the newspaper about a position in the travel company."

"Yes, I see. Do you have any experience as a travel agent or in the business?"

"No, but I'm a quick study and willing to learn."

"Why don't you come to our office so we can discuss this in more detail?"

Desperate, Edwin agreed to meet the person at his office later that morning. Wanting to make a good first impression, Edwin put on his navy blue suit, white shirt and a skinny red tie. He looked at himself in his bathroom mirror to make certain he looked sharp. He hurried to the train platform to make his way downtown.

Global Enterprises, located in one of the many skyscrapers that populated the Chicago skyline, was on Randolph Street. Edwin's mind raced as he rode the elevator to the third floor. He hesitantly opened the frosted glass front door and stepped inside.

Edwin rang the bell sitting on the reception counter. A small receptionist area with a black leather couch separated the room from an area with a desk and filing cabinets.

A tall man in his mid-forties came out from an adjacent room. "May I help you?"

"Yes, I'm Edwin Goldberg and I have an appointment with Joseph Carter."

"I'm Joseph Carter. Pleased to meet you. Come on back and let's get started. Can I offer you a cup of coffee?"

"No thank you." Edwin felt a bit uncomfortable with the unimpressive surroundings and no receptionist or actual separate office. It didn't resemble a successful business, where someone could earn one hundred thousand dollars a year.

Carter sat behind the small, simple, walnut desk as Edwin took a seat in front of him. "So tell me young man, are you willing to work hard?"

"Yes, sir, I am."

Joseph chuckled. "Really? Well let me tell you that while I have heard hard work never killed anyone, I am of the belief why take a chance."

Edwin grinned not sure what to make of Carter's joke. "Sir, I brought my resumé for you." He gave the document to Carter, who perused his credentials.

"I see you're an MBA from Northwestern. What can I do for you today?"

"I saw your ad in the *Sun-Times* and intrigued about the travel company opportunity."

"Ah, yes. Obviously, with a MBA you must be intelligent and good with numbers. Do you know anything about playing craps?"

"Craps? Like in the dice game?"

"Exactly."

"I haven't a clue."

"Perfect. If you are willing to learn the game and put the time and effort to master the skills I teach you, I may have a position for you."

Edwin felt swindled. Uncertain as to what Carter meant, he cautiously asked, "Exactly what does the position entail? The ad does state this company is in the travel industry, and you just asked me about my playing craps."

Carter rubbed his chin and stared into Edwin's eyes. "Son, you seem to be a nice young man. I operate a junket business. Are you familiar with what a junket is?"

"No. Sir, I don't."

"A junket is where we arrange for guest to travel from Chicago to Las Vegas for free. The trip includes airfare and hotel accommodations at a few major casinos on the Las Vegas Strip. The trips usually begin on Thursday night with a red-eye flight and last until Sunday afternoon. I need a few assistants to help with the guests, and make sure all their needs are met.

"While you are in Vegas you will have a lot of down time. During this time, you are expected to be at the craps table playing to make extra money. Your investment will be your time. You do not need to *invest* any money. I will provide you with the necessary bankroll.

"You will be paid five thousand dollars per month, plus a portion of the money you win at craps. Since I am providing all of the capital to risk, you will receive a certain percentage of the winnings, which should be a minimum of another four thousand dollars per month."

Edwin glanced around the shabby office. "If I understand you correctly, my responsibilities as your assistant would be to fly to Vegas to *babysit* junketeers, and play craps to make money for the business, and for this I would earn nine thousand dollars per month?"

"That is correct. Do you want the position?"

"What happens if I lose at the craps table?"

"Not to worry. I can absorb any losses. Besides, with the betting method I will teach you, you should win most of the time. Do you want the position or not?"

"Yes!" Edwin said excitedly.

"Good, when can you start?"

"First thing Monday morning."

"Excellent. I will see you at my other office at eight o'clock sharp. Here's the address." Carter handed him a business card.

They rose and shook hands. "We have a deal," Carter said softly.

Edwin left Carter's office feeling both excited and nervous. He thought, *What did I get myself into? I didn't even ask about benefits or medical insurance!* He pondered how Valerie would react to his new position. Would she value him more now? He had to find out.

****

The ringing telephone broke the silence of the afternoon doldrums. At one o'clock, Valerie was still lying in bed after a long night of clubbing with her new beau, Johnny. She slowly reached over and grabbed the phone off the night stand. In a slurred voice she said, "Hello?"

"Hey Val, its Edwin, I've got some great news. I got a job today. Can I take you to dinner tonight to celebrate?"

"Edwin?" Valerie said still trying to collect her wits as she woke herself up. "No, I told you I'm done with you. Besides I met someone else. Please don't call me anymore." With that, she slammed the receiver on the cradle.

Shocked at Valerie's response, Edwin gingerly placed the receiver back onto the cradle. After a few minutes, he regained his composure. Something inside his head snapped. At that moment, he decided to make the most of his opportunity with Carter. He thought, *I'm going to show that bitch she'd just made the biggest mistake of her life and become extremely rich.*

CHAPTER FOUR

Valerie Taylor and Johnny Accardi strolled down Michigan Avenue, window shopping on a dreary afternoon as a slight drizzle fell.

Johnny Accardi, a handsome young man, stood six foot two, with dark brown hair, a muscular build and striking facial features. He had warm dark brown eyes. Introduced to Valerie by a mutual friend, Johnny told Valerie he worked in his family's business without going into any detail.

Valerie didn't care what he did so long as he had money. The truth of the matter was that Johnny, a 'wise guy,' was a member of the Chicago Outfit crime family, and the nephew of Tazio Accardi. People knew Accardi, born Tazio Joseph Accardi, as "Joe Batters" or "Big Tuna." Accardi ran the day-to-day operations of the Outfit. Smart, he preferred to keep a low profile, and let Sam Giancano attract attention.

Johnny turned to Valerie. "Hey babe, would you mind if we stopped in at my apartment for a moment? We are close by and I'd like to show it to you."

He wanted to impress Valerie with his apartment and lifestyle. It was located in a nearby building on the portion of Michigan Avenue called the "Magnificent Mile." Besides, Valerie, unlike the other women Johnny dated, was smart as well as beautiful. His father made it clear to Johnny that he needed to settle down and start a family. Johnny had a hunch that his days of being a womanizer were coming to an end. He believed Valerie might just be the perfect wife for him. She never asked any questions about his business and appeared to have a demeanor suggesting she would appreciate being spoiled.

"Sure, I'd love to see where you live."

As Johnny and Valerie entered the building, the doorman greeted him with small talk and forced pleasantries. The doorman knew of Johnny's reputation and did not approve, especially since Johnny's uncle paid him to keep an eye on the young man. He smiled suspiciously at Valerie, showing his gapped off-white teeth. Valerie, too enthralled with the apartment building, was oblivious to the doorman's probing gaze.

Johnny's apartment, on the forty-fifth floor, topped twenty-eight hundred square feet in size. With three bedrooms and three full-sized baths, it was impressive. Valerie's eyes grew wide as saucers as she entered the abode. The bronze statutes and stylishly appointed furniture defined the room with an elegance and grace fit for royalty.

With a slight tug, Johnny pulled open the curtains covering the living room window to let the daylight shine through. The view awed Valerie. The large window was placed perfectly, so the Magnificent Mile and Lake Michigan could be seen simultaneously. "Breath taking isn't it?" Johnny whispered into her ear as he put his arms around her waist.

"Yes, it is." Johnny pictured Valerie's broad smile and was delighted when she swung around with a sparkle in her eyes.

"May I offer you a drink?"

Valerie did not want to start drinking so early in the afternoon. "No, thank you. Besides, I'm enjoying being held by you," as she snuggled back against him.

After a few minutes of staring out the window, Johnny proudly showed Valerie around his abode. When he finished giving her the tour, he suggested they go out for dinner.

Valerie got excited. She was not often to be treated to dinner at a restaurant.

"Hey, Valerie, you want to take a ride over to Gene and Georgetti's Steakhouse?"

"Sure."

The crisp afternoon air was a pleasant seventy degrees, and the drizzled had stopped. It was a perfect time to drive in

Johnny's convertible, a gorgeous 1960 Burgundy Red Corvette with a black leather interior and black canvas top.

They made their way to the building's underground parking garage to get his car. Valerie's mouth dropped when she saw the vehicle. "Is this your car?"

"Yes, it is," he said. His smile widened, sensing she was impressed. "Come on, get in and let's go for a drive."

The other few times they went out, they'd met at the bar. Valerie saw Johnny's wealth for the first time and became excited about the prospect of developing a deeper relationship with him. He opened the door for her, and she slid into the passenger seat.

They drove down Michigan Boulevard with the top down. Valerie smiled, as people on the street admired the car she rode in.

★ ★ ★

Several patrons waited in the lobby area of Gene and Georgetti's. Many of them had waited more than an hour to be seated. This was typical for a Saturday night crowd. Johnny and Valerie entered through the front door of the establishment. The hostess did not appear to recognize Johnny, asking him if he had a reservation.

Johnny's face lit up as he saw the approaching manager. "No, but do I really need one?"

Before the hostess had a chance to respond, the manager came over, and immediately greeted him with a warm hug and a strong handshake. "I'll take care of this guest," he told the hostess. He then escorted Johnny and Valerie to a secluded booth. The manager said, "Enjoy your meal," and quickly departed.

Within a minute of being seated, the maître D, Walter, arrived. "Would you care for a bottle of wine, sir?" Although Johnny was a frequent guest of the restaurant, Walter, always spoke to him formally.

"Yes, we'll have a bottle of Chappellet Napa Valley Merlot."

"Very good."

Valerie took note of everyone staring at her and Johnny. The staff treating them as if they were royalty. She loved it. This was the life she wanted, and Johnny was the guy to give it to her. Trying to hide her giddiness, Valerie perused the menu. With so many choices, she could not decide what to order. When the waiter asked if they were ready to order, she asked if he had a suggestion.

"The veal scaloppini with a creamy saffron sauce is excellent, if you would like to try something unusual?"

"That sounds tasty."

"And for you sir?"

Johnny ordered his usual, surf and turf with the lobster mashed potatoes.

During dinner, a gentleman in his late fifties, wearing a suit and tie, came over to say hello to Johnny. His wife, dressed in an elegant evening gown and adorned in a stunning diamond necklace, made it obvious they were out for a night on the town. The man introduced himself and his wife to Valerie, then he whispered something into Johnny's ear. Johnny smiled in an affirmative motion and made a gesture indicating his agreement.

After they left the table, Valerie asked, "What was that all about?"

"Nothing, just some business. How's your meal?"

"Delicious. This is the best meal I've had in a long time. Thank you." She did her best to keep a cool demeanor.

They finished their meal without further interruption. Johnny, intrigued with Valerie, inquired about her family, her interests and if she had a career. Valerie, more than willing to talk about herself, told Johnny all about her friends and family, and that she just started her career, albeit; she did not have a job *per se*. It didn't bother Johnny that Valerie wasn't curious about him or asking for details as to what he did or about his family. He preferred to keep his life private for the moment.

★ ★ ★

It was after midnight when Johnny suggested he take Valerie home. She reluctantly agreed as it was late in the evening. The evening had been a magical one for them both. Valerie made a feeble attempt to persuade him to let her spend the night with him back at his home. But, Johnny liked Valerie, and he wanted his budding relationship with her to develop slowly. She acted different from all the other women he had dated. She was more than just another pretty face that caught other men's eyes.

The night ended with Johnny dropping her off at her apartment and giving her a passionate kiss good night. "I'll call you soon," he said.

Valerie, confident he would keep his word that he'd call her soon, jokingly said, "We shall see."

Johnny did not disappoint her. The next morning two dozen perfect long stemmed red roses were delivered to her apartment with a note from Johnny. The note read, "I enjoyed last night and want to see you again soon—maybe tonight if your free." She immediately called him, "Hey Johnny, thank you for the roses. They're beautiful."

"I'm glad you like them. Did you want to have dinner and then go dancing afterwards?"

"Yes, that would be awesome. What time will you pick me up?"

"About seven."

"See you then." She heard the phone line click before she placed the receiver on the phone's cradle. *He's perfect!* She thought.

CHAPTER FIVE

Edwin walked through the door of the office at the address given to him by Joseph Carter. A receptionist greeted him, "May I help you sir?"

"Yes, I'm Mr. Carter's new assistant, Edwin Goldberg."

"Mr. Carter is expecting you, go on in."

Edwin noticed a small plaque sitting on the credenza behind the receptionist. It read, "Always be competitive. But as for our peers, always find resolution. And if that fails, kill them with kindness.—Author Unknown."

Edwin opened the door to the next room. The room, set up like a classroom with a chalk board and several desks, also housed a full size craps table.

"Welcome," Mr. Carter said to Edwin, extending his hand. "You are the first one to arrive. There will be three other new staff members today." Carter noticing the puzzled look on Edwin's face asked, "Confused?"

"Yes sir, I am. What exactly is going on?"

"This is where I'm going to teach you and the other new associates how to play and win at craps. You will also learn about Las Vegas casinos and what it takes to host our junketeers. Take a seat and we'll start once the others arrive."

"Others?"

"Yes, I hired four new associates to train. You are one of them."

Before taking his seat, Edwin looked around the room. He observed several flip chart pages taped to the wall. Each had something related to craps and Las Vegas.

The other associates arrived a few minutes later. They introduced themselves as Gwenn Alexander, Herbert Shoemaker, and Richard Esposito. Carter chose each person carefully.

Gwenn Alexander stood five foot five inches and had a slender, athletic build. Her shoulder-length brown hair was pulled back into a pony tail.

Gwenn, a market research analyst at Kraft Foods, hailed from Milwaukee, Wisconsin. She answered Carter's ad because she wanted more excitement in her life. It would be a lifestyle more then she could have ever imagined in her wildest dreams.

Herbert Shoemaker wore a navy blue suit, white shirt and solid dark blue tie. His shoes were polished. Standing six foot three, he stood out in a crowd. Clean-shaven, his short blond hair offset his dark brown eyes. Shoemaker had just returned from a tour in Vietnam. Honorably discharged from the Army, he was quiet and soft spoken.

Richard Esposito, slightly overweight, did not attempt to hide the belly that hung over his bell-bottom blue jeans. Wearing a green polo shirt, he did not seem to fit in with the other associates. Esposito, talented and charismatic, had the ability to charm just about every person he met. His boisterous demeanor, using profanity and being loud, did not go unnoticed by the others.

After everyone introduced themselves, Carter pulled out a revolver and waived it in the air. It was a Smith and Wesson Model 13 Military and Police .357 Magnum. The Model 13, a double-action revolver with a six-round capacity, had a three-inch barrel and a stainless steel blued finish. As Carter waved it he said, "This is Kindness. If I ever need to use it on a person, I want it known that person was killed with Kindness." Carter chuckled as his hand twitched.

Every associate in the room remained silent. Not one person cracked a smile. Gwenn twisted her hair with her finger. Edwin squeezed his eyes shut. Herbert turned away from Carter, while Richard eyes bulged in amazement.

Carter continued, "The reason I'm introducing you to Kindness is because you will all have access to a lot of cash—my cash. And although you'll all be generously compensated, I don't want any of you to get any ideas of keeping some of that cash for yourself. Do I make myself clear?"

Almost in unison, the associates said, "Yes sir!"

"Good." With that acknowledgment, Carter put Kindness away. Immediately, the tension in the room lifted as if a dark veil was removed.

Carter paced the room—"During the next four weeks, I'm going to teach you not only how to play the game of craps, but how to win. You will also learn how to treat our junketeers, whom you will be traveling to Vegas with every other week. Take notes. Ask lots of questions. Alright, let's begin, there are thirty-six combinations using two six-sided dice. The seven has the most combinations. There is six ways to make a seven: one and six, two and five, and three and four. Since there are two dice, there are two ways to make each of these combinations. On the wall to your left is a sheet which shows the various combinations. Memorize it."

Carter went over the basics of the game which were simple. "At the start of a new game, a puck, turned indicating 'OFF,' generally placed on an area of the craps layout marked 'Don't Come.' A person could make a wager on an area of the layout marked 'Pass Line' or 'Don't Pass Line.'"

"Most craps players bet on the Pass Line. The opposite bet of the Pass Line is the Don't Pass Line. If the person rolling the dice, called a shooter, rolled a seven or an eleven on the first roll of the game, the Pass Line was an immediate winner; and the Don't Pass bets lost. If the shooter rolled a two, three or twelve, the Pass Line lost and the dealers collected the bets. Don't Pass bets were only paid if a two or three was rolled. Casinos deemed twelve a push. Any other number, e.g., four, five, six, eight, nine, or ten; these are called box numbers, the dealer marked that number with the puck indicating 'ON' and it became the shooters point.

"For the Pass Line to win, the shooter had to roll the point number before a seven. Nothing else mattered. For the Don't Pass to win, the shooter had to roll a seven before the point. Any other number rolled was irrelevant, unless side bets were made. Any questions so far?"

Carter could see he was losing a couple of his associates, so he switched tactics. He instructed the associates to gather around a full size craps table with authentic looking chips, a dice bowl, stick and pucks to indicate the point number, he'd set up in the office. There, he demonstrated the basics of the game for about an hour.

He kept the game very simple. Each associate had the opportunity to roll the dice. Some of them were instructed how to bet on the Pass Line, while the others were taught how to bet on the Don't Pass. They all took turns betting on both sides of the game. Once Carter became convinced that every person got how to play the Pass Line and Don't Pass, he ended the session.

Before Joseph let everyone leave for the day he gave them these words of advice: "If you treat playing craps like a business, you'll get paid like it's a business. If you treat it as a hobby, you'll get paid like it's a hobby. If you treat it as entertainment, well . . ."

Edwin took Carter's words to heart. After leaving Carter's office, he immediately went to the library and checked out several books about craps. That evening he read as much as he could. Enthralled with the mathematics of the game, he started to apply his business background to winning the game.

One book in particular stood out to Edwin amongst the rest. It was John Scarne's book titled *Scarne on Dice*. The actual quote in the book that started Edwin to think deeply about the game read, "*You may beat a game, but you can't beat the game.*" In other words, the game of craps could not be beat. Still, Edwin, intrigued with it all wondered what else Joseph Carter would teach them, and if there truly was a secret to winning.

In addition to reading books about craps, Edwin read as many books on trading commodity futures and options. The more he read about trading futures and options, the more similarities he noticed it had to playing craps. He studied charts on the various commodities.

It occurred to him that Valerie's father might be able to help him understand the trading process better. Without hesitation, he made a phone call to Aaron Taylor.

"Hello, Mr. Taylor, Edwin Goldberg, do you have a moment?"

Aaron Taylor did not like Edwin. Valerie had poisoned him against Edwin when she dumped him. In a crotchety voice, he asked, "What do you want?"

"Well, sir, as you know, Valerie broke off our relationship. I'm not calling about her. I have a position that pays extremely well and I had some questions about trading at the Board of Trade and how it all works. Do you think you could teach me?"

Aaron, caught off guard, never expected to hear from him again, let alone ask him about trading options. His jaw tightened and he pressed his lips together. After he thought about the situation he said, "Sure, why not. Give me a day or two and I'll call you when I can meet."

"Thank you." Edwin gave him his telephone number, and said, "I'll look forward to hearing from you."

A few days had past. True to his word, Taylor called Edwin. "Okay, let's meet after the Fourth of July Holiday. Does July 8th work for your schedule?"

Edwin quickly glanced through his day planner. "Yes, that works for me. What time and where do you want to meet?"

"Meet me at the Board of Trade at 1. We'll talk more then."

With that, the conversation abruptly ended. Edwin quickly penciled-in the meeting in his planner. His heart raced with excitement thinking about the possibilities of learning to be a floor trader. He remembered some of his college classmates that bragged about the amount of money they were going to make at the exchange. The conversation deepened his conviction to show Valerie she had made the biggest mistake of her life.

CHAPTER SIX

The vision of a dimly lit room with shadowy figures loomed in the back of Edwin's mind as Joseph Carter spoke during training the next day. Carter assigned each associate a specific casino to escort the firm's junketeers. Gwenn Alexander had the Riviera assigned to her. Herbert Shoemaker got the Sands, while Richard Esposito drew, Caesars Palace. Carter reserved the Dunes for Edwin. Each associate had their own special casino host to assist them with the junketeers.

More importantly, Carter informed them, "Arrangements have been made for each of you to have a twenty-thousand-dollar line of credit with the specific casino to which you are assigned."

Gwenn, speechless upon hearing that she would be given a line of credit for twenty-thousand dollars, looked stunned. Her skinned tingled as her heart raced. She began to weigh the danger of the situation.

Esposito and Shoemaker were ecstatic. Unable to contain their grins, they looked down at the desk to avoid eye contact with Carter. Edwin remained suspicious. His gut, balled up in a knot, told him something was amiss. Edwin remained vigilant listening to Carter and all of the responsibilities involved in making certain the junketeers were well pampered.

Gwenn, more astute than Esposito or Shoemaker, asked "Why do we need a line of credit with the casino?"

"Because you will each ask for a marker for ten thousand dollars at the craps table. You will use this money to play. How you play will determine your bonus."

"But Mr. Carter, what if we lose?" Gwenn persevered.

Carter paced the room deliberating whether or not he could trust the new recruits with what they were really hired to do. After a moment, he decided to tell them the plan. "Each of you was told you will be paid five thousand dollars per month plus a bonus of a minimum of four thousand dollars, a total of nine thousand dollars. Do you all agree this is what I offered as your compensation?"

Edwin and the other associates nodded and verbally concurred to the amount of the compensation offered.

Cater continued, "You are required to take out a ten-thousand-dollar marker at least once per day for each of the three days you are in Vegas. You are not to lose more than five thousand dollars. If you win, excellent! You are each to bring me five thousand dollars per day for three days, a total of fifteen thousand dollars, in cash. Anything above that is yours to keep."

Each person in the room simultaneously gasped. Edwin, first to speak, asked the question that was on everyone's mind, "What about the marker, won't they need to be repaid?"

Carter, in a dead-pan voice, said, "An excellent question. I have made arrangements with certain dealers, pit bosses and people in accounting to have the markers handled. They will not need to be repaid and you will never need to worry about them once you leave the casino. Let's just say they will be misplaced and mysteriously disappear as if they never existed." He continued, "Do you remember Kindness? If any of you think of keeping all the cash, I will find you. And I assure you, you will not like the consequences."

Carter changed the subject and began teaching his recruits more about the game of craps. Much of it went over the heads of all, except Edwin. He had an edge because he had read the books and studied the mathematics of the game. Gwenn, Esposito and Shoemaker, still caught up in what Carter had just told them, didn't focus on the task at hand.

After the training session, Edwin went straight to his apartment. He had to think about what transpired and how he'd handle the situation. The other three associates went out for pizza and beer at a local pizzeria. Edwin declined the invitation to join them. Deep down he had an uneasy feeling. The little voice in his head said, *"Ever feel like you're winning even though you're really losing?"*

★ ★ ★

Over the next three weeks Carter taught his associates everything about how to win at craps. There were a lot of various betting methods. Each associate chose their own favorite betting scheme.

Carter didn't care which betting method they used because in the end he got fifteen thousand dollars from each of them every two weeks. Of course, he could not keep all the money. He had to grease the palms of the casino employees in on the scam.

If things went south or the families got wise to him he needed an out and someone to blame. His new associates would be the patsies.

Carter made certain that Gwenn, Edwin, Esposito and Shoemaker knew how much to bet so as not to draw attention. He said to them, "My young associates, there is a delicate balance between not being too aggressive and betting too much, and not betting too little. Based on my experience, I suggest that you play between three and five in the morning. The casino floor will be the least crowded during this time. Do you have any questions?"

None of the associates asked any questions. Edwin's head spun from thinking about the wee hours he would be up and wondered when he would sleep.

Carter dismissed his staff, "If there are no questions, you can leave. I've got other work to do."

With that, everyone got up to leave. Gwenn, Esposito and Shoemaker had formed a close bond over the course of their training. They spoke amongst themselves about pulling all-nighters as they walked out of the building. Edwin kept to himself and remained an outsider to the group. This did not go unnoticed by Carter.

Carter continued to build his list of junketeers who wanted to travel from the mid-west to Las Vegas for "free." His list grew to more than fifteen hundred. He made it known that it was a select group of people for whom he would make travel arrangements. He told many of the junketeers that his group was closed, but that he would make an exception for them. Carter made each junketeer he spoke to feel special and important.

At first, many wondered how Carter made any money if he paid for all of their airfare, hotel accommodations, shows and food. Carter explained, honestly, that the casinos gave him a small percentage of what his guests were expected to lose. It was not that they had to lose, only what the casino anticipated winning from each guest. As Carter explained it, some junketeers would win, while others would lose. In the end, the casino expected to make a profit—-from who didn't matter.

The junketeers bought into Carter's line of persuasion. Each thought they were getting a *free* trip to Las Vegas and that the other guy who paid for it with his losses. For others, it provided a means to escape to pursue other endeavors, such as affairs of the heart.

★ ★ ★

At last, in late June, the day arrived when Carter's four new assistants traveled to Las Vegas. They were each assigned to be personally responsible for between twenty-five and thirty junketeers. Carter spent a lot of time grilling them, similar to a military boot camp, how to handle the needs of the junketeers to make sure they could handle any situation that arose. They all learned how to play craps proficiently.

Carter made it crystal clear to his assistants that they were not to discuss their markers with anyone, not even among themselves, especially if they were in public, and especially not with Big Julie. Big Julie had no idea about the swindle about to unfold. With raised eyebrows the associates agreed with visions of dollar signs in their eyes. Only Edwin was wary, but a master plan began to formulate in his mind, and he wanted this money to succeed.

After a long night of traveling on the red-eye flight from Chicago to Las Vegas, the Boeing 747 finally landed at McCarran Airport. A loud cheer rose from the passengers. Gwenn, Richard, Herbert and Edwin escorted their junketeers to their assigned hotels. They treated all of the junketeers like royalty. Once they were checked into their suites or rooms and all of their needs and wants were attended to, the four met at the Flamingo to take a deep breath. They chose to meet at the Flamingo, because it was a place none of them were going to play and because of its reputation.

Gwenn grew nervous about taking a marker for ten thousand dollars. Sitting in the bar lounge with the others she spoke up, "I'm having a hard time processing taking a marker for ten thousand dollars."

Richard said, "Come on Gwenn. Merely act like you've done it before."

Herbert attempted to calm her down and tried to convince her she could do it. "Yeah, don't think of it as money. They give you pretty colored chips. Pretend you're playing with fake money. It will be fine."

Edwin had a gleam in his eye and a slight smirk on his face. "What's with you, Mr. smug?" she asked.

"Nothing. Only wondering when I will sleep during the next few days."

The four departed to take a quick nap before they had to go to their real job—stealing money from the casino.

★ ★ ★

At three in the morning, Edwin approached the craps table. Two other junketeers were playing. Edwin wore a dark navy pin-stripe suit, white shirt and classic red tie. He calmly took out his driver's license and placed it in the Come area and asked for a marker.

The dealer handed Edwin's driver's license to the box-man. He looked at Edwin and made some notes. "I'd like a ten-thousand-dollar marker," Edwin said, as the box-man looked at his ID one more time. The box-man called over to the pit boss. He handed him the ID and whispered something into his ear. The pit boss glanced at Edwin. He stepped around the table to where Edwin stood, and asked him to sign a sheet of paper. The pit boss made some notes on the paper and told the dealer, "Please give Mr. Goldberg ten thousand."

"Yes sir," the dealer said. His hands moved lightning quick as he Edwin picked up the chips and placed them in the chip rail directly in front of him. The other junketeers, also making large bets, paid no attention to Edwin. If anything, they made him aware how perturbed they were that he interrupted the flow of the game. One of them said, "Hey schmuck, are you trying to jinx us. What are you doing buying-in in the middle of a hot roll?"

"I'm Sorry?" Edwin, excited about getting a ten thousand-dollar marker forgot that craps players are superstitious. Carter taught him not buy-in in the middle of a shooter's roll. He refrained himself from pissing-off his junketeers any further.

Another player shouted to the stickman, "Come on, the dice are getting cold."

The stickman passed the dice to the shooter. Edwin closed his eyes. He dared not make a bet. He prayed the shooter would keep the roll going.

Fortunately for him, the shooter made several more rolls before he sevened out. Edwin's mouth was parched. He swallowed hard, but it did not help. The player standing next to him saw him hesitating to make a bet. "You gonna make a bet or what?"

Edwin placed a five-hundred-dollar purple chip on the Pass Line.

"That's more like it. Ok shooter, let's go. Come-on, seven or eleven."

The new shooter picked up the dice and let them fly. Time slowed to a crawl. It seemed an eternity to Edwin, before the cubes settled on the green-felt. The stickman called out, "Seven, front line winner."

The table erupted with a roar from the players' hollering. Edwin sighed. His hands trembled as he picked-up the extra chip and placed it in his chip rail. The other players, giddy with the continued good fortune, forgot about Edwin's earlier transgression.

Within thirty minutes he was up more than three thousand dollars. He decided to color up his chips. The box person counted up the chips and instructed the dealer to give Edwin two large chocolate brown five-thousand-dollar chips, three yellow one-thousand-dollar chips, a purple five-hundred-dollar chip and two black one-hundred-dollar chips. Edwin picked up the casino chips, and left the purple chip on the table; "For the boys." He gave a generous tip to the dealers. Edwin then made his way to the cashier's cage and converted the chips into legal tender. No one said a word about the marker. The other junketeers paid no attention to Edwin coloring up and leaving. They were too engrossed in continuing to play craps.

Edwin made his way to his room. He immediately put the money into an attaché case, quickly locked it and, put it inside the drawer of the dresser under several articles of clothing.

At the Riviera, Gwenn Alexander had similar success. She won almost two thousand dollars when she colored up. Taking deep breaths, she felt euphoric. She hummed as she made her way back to her room to catch a few winks.

Richard Esposito did not fare as well. He lost more than four thousand dollars playing at Caesars Palace. Esposito cut his losses, relieved to walk away with six thousand dollars.

Meanwhile, over at the Sands, Herbert Shoemaker won several hundred dollars. He hired a lady of the night to spend the rest of the evening with him. Uncharacteristic for him to act in this manner, he succumbed to the enchanting spell of Vegas.

When he awoke the next morning, the hooker and all his money was gone. Despondent at his stupidity, beyond consoling, Gwenn, Richard and Edwin were unable to get him to shut up about losing his money to a hooker and reminded him of the consequences if he kept chattering. Upon hearing Edwin mention "Kindness," he looked at Edwin with sadden and sullen eyes. Finally, Herbert quieted down when the three other assistants offered to cover the five thousand dollars he owed to Carter. They also reminded him that he had two more nights to recoup his loss.

★ ★ ★

The rest of the trip went without any other incidents. Shoemaker made certain to stick to the plan. He did not hire any ladies to please him, having learned an expensive lesson.

After landing at O'Hare Airport late Sunday night and bidding farewell to their junketeer guests, the associates made their way to Carter's office. The weather had turned gloomy and it began to rain.

The clouds hid any light from the moon or stars. Carter anxiously waiting for his associates, having had the lights turned on. A smile crossed his face when they finally arrived.

Each associate handed Carter three stacks of one hundred dollar bills separated into five thousand dollars in each bundle. Carter counted each bundle. Before dismissing them, he said, "Get some rest. You're going to need it. We're meeting again this afternoon for debriefing."

The four associates departed the office building at approximately midnight. Gwenn grabbed Edwin's arm after making sure Shoemaker and Esposito had gone ahead. She asked, "So how much did you make this trip?"

Edwin, not sure why Gwenn would ask such a question, told her, "About twenty thousand dollars. How did you do?"

"Not quite as well. I had a few losing sessions, but managed to keep about eight grand. How did you end up with the twenty grand?"

"It was fairly simple, I only won about five thousand, but because I kept half of the markers, that added another fifteen grand. My play was conservative so as not to make a lot or lose a lot. Most of the time, I played the Don't Pass Line for one hundred dollars. If a shooter had a long roll and kept the dice, I would stay at the table for a longer period of time without making any other bets."

Gwenn, impressed, said, "Pretty cool. Do you want to get something to eat? There's a Denny's near my place."

Edwin, tired after the long trip, decided to decline her invitation. Even though Gwenn was an attractive woman, he remained cautious. "Not tonight. It's late and I'm tired. Can I get a rain check?"

Gwenn understood and did not take it personally, "Sure thing."

"Hey Gwenn, why the sudden interest in me? I thought you were tight with Richard and Herbert."

"Yeah, but this first trip revealed a lot about them. I'm not so sure I want to hang around them much longer. Especially Herbert."

"Okay, see you tomorrow." He left to go home.

Edwin did not feel comfortable keeping a lot of cash in his apartment. Early the next morning, before meeting with the others for debriefing, he made his way to a nearby bank where he had a checking account and paid for a safety deposit box. He placed a plain brown paper bag which contained twenty thousand dollars in cash in the box.

The afternoon debriefing revealed a lot about each associate. Carter asked them many questions that focused on the junketeers and what each associate thought about the experience. Herbert, grateful little had been mentioned about the markers, felt relieved no one had said anything about the hooker.

Carter told his staff that the casinos informed him the junketeers lost more than four hundred thousand dollars during the trip. The casinos and Carter were both pleased. He made sure the associates understood that so long as the junketeers had a good time, they would not be upset with their losses.

CHAPTER SEVEN

On a bright Thursday afternoon, Edwin drove down Cassingham Road past Bexley High School in his rented Mercedes-Benz toward his parents' home. Bexley was a geographic enclave of Columbus, Ohio, a tree-lined suburb located on the banks of Alum Creek next to Wolfe Park. He spent almost every July Fourth since age five in this town.

He enjoyed going home for the Fourth of July holiday. Like he remembered, the downtown street posts were adorned with red, white and blue bunting and American flags. During the drive, his mind conjured up images of days long past as his memory besieged him with familiar sounds and scents.

Edwin recalled how he coped with the transition from his blissful suburban life to attend Northwestern University. His parents were extremely proud he'd received a full academic scholarship. There was nothing more important to them than their son getting an excellent education. He often told people, "From day one, my parents told me that I was going to attend college. Day two, they told me I had to pay for my college expenses." His mind drifted as he dredged up memories of how he had to work during high school. And, the bitterness towards his classmates. Most of them from privileged families, drove new cars and were able to party.

In hindsight, Edwin loathed that he needed to work twice as hard as others to maintain his grades. He was smart, but not brilliant. He chose to focus on business because he wanted to become affluent and work for a Fortune 100 company. Edwin believed business would give him opportunities to become successful. He quickly learned that a college degree, even an MBA, did not guarantee success.

His parents, full of pride that their son had graduated with an MBA, were pleased that he had a job that paid him a lot of money. But they made it perfectly clear to him that they weren't happy with his chosen profession. They expected more from him.

Edwin dreamed of having the lifestyle of his high school classmates. Many of them would become doctors, lawyers and venture capitalists. They would have large homes, families, and lake houses. They already drove foreign luxury cars and traveled around the world.

Edwin had made enough on his first trip to Vegas to pay-off his student loans, but decided not to do so as he thought it would be too difficult to explain. He never told them the total amount of how much he made. His father already gave him grief for not moving out of his studio apartment and finding a nicer place to live.

The more Edwin thought about telling his parents about babysitting junketeers and playing craps, the less likely it was that he would tell them the truth about the markers. Deep down, he understood what he did was possibly illicit. Or was it? The way Joe explained it, they were doing Vegas a favor by bringing sheep to the casinos to be fleeced. Joe always emphasized to the associates that what they took was a pittance compared to the amount of dough they brought into the casinos' coffers.

Edwin's parents invited many of the neighbors to join them for a backyard holiday picnic. Edwin's father, Sid, fired up the grill as the guests patiently waited for the burgers, steaks and hot dogs to cook. The sizzling of the steak made Edwin's mouth water. The men gathered in small circles, drank beer and grumbled about the sluggish economy.

Edwin's mother, Marlene, along with several other ladies, got the picnic table on the backyard patio set with paper plates, plastic silverware and napkins all decorated with an Independence Day theme. They placed Jell-O molds, potato salad, coleslaw, and other side dishes on the table. His mother fit, and trim, always smiled. Her eyes were kind, and she rarely raised her voice. Everyone adored her.

Once the guests had taken their food, they sat at the table. Sid sat at the head of the table. Edwin sat next to him. Unfortunately for Edwin, Rodney Rosenthal, chose to sit next to him. Rodney, made a lot of money in the oil industry working for Standard Oil. The truth be known, Rodney inherited most of his fortune. He pretended he acquired his wealth through hard work, not his inheritance. Rodney, inquisitive, questioned Edwin about his new position, "What exactly does Global Enterprises do?"

Edwin, not sure how to answer the question because he wanted to make a good impression for his parents' benefit, decided to be honest. "We represent a number of casinos and arrange for people to travel to Las Vegas as their guest."

Rodney raised an eyebrow and swirled the scotch in his glass. He took a sip and said, "You're a pimp for the casinos."

"We prefer to think of it as being their marketing firm." Edwin took another bite of his steak and drank some water.

Rodney finished stuffing the rest of a hot dog into mouth. He took a large gulp of his scotch. His face turned red as he swallowed. "Do you make any money working for this company?"

"Of course I do. Why do you ask?"

"Just wondering. Hey, Sid, do you have any Glenmorangie Single Malt Scotch? This stuff you're serving is like piss water."

Edwin glanced over at his father. Sid shook his head as his voice quivered, "No, Rodney, I don't. You're just going to drink the cheap stuff."

"I didn't think Chivas Regal is considered cheap," Edwin said.

Rodney, undaunted by Edwin, swirled the scotch around his glass before taking another swig. "It's not. But, it's not the expensive stuff that I'm used to having. Hey, kid, is that your Mercedes parked out front?"

Edwin's face glowed from the smile that brimmed from ear-to-ear. "Why yes, it is. Do you like it?"

"Yeah, I do. I guess you must be making decent money to afford that car."

Edwin quickly changed the subject. He didn't want Rodney to know it was a rental. "Do you like stories, Mr. Rosenthal?"

"Yes, I do."

"Can I tell you one of my favorite stories?"

"Sure. I'm all ears."

Edwin wiped the corner of his mouth with his napkin. "An elderly man walked into a pet shop on Michigan Avenue. He sought a companion to keep him company. He saw a bright blue and green parrot. The parrot tilted his head and eyed the man with a sadistic look.

"Intrigued, the man inquired of the store owner as to how much the bird cost. The owner informed the man that the bird was not for sale.

"'Why not?' the man asked.

"'Because he has a foul mouth and swears worse than a drunken sailor after shore leave.'

"'That won't bother me.' The man persisted. Determined to purchase the winged feathered friend, and after much dickering, the man made an offer to the store owner for more money than he ever dreamed he would receive. The parrot had observed the two men haggling. It never made a sound.

"The shop keeper made it clear to the man that there could be no returns or exchanges. That once he walked out of the shop, the parrot would be his problem to deal with. The man looked at the bird, who still remained silent, and thought 'Why not?' The bird turned his head at an angle, looked at the man and opened his beak. Not a sound came out. 'Okay, it's a deal.'

"The man brought the parrot back to his apartment. Within ten minutes of getting back home, the parrot began a tirade of foul and vulgar swearing unlike any that the man had ever heard.

"The man did everything he could to get the bird to shut up. No matter what he did, nothing worked. If anything, the bird became more vulgar and abusive. Much to the dismay of the man, he lost his temper. Frustrated, he grabbed the parrot and threw him into the freezer. The squawking continued for another five minutes. Finally, the room became quiet again. The man, distraught at what he did, thought, Oh, my God. What have I done? I've killed the poor thing.

"He quickly opened the freezer door. The parrot staggered out, looked at the man and asked, 'What did the chicken do?'"

Rodney bellowed a loud laugh and slapped his knee. "What did the chicken do? I like that story young man."

The other guests also laughed at Edwin's humor.

Rodney asked, "What happens if a junketeer gets out of line or creates a problem?"

Edwin did not know why Rodney showed so much interest in the junket business. "We kill them with kindness," he blurted out.

Rodney's eyes grew wide and his jaw dropped. He was speechless. The room grew quiet as the other neighbors waited holding their collective breath for something to happen. "You kill them with kindness," Rodney restated. He shot Edwin a quick, curious look and laughed. "How can I get an invitation to be a casinos' guest? A free trip to Vegas sounds like a lot of fun. I'm certain I have a large enough net worth to qualify."

Edwin slyly smiled. He knew Rodney had no idea what he meant with the reference to "kindness." "I'll have my boss, Joseph Carter, call you. He makes all of the decisions about those who get the invitations. Would you like another scotch or a steak?"

"Sure that would great."

Sid glanced over to Edwin, and smiled. The look on his father's face indicated he had done well. The people resumed talking amongst each other.

Edwin did not say another word. He rose up from the table and brought Rodney another scotch and a plate with three steaks on it. He decided not to sit back down. He'd lost his appetite. He excused himself and went to sit on the porch swing. He could hear Rodney boasting about his investments and the new speed boat he bought. Rodney's arrogance and superior attitude sickened Edwin.

* * *

Once the guests had left, and the kitchen cleaned, Edwin sat in the family room reading a book about options. Sid sat down next to his son. "What kind of career do you envision for yourself working for a junket business?"

"Dad, they pay me a lot of money. I have an opportunity to put money aside and invest it in some franchises."

His father noticed the book about options. "What is that you're reading?"

"It's a book on how to trade commodity options. I want to utilize what I learned in business school and see if I can apply the same principles to make money trading."

"Edwin, it's a waste of time. Trading options is gambling. You'll never make any money. You'll probably end up losing money."

The words stung. "Dad, why do you always doubt me? Why do you always think I'm not good enough?"

"Because, you've never done anything to prove yourself. Your mom and I are proud you graduated with your MBA. But you're wasting your degree working as a glorified travel agent. You should be doing better than that. No wonder Valerie dumped you. As far as I'm concerned, you're a loser."

"Thanks for the vote of confidence, dad."

At that moment, Edwin's mother walked in. "What's going on?"

"Dad thinks I'm a loser because Valerie dumped me."

"Well, son, I was surprised that she dated you to begin with. She was such a smart, beautiful young lady."

"Really? That's what you both think of me. That your son is a loser?"

"Edwin, we love you, but . . ."

He was cut-off in mid-sentence. "I'm outta here." Edwin stormed out of the house, frustrated, that his parents didn't understand his point of view.

Unlike his father, Edwin never considered that trading was gambling at all. He saw it as a math problem, a question with a solution. That solution led to easy money. He also couldn't believe that his mother thought Valerie was too good for him.

After careful deliberation and thought, Edwin decided not to mention about making money playing craps. It would be impossible to explain how it wasn't gambling since the game was fixed for him to win no matter what happened. He knew his parents, especially his father, would never comprehend what he did or why he did it. He became more determined to prove them all wrong.

CHAPTER EIGHT

The Chicago Board of Trade, one of the world's oldest future and option exchanges, located on Jackson Boulevard in the heart of Chicago's financial district, towered at 605 feet. The landmark, Art Deco building remained the tallest building in Chicago until superseded by the Richard J. Daley Center in 1965. A thirty-one-foot statue of the Roman goddess Ceres capped a pyramid roof on top of the building. Ceres referenced the exchange's heritage as a commodity market. Because the sculptor, Alvin Meyer, believed no one would be able to see her face sitting on top of the forty-five story building, Ceres did not have a face. The front fascia of the CBOT building had massive engraved "Chicago Board of Trade" letters adorned by a large clock placed between a carved relief of an Egyptian with a sheaf of wheat and a Native American carrying an ear of corn. A carved American Bald Eagle sat perched just above the clock.

Aaron Taylor gave Edwin a tour of the place. He explained that more than fifty different options and future contracts were traded daily by the thirty-six hundred Board members through an open cry process in many of the pit areas. The pit, a raised octagonal platform, where traders yelled out trades, either selling, referred to as offering, or buying, used various hand signals to denote the quantity and price for the contract.

Aaron stopped for a moment and gazed through the glass window overlooking the trading floor. As Edwin looked out, Aaron said, "Nothing you have ever experienced will prepare you for the total bedlam you are about to witness. In the pits, it's every man and woman for themselves. People make and lose massive amounts of money in a matter of moments. Stay here and watch. I've got some work to do. When I'm done I'll introduce you to some people who can explain what you're seeing."

The frenzy on the trading floor was indescribable. Men and women shouting and making all sorts of different hand signals, Edwin wondered how anyone could understand the trades being made. He stood in awe at the melee unfolding before his eyes.

About an hour later, Aaron returned to where he left Edwin. "Come with me. I want to introduce you to Bill Beckwith. He's my boss."

Edwin followed Aaron to an office on the thirty-fourth floor. The office, sparsely decorated, had a large cherry wood desk with several charts spewed about, a large desk chair and two smaller office chairs in front of the desk. Bill Beckwith sat in the chair behind the desk looking over several charts as Aaron and Edwin entered.

"Hi Bill, this is the young man I told you about. Edwin Goldberg, this is William Beckwith."

Bill rose from his chair, stretched out his arm and gave Edwin a firm handshake. "So why your interest in trading options young man?"

"Well, sir, I accepted a position with a company that provides junkets to Vegas and part of that position required I learn how to play craps."

"As in the dice game?" Beckwith interjected.

"Yes, sir. I started reading books about playing craps and with my MBA I thought about applying business principles to the game. At one time I dated Mr. Taylor's daughter. She mentioned that he worked at the Board of Trade for you. I started to read books about trading options, but found it confusing. So I thought I would ask for some guidance."

Beckwith eyed Edwin amused that he wanted to learn about trading options. Not many people knew about options or even if they did, they weren't interested in them. "Okay. Tell you what I'm going to do. Do you work out?" he asked Edwin.

"No sir. I jog a little when I have time."

"Ever heard of the Lawson YMCA on Chicago Street?"

"No."

"I work out with a bunch of other guys there with a man named Dick Woit. Meet me there tomorrow evening and be prepared to work out. Woit's workouts require a lot of mental discipline. If you can handle the abuse and have the discipline to stick with it, I'll teach you how to trade options. You need to have a strict discipline to trade options. Otherwise, you end up like Aaron working for some jerk like me." He looked over at Aaron who stood quietly observing the interaction between Edwin and his boss.

"What time?"

"We start at 6 p.m. sharp. Make sure you're there and ready to go by 5:45. I'll see you tomorrow. Aaron will escort you out."

"Thank you Mr. Beckwith. See you tomorrow."

Aaron escorted Edwin to the building's exit. "Thank you Mr. Taylor for the tour and for introducing me to Mr. Beckwith. I appreciate it."

"Don't thank me yet. You have no idea what you're in for tomorrow."

In deep thought, Edwin departed and made his way back to his apartment.

★ ★ ★

Dick Woit, a defensive back with the Detroit Lions in the mid-1950's, was from the "No Pain, No Gain," school of physical fitness. A closet ascetic, his weight had dropped from 175 pounds to under 100 pounds. On his five-foot-eight frame, his ribs were as neatly defined as the bars on a xylophone. Woit ran an unusual, eccentric fitness class for professional athletes, middle-aged businessmen and politicians. Those who trained with him had to endure the verbal abuse he dished out upon them as they struggled through sets of push-ups, sit-ups, presses, arm curls and sprints. Members who survived the ordeal and remained a part of the elite group called themselves "Woit's Warriors."

Bill Beckwith met Edwin in the locker room of the Y.M.C.A. He introduced Edwin to several others who were getting ready to endure another punishing work out. Edwin moved from the locker room to the odoriferous exercise room. It wasn't much—a few barbells with light weights ranging anywhere from forty-five to one-hundred pounds, a few exercise mats and several benches along the wall.

At exactly 6 p.m., a middle-aged businessman called out, "Ready, begin." With that everyone in the room began doing bent knee sit–ups. One hundred bent knee sit-ups, followed by five sets of sixty-second leg raises wherein they held their legs about six inches off the ground for one minute, followed by fifty more bent knee sit-ups. Then the men did four more sets of sixty-second leg raises, followed by thirty-second leg kicks. Edwin felt his stomach tighten. Not even half-way through the routine, he was nauseous. Finally, after another eighty bent knee sit-ups, the stomach portion of the workout was finished.

Woit walked into the room. Dressed in a grey sweat shirt and pants, he looked like a prisoner straight from the Auschwitz concentration camp. He immediately saw Edwin gasping for breath. In a high-pitched, raspy voice, he shouted, "Hey, mother-fucker, anyone who looks like you should be dead."

Edwin, earlier advised not to say a word no matter how much verbal abuse Woit dished out, remained silent. He was told, if Woit didn't like you, he ignored you. The verbal abuse let you know he cared.

Woit picked up a set of weights. They were "his" weights. No one touched them. He did every work out with each group. Some days he had as many as six groups. Some were men, and some were women, but the sessions were always done separately. No co-ed groups. He moved the weights out of the way and put his feet on the bench to begin doing push-ups. "Down one, down two, down three, down four . . ." The men did two sets of ten fast and five slow elevated push-ups to Woit's count, followed by three sets of eight fast and seven slow elevated push-ups.

After the push-ups, each man grabbed a barbell. They did two sets of ten presses followed by five curls. Grunts and groans could be heard each time the men lifted the weights. The barbells were set gently on the floor between each set, and God help the person who dropped the barbell. Although Edwin only lifted a forty-five-pound barbell, he could not finish the work out. He put his barbell on the floor; went out onto the fire escape balcony and puked his guts out. Beckwith quickly checked on Edwin.

"Hey, are you okay?"

Heaving between breaths, Edwin managed to utter, "Yeah."

Once Bill knew Edwin was okay, he immediately went back inside to finish the routine.

The group did more push-ups and weights before heading outside for a one mile run around the block.

Edwin sat in the steam room listening to the other fellows talk about business or marital issues. His weakened body trembled and shook from the work out he just experienced. He remained silent, letting the heat ease the pain in his joints, grateful to be able to sit for a few moments.

Afterwards, once Edwin showered and got dressed, Bill Beckwith approached. "So what did you think?"

"Oh man, I didn't realize how out of shape I am."

"Well, if you want to continue, we meet every Monday, Wednesday and Friday. I will see you Monday if you still want to work out with us."

"See you on Monday," Edwin said as he shook hands with Beckwith and left the Y. Despite being fatigued, he managed to get to his apartment and collapse on his bed fully clothed.

The next morning, Edwin could barely move. Every muscle screamed with the slightest movement. He felt excruciating pain unlike anything he had ever experienced. Edwin stayed in his apartment all weekend dreading having to go back to Woit's workout on Monday.

He realized he had to show up Monday evening if he had any hope of Bill teaching him how to trade options. Notwithstanding the pain, Edwin wanted to get into better physical shape for several reasons; one benefit being that in better shape he could endure the grind of standing at the craps table and of traveling to and from Vegas every other week.

★ ★ ★

Edwin returned to suffer though the workout over the next several weeks. With each week that passed, he was more able to keep up with the other members. New people would come; most of them did not stay. Edwin formed relationships with the other professional businessmen. He enjoyed a special camaraderie with them. As Beckwith explained it, "Woit preached that exercise was eighty percent mental. Everyone had the ability to meet demanding challenges of the intimidating workout."

During several workouts, Edwin watched as another participant, Alex, held the bar bell weight as sweat profusely dripped off him. He always appeared to be standing in a small pool of water. Each time, he dropped his towel to soak up the perspiration. No matter how much Woit yelled at Alex, he never said a word, but always continued with the routine.

Edwin reminisced about his first workout. He thought lifting fifty-five pounds would be easy. It didn't seem like much for a physically fit person, but as everyone learned, the repetitions and altering between presses and curls made it difficult— even for many of the professional athletes who attended the workouts.

Edwin learned that most of the men who participated on a regular basis were those who had had heart attacks or other physical ailments. These men were in their late forties and fifties. Edwin felt embarrassed and ashamed that they were in better physical condition than he was.

Woit charged each member three dollars, cash, per workout. Woit expected each participant to pay either before the class or immediately afterwards. No exceptions. Edwin paid Woit nine dollars per week. Edwin estimated that each week about one hundred people worked out with Woit. Edwin learned a valuable lesson from both Joseph Carter and Dick Woit. Cash was king.

Bill kept his promise and began to teach Edwin how to trade options to make money. Edwin, for the first time, felt mentally tough. It showed in his handling of the junketers and in his craps play. Edwin quickly realized that the option market was similar to a casino—it was rigged so that the general public would lose while floor traders got rich. Aaron was the only person annoyed with Beckwith's relationship with Edwin. He never expected Edwin to last this long or be befriended by Beckwith. Jealousy, the green-eyed monster, reared its ugly head.

CHAPTER NINE

NOVEMBER, 1974

The next four months flashed by at warp speed for Edwin. He lived modestly, saved all of his money and worked out at the Lawson Y.M.C.A. religiously.

His peers were not so frugal. Their Vegas trips proved to be lucrative. Gwenn purchased a red Mustang convertible, designer clothes, a new home, and expensive jewelry from Tiffany. Herbert bought a black Mercedes Benz 280C, an 18k gold Rolex watch and Brown Stone in Evanston. Richard drove a new silver Corvette. He too bought a Rolex watch, as well as a new home in Rosemont.

Gwenn, being observant, noticed Edwin had not purchased anything substantial. Curious as to what he did with his money, she decided to invite Edwin to dinner to show him her new residence and ask him. She wondered if Edwin knew something the others did not.

Edwin sat in his cubicle when Gwenn broached the subject of inviting him to join her for dinner. "Hey Edwin, how's it going?"

"Excellent! What's up?"

"I was wondering if you'd make good on that rain check and join me for dinner at my place tonight. I'd like to show you my new digs."

"Will Herbert and Richard be joining us?"

"No, just the two of us. Is that alright?" She said with a wryly smile.

"Sure, why not. Where do you live?"

Gwenn jotted down her address on a piece of paper and handed it to him with her telephone number. "Let's say about eightish?"

Edwin, pleasantly surprised with Gwenn's invitation, looked forward to the dinner. "Is there a reason why you only invited me and not the other two?"

"Yeah. I don't like Richard. He's too crude and opinionated for my taste. Plus, he's a slob. I lost all respect for Herbert when he hired that hooker during our first trip to Vegas. I can't understand why he keeps hiring hookers. As far as I'm concerned, you can't fix stupid, you just have to live with it."

Edwin, like the other associates, all knew Herbert hired sexy women to satisfy his sexual desires. He'd learned what to do and not to do from some of the other junketeers who indulged themselves while away from home.

"Got it." Edwin said. He wasn't sure what else to say.

She eyed Edwin as he left. He intrigued her. He kept mostly to himself. Although she never again asked him how much he made, she knew for certain he did better than the rest of them. Tonight, she made it her mission to find out what he did with his money.

★ ★ ★

Just before Edwin arrived, Gwenn set the table with fine china, wine glasses and candlesticks. She lit the candles. The flames flickered to and fro, flickering every now and then. Every once in a while, the flame would hiss, and black smoke rose for a brief moment into the air. A bottle of Pinot Noir sat on the table.

Edwin arrived on time. Gwenn invited him inside her home. "Come on in. I want to show you my humble abode."

"Thank you." Edwin noticed every detail of Gwenn's decorum. As she showed him around, he said, "Very impressive. Who'd you use to help decorate, it's gorgeous?"

"A friend recommended this amazing interior decorator. I love what she did with the place."

After the tour, she asked, "Will you open the bottle of wine, please?"

Edwin uncorked the bottle and poured each of them a glass. He sniffed the purple stained cork. It had a faint floral smell of roses and violet, and a fruity aroma.

"Go ahead and have a seat," she said.

Edwin complied. He sat as she served the meal. Gwenn had prepared a simple baked chicken with a lemon sauce, baked potato, green beans and mixed greens salad.

Before they ate, Edwin raised his glass. "To profitable journeys."

Gwenn also raised her glass, "To profitable journeys." They clinked their glasses and each took a sip of wine.

"This is superb," Edwin complimented Gwenn. "Where did you learn how to cook?"

"My mother taught me."

After a few minutes of small talk and having given Edwin a few moments to enjoy his meal, Gwenn asked, "I noticed that you haven't purchased anything with your money. Why?"

Edwin almost choked on his food. He finished chewing, and swallowed hard, before he spoke. "I'm investing it. I don't believe this good fortune will continue. There is something odd about Mr. Joseph Carter. I tried to do some research on him. I couldn't find anything about the man. He doesn't have a past. Besides, I don't want to spend the rest of my life babysitting his junketeers."

"Where are you putting your money? In the stock market?"

"No, my goal is to purchase a seat on the Board of Trade. I've been doing some research about traders. It appears that a floor trader has the deck stacked in his favor, much like us with the casinos."

"How so?" Gwenn became intrigued with Edwin and his knowledge of being a floor trader.

Edwin explained how a floor trader made his money. He said, "If done correctly, it's a lucrative profession with little risk. The way it works, a floor trader watches the trend in any given commodity." He gazed at Gwenn as he talked. Was she interested? "Commodity futures price movements are measured in a unit called a tick. In other words, a tick represents the minimum increment in which prices changed. Each commodity has a tick size that is specific to the instrument." He paused to see if she had any questions, but she remained silent, her blue eyes wide and curious.

Edwin continued, giving an example to Gwenn. "A corn contract represented five thousand bushels. The tick size for corn is twenty-five cents per bushel or twelve dollars and fifty cents per contract. If the price of corn moved in the direction you *bet* on, up or down; you made twelve dollars and fifty cents per contract. Most profitable traders bought and sold contracts to make two ticks, or twenty-five dollars per contract per trade. If you wanted to make more money, you made more trades or purchased more contracts. Because a floor trader had immediate access to price changes as they occurred, they could buy and sell quickly, ahead of the retail customer. This is known as *front running*. Plus, they paid only a tiny fee for each trade, wherein the general public paid a broker a commission. The broker's commission eats up most of the profit of a retail customer. They have to assume more risk to make less money."

Gwenn's head was spinning. Edwin could see the confusion on her face and stopped speaking. "Oh, Edwin, this is far too complicated for me. How much is a seat on the Board of Trade anyways?"

"About one hundred and ten-thousand dollars. Plus, you need money to make trades."

"How did you ever get interested in options?"

"My ex-girlfriend's father worked at the Board of Trade for a floor trader. I'm not sure exactly what he did. He had a seat at one time, but made some bad trades and lost everything. Just as in playing craps and what we do in Vegas, you have to make right the decisions and use sound judgment. Apparently, my ex's father did not exercise good judgment."

Gwenn, surprised that Edwin shared his past with her, as this was the first time that he had opened up. She never knew he had a girlfriend or why they were no longer together. She wanted to learn more about Edwin's relationship. "Whatever happened to your girlfriend—what's her name?"

"Her name is Valerie. She wanted to marry someone who had a lot of money."

Edwin's voice changed. He became serious talking about Valerie. Gwenn sensed that Valerie hurt him.

"Valerie dumped me because I didn't get a job right after graduation. When I called her to tell her Carter hired me, she said it was too late. She'd started dating someone else. I made it my mission right then to become extremely wealthy and make her regret her decision."

Edwin's demeanor became dark and bitter. Gwenn got frightened the way he got so upset about Valerie. She did not like how quickly angered and enraged Edwin had become. She surmised he still loved Valerie and was deeply hurt.

She immediately changed the subject. "What other investments are you making?"

Edwin snapped out of his belligerent frame of mind and smiled. "Actually, I'm seriously thinking about purchasing a McDonald's franchise."

"A McDonald's franchise? Why in the world would you want to do that?"

"Why not? Besides, from the looks of this place you're enjoying our Vegas spoils."

Gwenn smiled. "Yeah, right? You probably have more money than Richard, Herbert, and me put together. Look, I bought this home and made a large down payment to have a small mortgage. I paid cash for my car."

"I hope you put some away for taxes," Edwin said sarcastically.

"Yep, I'm a rich bitch and enjoying every moment."

Edwin laughed. He then helped Gwenn clear the dishes. She was not used to having a man help her with domestic chores. After helping to clean up from dinner, Gwenn suggested the two of them sit in her living room. She wanted to talk to Edwin and find out more about him.

Initially, Gwenn had not been interested in Edwin in a romantic sort of way. She did not find him physically attractive, even though he had toned down and looked to be in excellent physical condition from his work out at the Y. But the more she spoke with him, the more interested she became. And not because of how much money he had. She had her own money. No, Gwenn liked that Edwin was educated and could talk about things most people never thought about. After all, how many people, let alone a twenty-three-year old, thought about options or purchasing a McDonald's franchise? She could now tell that Edwin had many layers to him and she wanted to get to know him more deeply.

"So, where do you lived?"

"I still live in my studio apartment."

"You're kidding, right?"

"Nope. I'm still in the same place as when I attended school and had no money."

"I don't understand. Why would you want to live in such a small place?" She pressed the issue. "You can live anywhere you want with what we make!"

He looked her in the eyes boldly. "Because I want to invest my money and have it work for me rather than worrying about Carter and the junket business. Doesn't it bother you that we are stealing from the casino and nobody seems to care?"

"No, not really, I hadn't thought about it much. I'm just happy to earn more than ten thousand dollars each month and travel to Vegas. But, I think I understand what you're saying."

Edwin stood up. "It's late. I'd better get going. Thank you for the delicious meal."

"Do you want to stay the night?" she asked.

Edwin smiled. "As much as I'd like to, it's probably best if I don't. I'm not sure dating someone at work is such a good idea. Besides, I think it's the alcohol talking and you'll regret it in the morning."

"Yeah, you're probably right. Just to let you know, I don't like being rejected." Gwenn escorted Edwin to the door and gave him a long passionate kiss good night. "Are you sure you don't want to stay?" She squeezed his ass.

"Oh, you're such a tease. Thanks, but no," Edwin said.

"Why? Are you still thinking about Valerie? Get over it already."

Edwin turned away from her. "I'll see you tomorrow." He left pondering the events of the night. He found Gwenn attractive and wondered why he did not sleep with her. Deep down, he still loved Valerie.

Edwin had not seen nor heard from Valerie since she slammed the receiver down the last time he called her. He wondered about her and her new beau. He had not thought about Valerie until Gwenn broached the subject. It pained him to think of her and why she did not want to be with him any longer. Her father never mentioned anything about Valerie and he chose not to ask him about her. All in all, it was probably for the best.

As Edwin made his way home on the train, he began to reflect on his life. Traveling to and from Vegas every other week along with working out at the Y and learning about trading options on the floor of the Board of Trade had occupied all of his time. It left only a few moments for a social life. Tonight was the first time he'd engaged in any social activity in months. He grinned, grateful that Gwenn invited him to her home for dinner and wanted to sleep with him. It was a nice change of pace from his dullish routine. He felt lonely.

CHAPTER TEN

Richard arrived at the office early in the morning, shortly after six o'clock. The room previously used for training, had been transformed into an office with four cubicles. Each associate had their own work station. Richard hung a few photos and quotes to keep him inspired as he handled the daily drudgery of calling junketeers. He made a fresh pot of coffee and began listening to his messages and take notes.

Gwenn arrived shortly after Richard. She put her purse down at her work station. She decorated it with some photos, a small potted fern and a few knickknacks; souvenirs from Vegas. She leaned over the cubicle and greeted Richard with her usual salutation, "Hey tricky Dickey, what's up?"

Richard smiled and replied, "My pole, you want a ride?"

"You're a pig. No thanks."

Richard, not the least ashamed of his crude remark said, "I made coffee."

"Great, thanks."

Gwenn made her way to the small kitchenette and poured herself a cup of the black brew. She looked forward to her morning jolt of caffeine.

Back at her cubicle she began to make phone calls to her list of junketeers. "Hello, Neil, this is Gwenn with Global Travel. I'm calling to confirm your itinerary for your Vegas trip this weekend."

"Hi Gwenn, thanks for the call. What's the schedule?"

"We depart on United Flight 621 at 1 a.m. and arrive in Vegas at approximately 6 a.m. Vegas time. Do you need any show tickets or restaurant reservations?"

Neil laughed. "Gwenn, you know I'm a gambling junkie."

"Okay Neil, I'll see you at the airport on Thursday night."

Gwenn looked at her notes about Neil. A compulsive gambler, he would gamble on anything and everything for fifteen to eighteen hours a day. It didn't matter if Neil won or lost. Being rich, he seemed to care less about the money. He had a fifty-thousand-dollar line of credit with the casino. The action seemed to energized him. She once observed that once he started playing, he had no control over himself. He rarely would go to his room to change clothes. He didn't care about seeing shows or eating at any restaurants. According to the casino's records, Neil consistently lost on each trip. Gwenn attributed his losing each time to the fact that no person could play for that many hours, without making bad betting decisions. She noted that Neil ate one meal a day, and usually he had it served to him at the blackjack table.

Before making her next call, she overheard Richard talking to one of his junketeers. It was pretty much the same. He confirmed the flight number and departure time with his client. He then asked if the guests needed show tickets or dinner reservations. Invariably, most of them wanted show tickets, dinner reservations, or both.

A few of the male junketeers would hit on Gwenn or make inappropriate gestures towards her. They quickly found out that she was one tough bitch who would just as soon gouge their eyes out then spend any alone time with them. On one occasion a guest got too drunk and rowdy. She had casino security escort him to the airport. Despite profusely apologizing to her and Carter, he was never allowed on another junket.

Herbert and Edwin arrived at the office within moments of each other. Once settled, they began their routine of calling their guests. It was mentally draining keeping track of each person's particular needs and wants. The associates trained by Carter made each guest feel important. If the associate failed to coddle the whims of the guests, they would need to answer to Carter for the short falling. After all, if it weren't for them, they wouldn't have a job—albeit, a very lucrative job.

Shortly before one p.m., Gwenn stood up and leaned over to Edwin's cubicle. "Got time for lunch?"

"Is it that time already? Yeah, let's get out of here. I need a break."

Richard overheard Gwenn's invitation to Edwin for lunch. "Hey, where you guys going? Can I join you?"

Edwin said, "Sure. We're heading over to Berghoff."

Richard slipped a note in front of Herbert as he spoke with a client. Herbert motioned that he didn't want to join the others for lunch.

Berghoff, a Chicago landmark, opened in 1898. The iconic restaurant served German-American cuisine and steins of their own brewed beer. Located on Adams Street in the heart of downtown Chicago, it was only a short walk from Carter's office.

The three associates were seated at a table. Gwenn ordered the classic Berghoff steak salad; Edwin ordered sauerbraten and Richard chose to have a Reuben sandwich with mashed potatoes. Gwenn also ordered a Diet Coke, Edwin just had a glass of water with lemon, while Richard ordered a stein of Berghoff's famous brewed beer.

Edwin felt awkward being with Richard at lunch. They hadn't spent much time together, as Richard usually spent his time with Herbert.

"So Gwenn, how come you don't hang around with Herbert and me anymore?" Richard started the conversation.

"Nothing personal, but you're boring. Not to mention you're a male chauvinist pig."

Richard took her comments in stride and smiling, said, "Tell me how you really feel."

Edwin sat quietly listening to Gwenn and Richard banter back and forth.

Once the food arrived, the three ate in relative silence. Each felt an uneasiness being together. Other than the first day they all met, the four never took the time to learn about each other. Only Gwenn made the effort to get to know Edwin. Edwin and she decided to keep their relationship private. Richard or Herbert didn't need to know they were friends outside of work. After all, it wasn't like it was a romantic relationship. At least not yet.

After lunch, Gwenn, Edwin and Richard returned to the office. Herbert sat at his desk eating a sandwich. They all spent the rest of the afternoon doing the same doldrums of calling junketeers.

CHAPTER ELEVEN

On a blustery cold January day in Chicago, the wind swirled between the buildings, howling like a wild animal in pain. Valerie Taylor, though layered in warm clothing and a full length fur coat, felt chilled to the bone. The wind in Chicago could cut through a person like a knife. She'd only walked a few blocks through the streets covered with grayish, black slush. Everything looked gloomy to her.

Once she entered the restaurant next to the Board of Trade, she immediately she saw her father sitting in a booth. He waved to her. She hesitated before she removed her fur coat and sat down. The heat in the eatery warming her chilled body felt good.

"How are you, daddy?"

"I'm doing fine, sweetie. Look at you. You look stunning! How is everything with Johnny?"

"Oh, daddy, Johnny is the best thing that I could have wished for. He bought me this beautiful coat as a Christmas present. He lets me drive his Corvette, and he's paying for my apartment. He told me he doesn't want me to work or worry about money."

Aaron Taylor raised an eyebrow, his face doleful, with a haunted, hollow expression. "What are his intentions with you? Have you discussed marriage?"

"Yes, of course, why do you ask?"

"Because, the way you just talked about how Johnny treats you, it's as if you're his mistress."

"How dare you say such a horrible thing!"

Aaron's lips tightened and his eyes narrowed. "I just want to make sure you're happy, and that he's not using you."

"No, daddy." Valerie said emphatically. "He's said he loves me and that he wants to marry me. He's wants to wait until May to surprise his parents. It will be his father's fiftieth birthday, and he wanted to surprise him with our engagement announcement."

Valerie's father let out a low whistle and smiled. He kissed his daughter's cheek. "I guess I under estimated this Johnny. I'm so glad for you." He had a broad grin. "So what do you do all day?"

"I'll shop, or go to the gym to work out. Sometimes I'll meet my girlfriends for lunch. Other days I'll prepare dinner for Johnny. I don't know. I keep busy. Johnny says once we're married, he wants to buy a house in the suburbs. He's thinking maybe in Northbrook or Highland Park."

The waiter interrupted the conversation. "Would the lady like to order a drink, or are you ready to order your meal?"

Valerie ordered a glass of Chardonnay and a Caesar salad with grilled chicken. Her father ordered a grilled salmon and baked potato.

Once the waiter left, Valerie and her father carried on their conversation. Aaron made the mistake of mentioning Edwin. "Has Edwin tried to call you?"

"Not that I know of, why?"

"No reason. Did you know he's working for a junket outfit? He's making a lot of money. He asked me to introduce him to my boss."

"Did you?"

"Yeah, I did."

The waiter brought the glass of Chardonnay and placed it in front of Valerie. After she took two sips, she asked with feigned interest, "And?"

"Bill Beckwith told Edwin he would teach him how to trade options if he worked out with him at the Y. The son-of-a-bitch.

Edwin not only works out regularly with Bill, but he's teaching him the ins and outs of floor trading."

"Oh? So why does that bother you?" Valerie wondered why her father would care.

"I don't know. It just does. I'm pissed because I couldn't keep up with the other fellows and stopped going to the workouts. I know Edwin is making some great connections. A bunch of pro athletes, politicians, lawyers, doctors. You name it, they're talking to him."

Valerie, thankful the waiter had brought their food, took a forkful of the salad and said, "Delicious. How's yours?"

"Excellent." He said, as he put another forkful into his mouth.

"I'll tell you what, daddy, I'll find out what Edwin is doing and give you a full report. I bet it's not much. He's so socially awkward and boorish."

Aaron chuckled. "Yeah, you're probably right."

◆ ◆ ◆

The black sedan parked across the street from Edwin's apartment had two male occupants. They drank coffee and ate donuts trying to stay awake by making small talk. They watched as Edwin went in to the apartment carrying his gym bag.

Edwin didn't know he was under surveillance. He went through his normal routine of reading and studying the information Beckwith taught him. He wanted to master being a floor trader. He knew deep down he could make more money than his wildest dreams at the exchange. His heart still bruised from how Valerie had treated him, finished reading, turned in for the night and went to sleep.

The next morning, another black sedan parked in the same spot across the street as the first. Two other men watched as Edwin walked to the "L" and boarded the south bound train. The two men abandoned their vehicle to follow him. Edwin carried his gym bag and brown bag lunch.

Once Edwin arrived at his stop, he left the train and walked to the Global Enterprises office. The two men followed only as far the office door. They didn't enter into his place of work. They waited, watching the door. Edwin did not leave his office all day. Finally, at five p.m. Edwin left work and went to the Lawson YMCA.

The people watching Edwin's every move expanded their observation to Las Vegas. They noted nothing unusual. They had no idea however, how much Edwin bought-in for at the craps. They kept their distance to keep from being spotted. Nor did they see how much he collected at the cashier's cage. Edwin always handled his money discreetly.

After six weeks of the same drudgery, the P.I. filed a report with Johnny Accardi. Johnny reviewed every detail. *Boring* was Johnny's first impression of Edwin.

Johnny called Valerie's father to fill him in. "Aaron, Johnny Accardi. I've got the report on Mr. Goldberg."

"And?" Aaron waited, anxious to hear the details.

"I don't understand why you thought this douchebag warranted investigating. He's a nothing, a no body."

"Really? Huh. I'd like to read the report myself."

"I'm telling you. This guy is a nothing. He goes to work, goes home, and works out. He has no social life. He doesn't spend any money. He lives like a pauper. Hell, even in Vegas he's a stiff."

"Humor me please," Aaron said. "Let me look through the report myself. I'll sleep better. And, I do appreciate everything you've done and do for Valerie."

"Okay, I'll have a messenger deliver you a copy this afternoon."

Once Aaron got the report he read every note and detail. He examined every photograph. Nothing. Edwin's life amounted to absolutely nothing. Aaron threw the file on the floor. *I know that little prick is up to something*, he thought. His jaw hurt from clenching his teeth and he had a burning sensation in his stomach.

Aaron approached his boss about Edwin. Maybe Beckwith would be able to shed some light on the mysterious Mr. Goldberg. He waited until after hours to talk to Bill. "Hi Bill, can I ask you a question about Edwin?"

"Sure, what do you want to know?"

"How's he doing learning the business?"

"Edwin, he's doing excellent. He's a bright young man; polite, nice and sincere. I think he could make a lot of money as a trader if he weren't so naive. I'm not surprised your daughter dumped him."

"Yeah, but does the schmuck have any money to trade for his own account?"

"I don't know. Why the sudden interest?"

"Oh, just curious."

"Oh, well, all I can tell you is that I see him during the workout and we meet a few hours every Tuesday evening to talk about charting the various commodities and the best way to trade."

"Does he know how things truly work in the pits?"

"No, not yet. He still believes we have to chart to trade."

"Are you going to let him in on how you actually make money?"

"I'm not sure. Maybe. We'll see."

"Okay, thanks. Sorry to have bothered you."

Aaron walked out of Beckwith's office satisfied Edwin Goldberg was a loser who would never amount to anything. The pain in his jaw subsided.

Valerie walked into Johnny's office. She had a big smile. "Hi honey. How's it going?"

"Hi Valerie. Why is you dad suspicious of Edwin and why do you want to know so much about him."

"What? What are you talking about?"

"I got the report back on Edwin Goldberg. He's a nothing."

"Johnny, I'm sorry. I wished I'd never asked you to spy on Edwin. I only did it because my father inquired about him. I could care less about the jerk." Tears welled-up in her eyes.

"I think we should postpone the announcement of our engagement," Johnny said.

"Why? I told you I have no interest in Edwin."

"I'm not sure you don't have feelings for the guy. With everything I've given you, I don't understand why you dated him in the first place. I just want to be sure you're over him"

"I'll never understand why my father cared about him to begin with. They were never close. I love you." Valerie hugged Johnny and gave him a long passionate kiss.

"Okay. I'll see you later tonight. I've got work to finish."

"See you at home tonight. I love you." She walked out of the office still upset with her father.

CHAPTER TWELVE

MARCH, 1975

On a few occasions, Carter travelled with the junketeers to observe how his associates handled themselves with them and to watch their play at the tables. During one trip he introduced Gwenn, Edwin, Herbert and Richard to Big Julie.

"This is my New York counter-part with the junket business," Carter began. The group enjoyed a nice meal at a secluded steakhouse off the Strip. Carter did not want any of his junketeers to interrupt the private meeting. Big Julie, was not pleased with Carter's choice of restaurants. He preferred to be close to his junketeers in the event they needed him.

After a few glasses of wine, Big Julie began to relax and tell the associates how he met Carter. He then told an interesting story about one of his junketeers.

Big Julie began, "Joe Bernstein was seventy-six years young. He's been married to his wife Rachel for more than fifty years. At his fiftieth wedding anniversary party I asked Joe how he managed to stay married for fifty years. Joe looked at me and said, 'When Rachel and I got married, we went to the Grand Canyon for our honeymoon. We took a day-long horseback ride down the canyon trail. At the start of our trip, my wife's horse would not move. So she got off the horse, looked it straight in the eye and in a stern voice said, "That's one." She then got back on the horse and we made it about half-way down the trail when the horse stopped and again, refused to move. My wife got off the horse a second time, looked it straight in the eye and said, "That's two." She got back on the horse and we made it to the bottom of the trail. The horse refused to move once we were at the bottom. So my wife got off the horse again, looked it straight in the eye and said, "That's three." She then pulled out a pistol and shot the horse in the head. I was horrified, so I asked my wife why she shot the horse. She smiled and said, "That's one."'"

The grouped laughed at Big Julie's joke.

Richard asked Big Julie about his career. "So Big Julie, how did you get interested in the junket business?"

"I'm a degenerate gambler," Big Julie began. "I got to Las Vegas by sheer accident. The first time I went to Las Vegas was in August, 1955 to attend the wedding of my close friend, Ash Resnick. Ash had moved from New York to Las Vegas as an executive at the El Cortez Hotel. He met a showgirl from the Tropicana and brought her back home to New York to meet his friends and relatives. Ash asked me to fly back with him to Vegas to attend his wedding. So I did. When we got to Vegas, Ash said to me, 'Go take a shower and get dressed. We're going to a party.' The party was at George Duckworth's home. George was one of the owners of the Riviera. The other guests at Duckworth's home were all very influential people, owners, executives and floor managers. The party went from six o'clock in the evening to nine o'clock the next morning. I never saw so much food, booze and beautiful women. This was my introduction to Vegas.

"I was in the jewelry business. I brought a case of my jewelry along with me. The next day, Ash took me around town to introduce me to various casino owners. Beldon Katleman, the owner of the El Rancho, as well as a few other owners bought some jewelry from me. I sold out my inventory.

"Two months later, the first week of December, I went back to Vegas with everything I could get my hands on. Immediately I discovered that the first three weeks of December in Vegas were the slowest weeks of the year. It was like a crypt. You could have driven a Mack truck through the town and not hit anybody. The place was deserted, a ghost town. I went from casino to casino—all of them were empty."

"So what did you do?" Richard asked.

"I went back to New York. I told all of my friends about Vegas and its glamour. One day, while preparing for my next trip to Vegas, out of the blue, I got a long distance call from one of my friends. He tells me he has thirteen friends who are all gamblers that want to fly to Vegas to see with their own eyes if everything I claimed about the place was true."

"So I called Katleman at the El Rancho and asked him to reserve thirteen rooms for my high roller friends. At the end of our five days all of my friends were busted—broke. But they had a blast. The El Rancho probably won one hundred grand from my New York friends and they easily dropped another two hundred grand or more around the town."

"These were the types of players the casino owners are always looking for to patronize their establishments. Without realizing it, I steered my friends to certain casinos and restaurants. In the five days we were there I helped turn the three weeks in December from a losing proposition into a profitable one.

"In those days, the hotels only picked up the hotel bill for the highest players, but when Katleman heard my guys were all busted, he raised his hands and said, 'They'll be my guests. You can tell them it was my pleasure.' Before anyone had heard of a junket, I had in fact, run one. I did well too, because before the guys lost all of their money, they bought a lot of my trinkets, such as rings, necklaces and bracelets to take home for their wives and girlfriends.

"Fast forward to May, 1962. My friends George Duckworth, Charlie Rich, and Sid Wyman bought into the Dunes. They asked me to become a part-time representative for the Dunes at one thousand dollars per month. My duties were to encourage my New York friends to stay at there. And since I went back and forth anyway they wanted me to pick up money owed on markers from the general East Coast area."

Big Julie paused and took a sip of wine. For an extended moment his eyes remained steady and unblinking. The smile on his face transformed from cheerful to dismal. He said, "The Dunes, unfortunately, was a dump, a real toilet. I felt I took money under false pretenses. In December, I asked for a meeting with the owners. I got the idea to run junkets from the Flamingo. They were the first Las Vegas casino to run junkets—but strictly on a seasonal basis. Bernie Cohen ran the junkets every four months or so. I knew as many people as Cohen and I knew I could do what he did.

"I persuaded the owners to give me a chance on my idea. I told them it would cost them twenty-five thousand dollars to charter a plane, plus whatever it cost for the hotel to feed them and give them their rooms for free. Charlie Rich opposed the idea. He kept the other owners from implementing my plan. But, when he became ill, and wasn't around, the other owners reluctantly agreed. I promised them I'd bring a hundred and twenty guests. We were over-booked." Big Julie's face exploded into a radiant smile, his eyes sparkling. "A hundred fifty of my friends all wanted to go. Initially, the owners balked paying for the extra plane seats. But by Sunday afternoon, the casino had raked in more than six hundred-thousand dollars. I was a hero to them."

Gwenn interrupted, "Excuse me, did I hear you correctly? Did you say 'six hundred-thousand dollars'?"

"Yeah, I did. Six hundred grand."

Gwenn sat stunned at the amount Big Julie said the casinos had taken from the New York guest. "How is that possible?"

Big Julie smiled. He looked directly at her and said, "On average, each junketeer lost six thousand dollars. I have more than a hundred and fifty junketeers on each trip. You do the math.

"I ran another junket in March, 1963. The casino did almost as well. Eventually, they realized the gold mine they had in hand. To this day, they never had a losing junket. The casinos generally take-in between five and six hundred-thousand dollars each weekend I run a junket. So yeah, they're happy to pay me, and let me tell you, it's a lot more than a mere thousand dollars a month."

Everyone sat silent listening to Big Julie and how he got started. They were awe struck by the amount of money people lost and the fact that they were not unhappy about losing. Big Julie told them, "If I can give you one piece of advice it's that the most important part is that they all had a great time. People do not get upset if they lose, so long as they had a good time. To them, it's entertainment money."

Gwenn, Edwin, Richard and Herbert realized the amount of money they took from the casinos each trip was a small pittance compared to what the casinos took from the junketeers. Their eyes were opened to the enormity of the operation.

Big Julie saw Edwin's expression of mixed emotion on his face. "Look," he said, "Irwin Gordon, the pit boss at the Dunes, did not feel ashamed taking the junketeers' money. Irwin told me, 'Cater to a winner, leave a loser alone. What am I going to tell him, that I'm sorry? He knows I'm not sorry. That's what we're here for; to take his money.'

"You must understand that the owners of the casinos are callous people. They're in business to make a profit. They're only concerned about how much they can take from you. They are in the gambling business; they can't afford to be soft-hearted. Think of it like an adult Disneyland. Parents don't care how much the little rodent sucks from their wallets so long as their kids are having a great time. That's how Vegas view the junketeers."

Herbert, saw Big Julie living his dream. He wanted to be like Big Julie. Beautiful women, people admiring and respecting him and treating him like royalty. Not to mention Big Julie being connected to powerful people. Joseph Carter sensed that Herbert became infatuated by Big Julie's stories. Herbert asked, "How did you and Mr. Carter become partners?"

Carter spoke before Big Julie had a chance to answer. "I met Big Julie in Europe in May, 1972. We were both traveling on a North Atlantic cruise that took us from Lisbon, Spain to several ports in France, including Bordeaux, and then on to Dublin, Ireland. It was an incredible holiday. I sampled the most delectable cuisine and spirits of Spain and France. They had daily wine tasting, and I treated my palate to Europe's best seafood."

Carter sat, dazed, remembering his past. Big Julie smiled, and said, "We were seated at the same table for dinner. The conversation revolved around, what else, craps and Vegas. Go ahead, Carter, tell them what you told me about money being the inventory of Vegas."

Carter swirled the Merlot in his wine glass before taking a swig. He took a drag from his cigarette and watched the smoke curl above his head before he spoke. "The kind of business Big Julie operates is based on credit. Back in the early days, a player needed cash to be comped by the casinos. A comp is the free room, food, beverages, and shows. Big Julie persuaded the casinos to give credit to the players. In Nevada, a gambling debt is legally uncollectable. The Nevada legislature made gambling a 'privileged business', with various extra legal rights including the right to bar a player at any time. The legislature felt compelled to follow conventional morality and passed a law that a gambling debt was a debt of honor because the marker isn't worth the paper it's written on."

Big Julie chimed in, "After all is said and done, the only contract you have is a handshake."

Carter continued his rendition of the gambling debt being unenforceable in Vegas. "At one time, the lawyers for the casinos got the brilliant idea of having customers sign a note for a cash advance. They reasoned that this would give them a written record that would enable them to collect from delinquent players. Not so. The courts wouldn't allow it. Undaunted, the casinos came up with a marker that is made out exactly like a check. Should a player fail to repay the marker, the casino

would simply put it through the bank, and if there were suffi-
cient funds in the bank, the marker would be satisfied. If there
were insufficient funds, the casino would get paid what was in
the player's bank account and turn the balance over to a col-
lection agency, or worse, they send Guido to collect."

Edwin had a sick feeling in his stomach listening to Carter
describe the marker policy of Vegas. He wasn't sure if the
markers he had previously signed would eventually be collected or if they were truly destroyed as Carter had told them.
Edwin thought, *All of us have given Carter cash each time we
returned from Vegas. I have no record to prove I gave him anything. Are we being used by him?*

Gwenn glanced over at Edwin. He sensed she had the same
gut wrenching feeling as he did. Herbert and Richard remained
oblivious to what Carter had just conveyed to the group.

Carter paused for a moment and took another swig of the
grape nectar. Big Julie allowed Carter more time to reflect and
interjected, "My junket business is like any other business. As
with any other business, the inventory has to keep revolving;
old merchandise out, new merchandise in. Simple, yes? By law,
the casino must keep enough cash in the cage to cover any
losses. Depending on the day of the week, this amount can
fluctuate between half a million and a cool million dollars.
All cash. If a player wins, all he has to do is walk up to the
cage and collect his money. If the player loses and has taken
out a marker, then the casino must be able to collect. Sometimes, players have to liquidate stocks or move funds around
to pay their marker. The casinos understand this. That's why
they give players a ten-day grace period, because if the money
doesn't keep revolving, the casino is in trouble. If the casino's
marker inventory goes longer than two weeks and they don't
collect, the amount can become astronomical."

Carter snapped out of his stupor and back to reality. He said,
"The reason Big Julie is successful where other junket businesses
have only been moderately successful is because he checks out
his people with intense scrutiny before they are allowed to

travel with his group. In order for a person to become eligible, the new applicant must be recommended by somebody who has been on a junket before and whom Julie knows he can trust. By insisting on a recommendation, if the player fails to repay his or her marker, Big Julie calls up the person who made the recommendation. This friend who made the referral will always call the person who owes the money and tell them 'You know you have embarrassed me. You made me look bad. I'm never going to be able to recommend anyone again.' And the referent will help collect the money."

Gwenn interrupted the conversation, "What about our guests, do you make them go through the same process as Big Julie?"

Carter smiled. He knew exactly why Gwenn asked. "No, I have a different method as to how our guests are eligible to be on our trips. But don't worry, that is my headache to worry about."

Gwenn decided not to push the issue. The pit of her stomach gnawed at her like some animal rumbling around inside her gut.

"Speaking of guests, we should probably be getting back to our casinos to make sure our guests are behaving themselves and not having too much fun," she said.

Herbert, Richard, Gwenn, and Edwin all chuckled as they each excused themselves from the table. Big Julie eyed Carter with a beam of gratification, "You have a great bunch of associates. I can see why your business is expanding so rapidly."

"Thank you," Carter said. Deep down in his twisted mind he thought, *If you only knew.*

CHAPTER THIRTEEN

Shortly after midnight, Joseph Carter sat at small table, swirling his scotch on the rocks. The air in the lounge at Trader Vic's in the Palmer House, stale from all of the cigarette smoke, lingered about. He was waiting to meet Johnny Accardi. The dimly lit room hid the customers' faces. A female vocalist in the band sang *Killing Me Softly* by Roberta Flack in the background. Only a few of the patrons paid any attention.

Johnny arrived fifteen minutes late. "You're late. Where have you been?" Carter asked in a condescending voice.

"I was taking care of a few personal matters. Sorry for the inconvenience. Besides, I wanted to make sure everything is in order," Johnny replied.

Carter, not amused with Johnny's demeanor and lack of respect, placed a large brown envelope full of cash in Johnny's lap. "You got something for me?"

Johnny placed the briefcase he carried next to Carter's chair. "Thank you. It's a pleasure doing business with you." With that, he got up to leave.

Carter said, "What, you're not going to have a drink with me?"

"Not tonight Joe, my girlfriend is waiting for me at my apartment. We've taken care of our business, now it's time for me to have a little pleasure."

★ ★ ★

Valerie Taylor sat on the corner of the circular bed in the elegant bedroom at Johnny's apartment. She wore a sexy red negligee revealing her large, well formed breast. She dabbed Channel

No.5 perfume on her wrist and neck and poured herself a glass of champagne, enjoying the bubbly brew when Johnny arrived.

"Where have you been?" she quipped having grown tired of being alone.

"I had to take care of business. Here, this should make you feel better. Shopping money." He tossed a wad of hundred-dollar bills at her. There was five thousand dollars in the wad.

Valerie smiled. She planted a long adoring kiss on Johnny's lips. He immediately became aroused. Within a few minutes the two were groping each other and ripping off their clothes. It was a night full of passionate love making.

$ $ $

The next morning, Johnny went to Carter's office. He felt he needed to clear the air about their arrangement. He got off the elevator and opened the door to the office. The receptionist greeted Johnny. "May I help you sir?"

Johnny, smugly said, "Tell Joe that I'm here to see him."

Joe heard Johnny in the reception area and came out from his office. "Johnny, good to see you. Come on in."

Meanwhile, Edwin had heard the commotion up front and walked from his cubicle to see what the ruckus was. He caught a quick glimpse of Johnny before Joe's door closed.

Carter sat in the chair behind his desk. "How can I help you Johnny?"

"That briefcase I gave you last night with the markers. The markers are for your employees. Am I right?"

"Yeah, so what of it?"

"Well I finally figured out who you are, Mr. Bazzoli."

Carter remained silent.

"I want a larger piece of the action. If my uncle finds out that I'm your inside man, I'm dead. I'm thinking about making other arrangements for someone else to handle the markers."

Carter sat quietly. Leaning forward in his chair, he rested his forearms on his desk. His finger tips touched together as if he was praying. He then intertwined his fingers together and said,

"Johnny, give my regards to Anthony Sindler. Your threats mean nothing to me. Do you think for one moment I give a rat's ass about those kids? Now get the fuck out of my office, you greedy little punk!"

The shit-eating grin on Johnny's face vanished. He realized that he'd messed with the wrong person. "My apologies; let's just pretend this conversation never happened." With that, Johnny rose from his seat and immediately departed Carter's office.

Carter took a drag from a cigarette and watched the smoke circle above his head. His right eye twitched at the thought of being shaken down by Johnny. He sat back, closed his weary eyes and reflected back to how he had gotten into this mess.

Carter enjoyed retirement. But Big Julie, always persuasive, convinced him to become his Chicago partner. Once Carter learned about the junket business, he made some inquiries about his friend and former boss of the Outfit, Anthony Sindler.

Sindler, agreed to meet Carter for dinner at a secluded place to discuss business. It was risky for Sindler to be seen with a "dead man."

"How are you my old friend?" Joe started the conversation.

"I'm doing well. And you? Where have you been hiding yourself?"

"Accardi still looking for me?"

"Yeah. If he finds out I'm talking with you . . ."

"I understand. What's going on in Vegas?"

"The families are hurting. Cash from the casinos is drying up and the Fed's cracking down."

"Do you know of someone who might help me with my junket business?" Carter asked.

Sindler raised an eyebrow. "Junket business? What junket business?"

Carter explained his fortuitous chance encounter with Big Julie and how he operated a legitimate, extremely profitable business for the casinos from New York. "Big Julie asked me to be his partner," Carter said.

"Joe, come on, be straight with me. What is it you really want?"

Carter looked heavenward, then directly at Sindler. His lips curled upward as his mouth formed a smirk. "I need someone to help markers vanish like we did in the old days."

"Are you outta your fucking mind?"

"No. It's a perfect cover. Besides, I have four eager beavers who don't know they're being used. Come on. You gotta know someone."

"Ah, I know the perfect person. Johnny Accardi, he's Tazio Accardi's nephew. He's volatile, often out of control, and likely to cause a lot of inadvertent damage. He's a hot head, but I think he may be interested."

"How much is Johnny involved with the casino business?"

Sindler knew the kind of information Carter looked for. "He isn't involved with any of the operations, but he has unfettered access to all of the casinos and their employees."

Carter had all of the information he needed to know. "Can you introduce me to Johnny? I'd like to confer with him about some ideas for my junket business."

Sindler did not approve of Carter's true motives for wanting to meet with Johnny Accardi, but, he was old and set with the family. They'd taken care of him and his family and rewarded him handsomely for his loyalty. "Yeah, I'll make the arrangements. Meet him tomorrow at the park bench near the entrance of Lincoln Park Zoo at noon. Keep me the fuck out of this."

Sindler delivered as promised. Johnny Accardi showed up at noon to talk with Carter. "Joseph Carter, my name is Johnny Accardi. Mr. Sindler told me you wanted to discuss some ideas about your Vegas junket business."

It was a warm spring day in Chicago, the temperature a pleasant seventy-eight degrees. The sun shone bright at noon. Carter dressed in a white shirt, black suit pants and a tie, kept his fedora on to keep the sun from his eyes. "Yes, I do."

The two men sat on the park bench watching mothers bring their children to the Zoo for a day outing. They rarely looked directly at each other. Carter explained his idea about the markers. "Johnny, could you make arrangements with people in accounting to divert the markers and make them disappear?"

"Yeah, But, what's in it for me?"

"A large percentage of the take. My plan is to have four associates assisting with the junkets. It gives them a reason to travel to Vegas every other week without raising suspicion. Each of them will bring back fifteen thousand; a total of sixty thousand each trip. You get twenty-five grand; ten-grand will go the casino employees to grease their palms, and I keep twenty-five grand for myself. So how does fifty grand a month sound to you?"

"It sounds too good to be true. But, let's say you're right, why do I need you?"

Carter turned and looked Johnny straight in the eyes. "You don't. But how are you going to explain to your uncle why you are traveling to Vegas so frequently? And what do you know about the junket business to make everything appear legit?"

Johnny wrung his hands, thinking about Carter's proposal. He thought, *fifty thousand each month is a lot of dough for doing almost nothing.* There didn't appear to be much of a downside. Johnny, acutely aware how much cash the family skimmed each month from the casinos, knew one hundred twenty-thousand was a drop in the bucket. "Yeah, I want in. We have a deal."

The two men shook hands. Each rose from the bench and went in the opposite direction. They would work out the details of the plan during the next few weeks.

$ $ $

The limousine drove up to the entrance of the Sands Casino. Johnny wore an all-white suit, white shoes, white shirt and a solid red tie. He walked into the lobby of the den of iniquity. The bright lights glowed from hundreds of slot machines that illuminated the enormous cavern. Johnny didn't remove his white hat with the black trim. His sun glasses hid his eyes. He made his way to the registration desk where a friendly clerk checked him into one of the luxury suites.

After unpacking and getting settled into the lavishly decorated suite, Johnny made his way to the accounting department. He had carte blanche in the most sensitive areas of the casino. He spoke to the head of personnel, Franco, to find out how casino markers were handled. He gave the pretense that the owners were worried not all of the markers were being collected in a timely manner. Franco then explained the procedure for the markers to be processed. He introduced Johnny to Nancy, who had been with the casino for over five years. She had extensive knowledge about how markers were handled and the issuing of credit to the casino patrons.

Johnny spoke to Nancy about his scam. They had a simple arrangement. Nancy removed the markers for the name of a certain person and gave them to Johnny. The markers were not to be recorded or entered into any books. As far as anyone knew, they never existed. In exchange for her cooperation, Johnny arranged to have Nancy's salary doubled. She received payment of the extra money in cash.

Johnny made similar arrangements with Lola at the Riviera, Beth at the Dunes and Gail at Caesars Palace. None of the women from the accounting departments at the casinos were aware of each other. Johnny presented the opportunity as exclusive to each of them.

Everything in place, all Johnny had to do was get the names of Carter's associate assigned to each casino and provide that information to the girls. He also made sure each of the associates had a large line of credit so that taking a ten-thousand-dollar marker would not arouse any suspicions. Big Julie had paved the way for the high rollers to be given lines of credit up to one million dollars.

Johnny had the idea to have the markers given to him once a month. He then delivered them to Carter in exchange for his share of the currency. The checks and balances between Johnny and Carter, allowed Johnny to verify how much money he should receive, based on the number of markers he delivered. In the event anything went south, Johnny always had the markers he could collect.

CHAPTER FOURTEEN

After the last trip to Vegas, Carter's revelation about markers, made Edwin melancholy. The darkness of his soul had become almost too much to endure, and he became depressed and calloused. He did not trust anyone. With no one to talk with, he kept all his emotions bottled up inside. In the background he could hear the words from Simon and Garfunkel's *Sounds of Silence*. Edwin thought to himself, "*The darkness is not my friend. The darkness is my black dog.*" Black Dog was the term used by Winston Churchill to describe his depression; an ever present companion, lurking in the shadows, out of sight, growling, sinister and unpredictable, capable of overwhelming a person at any moment. Edwin knew the black dog all too well. The dreary Chicago weather did not help his mood.

Shortly after 5 p.m., Edwin's telephone rang. "Hey Edwin, it's Gwenn. What are you up to?"

"About six two."

"Haha, very funny. Seriously what are doing tonight?"

"Nothing, trying to wrap my brain around Carter and Big Julie's conversation about the junketeers and how much money they lose."

"Yeah, me too. Do you want to come over for pizza and maybe talk about it?"

"Sure, why not. What time?"

"Say about eightish."

Edwin placed the phone's receiver back onto the cradle. In a better mood, he did not feel so alone in his small studio apartment.

* * *

Edwin arrived at Gwenn's place just as she returned from picking up a pizza from Lou Malnati's. She opened the door to let Edwin inside. Unlike the last time Edwin had been over, the table was not set. Gwenn placed the pizza on the table, "Are paper plates okay?"

"Sure."

"What would you like to drink? I have beer, wine or soda?"

"A beer will be perfect."

As Gwenn and Edwin sat on the black leather sofa enjoying the gooey cheese, fresh mushrooms and zesty pepperoni, Gwenn broached the subject about Carter. "Did you get the same uneasy feeling I did about Carter and Big Julie?"

Edwin winced, "Yeah, I'm fairly certain Big Julie has no idea about Carter and what we do for him. As for Carter, he knows a lot about the inside workings of the casino. I'm almost certain we're in over our heads."

The unique scent of the pan crust filled the room with the smell of a bakery. Gwenn finished her mouthful of food before speaking. "Do you know how Carter is supposedly taking care of our markers?"

"No, but I think we should ask him. He owes us at least that much. I'm curious, though: I know why you left Kraft Foods to work for Carter, but what do you want to do with your life? I can't imagine you want to keep up this lifestyle of flying back and forth every other week to Vegas?"

Gwenn, caught off guard by Edwin's question, said, "I hadn't really thought about it much until this last trip when Carter enlightened us about the markers being checks and the casinos being able to cash them anytime they wanted to." She paused contemplating Edwin's question. It seemed a fair question considering the situation.

"Actually, I always pictured myself in the corporate world as a high ranking executive. I graduated from the University of Chicago with a degree in marketing. How about you Mr. MBA graduate from Northwestern, what's your dream?"

"Well, prior to Valerie breaking up with me, I always thought I'd work for a large firm downtown and raise a family in the suburbs. After she dumped me, the only thought I've had is to accumulate as much wealth as possible. I'm beginning to rethink my priorities."

Gwenn took another slug of beer. "So are you going to ask Carter tomorrow about those markers we've been signing, or shall I be the only one with a pair large enough to confront him?" She flashed Edwin a wicked smile. She baited him to see if he had any balls.

He smiled, "Of course I'll ask Carter about it. What sorta of man would I be if I let you do the dirty work?" Edwin had just finished taking the last mouthful of pizza. He put his plate on the coffee table in front of him and downed his final swig of beer with one big gulp. After he finished his beer, he placed the glass on the coaster and sat back to relax.

Something about Edwin aroused Gwenn. She put her plate on the coffee table, leaned over and gave Edwin a long passionate kiss. Edwin reciprocated. Following the long embrace, Edwin looked deeply into Gwenn's beautiful blue eyes. Her eyes sparkled with a certain twinkle. Uncertain about the situation, he asked, "What are we doing?"

Gwenn placed her index finger on Edwin's lips suggesting he not say another word. She took his hand and stood up. Without saying a word, Edwin stood up and let her lead him into her bedroom. It was a night both of them needed to release their pent-up stress and tension.

★ ★ ★

The next morning, Edwin returned to his apartment to shower and change clothes before heading to the office. He arrived at the office as Carter entered. "Good morning, sir," Edwin said. "I wondered if I could have moment to talk with you about our Vegas trip."

Carter responded, "Of course, let me get settled."

Richard, Herbert and Gwenn arrived at the office within a few minutes of Edwin's arrival. They took their seats in their respective cubicles and prepared for the day's tasks.

Gwenn popped her head around the corner and gave a wink to Edwin. He smiled back. A few moments later, Carter called Edwin into his office.

Carter sat behind his large walnut desk. "What's on your mind?"

"Well, sir, it's about the markers we've all been signing in Vegas. I was concerned because we have no guarantee that the markers are being disposed of as you have told us. And, to be perfectly frank, we all give you cash, so there is no record of the funds being given to you."

Carter grabbed a cigarette from the pack sitting on his desk and lit it with a lighter. The end of the cigarette glowed red as he took a drag. He watched the smoke swirl about the room as he sat in his plush office chair. Carter took a few more puffs before speaking. "An excellent observation; I'm glad you were paying attention. It's important for a person to pay attention to his surroundings at all times. Have any of your colleagues made a similar observation?"

Edwin, not sure how to answer or what Carter was getting at, decided to take a chance and confide in him, "Gwenn mentioned to me she had similar feelings. We're just concerned we're being set up, sir."

"That makes perfect sense. I would have concerns too if it were me. Have everyone else join us."

Edwin left Carter's office, and within a few minutes, returned with the other associates. Gwenn looked at Edwin quizzically. Edwin shrugged his shoulders, indicating he had no idea.

In the meantime, Carter had several thick file folders sitting on his desk. He held them up to show everyone. "Only a few minutes ago, Edwin asked me about your markers from Vegas. Apparently, he and Gwenn have concerns that the casinos will take action to collect them. Rest assured, they will not. Your markers are in these files."

He handed each associate a file folder. Each folder had the name of the associate on it. Inside the file folder were the markers signed by the particular associate. "You are free to dispose of the files and the markers as you deem fit. You have earned my trust, and in return I want to earn yours. Unless there is anything else, you need to get back to work."

The four associates left Carter's office. As she left, Gwenn whispered into Edwin's ear, "Thank you."

He glanced over his shoulder and smiled.

Richard and Herbert did not realize what had happened. They were not paying attention to Carter when he talked with them in Vegas with Big Julie. To both of them, it was another day at the office.

A few moments later it dawned on Edwin that he never asked about the inside man at the casinos and how it might affect the group in the future. Edwin's feeling of triumph was short lived as he quickly perused the contents of his file and looked at each marker carefully. The same initials, "J.A." approving the marker appeared on each document.

Edwin marched back into Carter's office, and closed the door behind him. "I'm sorry to interrupt you, sir, but who is J.A.?" He wasn't sure how Carter would react.

Carter took the last drag from his cigarette before putting the butt out in the Baccarat glass ash tray. Edwin's heart pounded as he watched Carter reached into his blazer. His first thought was simply *Kindness*. Instead, Carter pulled out another pack of Camels. He tapped the pack of cancer sticks before opening it. "Would you like one?" offering a rolled white stick to Edwin.

"No thank you, I don't smoke."

Carter lit the cigarette and took a puff. He exhaled the white smoke. Edwin coughed a bit.

Carter said, "J.A. stands for Johnny Accardi. He's the nephew of Tazio Accardi. Tazio is in charge of the day to day operations of the Outfit. Have you heard of them?"

"No sir."

"The Outfit is a crime family. They are part owners in the casinos we take our junketeers."

"Are you shitting me?" Edwin blurted out. "We're stealing from the mob?"

Carter moved his hands directing Edwin to relax and calm down. "Hey, it's all good. Johnny and I have everything covered. Not to worry. With Johnny helping, it's as if we have permission."

Edwin immediately realized he was in deep trouble. Not wanting to let on to his true feelings he played along with Carter.

"Okay sir, I trust you. Thank you for sharing with me."

Carter said, "I trust you will keep this information between the two of us. I prefer not to worry the other associates."

"Understood," Edwin said. He walked out of Carter's office.

CHAPTER FIFTEEN

APRIL, 1975

The bright red sun illuminated the Chicago skyline as Herbert Shoemaker drove his silver Corvette with the top down; a gorgeous moment to be cruising down the "Magnificent Mile", otherwise known as Lakeshore Drive. Richard Esposito rode with Herbert enjoying the beautiful women they passed along the way. The two had formed a close camaraderie and often socialized together outside of work. Despite their sincere efforts to invite Gwenn and Edwin into their inner circle, both had declined. Neither Gwenn nor Edwin wanted to be a part of their mutual admiration society.

Richard devised a scheme to guarantee he and Richard would each win at least five thousand dollars from their markers. The simple plan worked perfectly, especially since they played not to win or lose any money at the craps table—only to break even. Herbert joined Richard at Caesars at the same time he played. He bought in for five thousand dollars with his own money. By now, they each had a significant amount of cash stashed away. Herbert would bet one hundred dollars on the Pass Line, Richard would make an off-setting bet of one hundred dollars on the Don't Pass Line. The only number that they could lose on was a twelve. In most casino, a twelve rolled on the Come-out roll was a push for the Don't Pass bet. To off-set the twelve, Herbert made a five dollar bet on Box Cars, aka, Midnight, a pair of sixes. This way, one of them would lose, while the other would win. At the end of the session they would pool their money. For the most part, they would be up or down no more than one hundred dollars. But since Herbert's marker never got repaid, they simply walked off with approximately ten thousand dollars of found money.

Upon finishing their play at Caesars, the two would play at the Sands implementing the same betting techniques. They each made approximately fifteen thousand dollars every trip. They cared less that they traveled to Vegas twice a month to appease junketeers. Thirty thousand dollars a month for each of them was a lot of dough.

One day at the office, Gwenn became suspicious of Richard and Herbert when she overheard them boasting to each other about their perfect play. She confronted them. "Hey guys, I overheard your conversation. How are you making so much each trip?"

Herbert was about to tell Gwenn, but was interrupted by Richard. "That's for us to know and for you to find out."

"Come on fellas, were all friends here."

Richard didn't fall for her bullshit. "Friends? You gotta be kidding. The only person you're close with is Edwin. Ask him. He's some sort of math wiz."

"Seriously? You're making all this dough and you won't tell me how?"

"Well, maybe we can work something out. A trade let's say. You give me something and in return I'll tell you."

"You're a pig! Forget it. I make enough I don't need to fuck you."

Herbert chimed in. "Yeah. You heard the man. We're not telling you nothing. It's our little secret. Unless . . ." Herbert could see the daggers coming from her eyes. He shut up before saying something he'd regret.

"Fine." She stormed off pissed that the two idiots had bested her.

Gwenn made it her mission that the next time they were in Vegas to watch Richard and Herbert's action at the craps table. She was determined to learn their method of play.

$ $ $

A beautiful woman wearing a tight red body con-high cotton mini skirt and matching six-inch-high heel single strap leather shoes stood at the craps table. Her shoulder length strawberry red hair framed her high cheek bones. Her blues eyes sparkled as her pirate smile showed her perfect white teeth. "Oh, I don't understand this game," she said speaking loudly to the dealer. The truth of the matter was, she wanted to get the attention of Richard and Herbert who had become visible at the table.

Herbert and Richard stood at opposite ends, pretending not to know each other. Richard bought in for five thousand dollars. Herbert signed for a marker and got ten thousand dollars in chips.

The lady in red winked seductively at Richard. He blushed not recognizing the woman—it was Gwenn. Gwenn watched the two other associates play as she made small bets on the Pass Line and a Place bet on the Six and Eight, unless that number was the point. It only took her about fifteen minutes to see how Richard and Herbert bet.

She left the table and made her way to a nearby slot machine. She watched as Herbert finished his play and colored up. Within five minutes, Herbert did the same. As they made their way to the cashier's window they did not realize she was following them. Standing right behind them, she asked, with a southern drawl, "So how did you fellows make out tonight?"

A smile slid up Herbert's face and immediately settled in, a magnetic, no holds-barred smile, and unmistakably sexy look. He assumed Gwenn had hit on him. "Excellent," he said. His face radiated as his cheeks turned red.

Richard, a bit more evasive, said, "Not too bad for a night's work. Speaking of a night's work, are you available?"

Gwenn slapped him on the cheek, leaving a red mark. "I'm not that type of lady. Besides, I'm just waiting for my husband to finish playing at the blackjack table." She marched off, leaving Richard flabbergasted.

During the several months that Gwenn had worked for Carter, she won some and lost some. Some nights she left the table with only a few thousand dollars more than what she had to contribute to Carter. She saw the advantage of teaming up with a partner to play. The approach taken by Richard and Herbert made a lot of sense. Very logical; as a matter of fact, it was brilliant. She wished she'd thought of it.

Once Gwenn returned to her suite at the Riviera, she quickly changed her clothes, removed the wig and colored contacts and transformed back to her normal self. Without further delay, she made her way to the Dunes and found Edwin at the craps table.

"Hi honey," she said as she stood next to him.

"Hi sweetie," he played along.

"Can we go somewhere and get a bite to eat? I'm hungry," she said.

"Of course." Edwin colored up his chips.

They made their way over to the cashier's cage so Edwin could convert his casino chips into legal tender. Before heading to the all night café, they made a quick stop at the front desk so that Edwin could deposit the cash into his safe deposit box.

Edwin and Gwenn chose a booth at the café. Gwenn wasn't really hungry, but needed an excuse to talk with Edwin alone. She ordered a cup of coffee and an English muffin. He ordered scrambled eggs, bacon, wheat toast and coffee.

"What's up?" Edwin started the conversation.

"I overheard Richard and Herbert in the office a few days ago bragging about having the perfect betting system. I asked them how they played, and they clammed up. So I went to the Sands, incognito, to watch them tonight."

Gwenn had Edwin's attention, curious if the two goofballs had actually figured out a foolproof way to make money at the craps table. With all of his studying and research, he could not figure a way to beat the table without cheating.

Gwenn finished explaining how Richard and Herbert bet. "Do you see a downside to this if we teamed up?"

Edwin already knew the downside. He did not hesitate with his reply, "Yeah, there is a downside. If Carter ever learned that we did team play he would probably freak out. He made it clear that we were not to be seen together at the same casino."

Gwenn interrupted, "Yes, but how would he know? Besides, how much are you making each month above our salary? According to my calculations, those two consistently make at least fifteen grand each trip."

Edwin thought about Gwenn's suggestion. She was persuasive. He made about twenty grand each month. If he could consistently make thirty grand every month, that would be a thirty-percent increase. "Okay, I'm in," he said.

Edwin finished his meal, and they left the café.

As they walked through the casino, Gwenn asked, "Do you want me to stay in your suite tonight?"

Before Edwin had a chance to answer, one of the junketeers yelled over, "Hey Edwin, how's it going? Who's your lady friend?"

Edwin waived to the man. He told Gwenn, "Better not tonight. I'll go over and see what they're up to. Let's talk tomorrow."

Edwin left Gwenn and joined the other junketeers as they headed over to the craps table. He knew they would want him to get in on their action.

CHAPTER SIXTEEN

JUNE, 1975

Bindi Maxwell, a young woman from a small town in Iowa, walked in a daze as she moved through O'Hare International airport in Chicago, Illinois. Bindi, in Chicago for a job interview with United Airlines, was traveling to Las Vegas to attend her cousin's wedding. Since there were no direct flights from Des Moines to Las Vegas, she decided to fly directly to Las Vegas immediately after her interview. Maxwell's friends described her as a sweat-heart of a person; an angel. Many of them told her she was too nice to work in a big city.

Overwhelmed by the sheer size of O'Hare Airport, Bindi, in a stupor, bumped into Edwin. Startled, she awoke from her trance. "Hey, watch where you're going," laying blame on him despite her being the one at fault.

"Sorry ma'am." He was not going to get into an altercation in the terminal, especially with his junketeers watching.

Edwin boarded the plane and found his aisle seat. While seated, much to his dismay, he noticed Bindi walk down the aisle watching as she approached his row. He thought to himself, *Please, I hope she is not sitting next to me.*

Bindi placed her small suitcase in the overhead bin above his seat. She looked directly at Edwin and in a gruff voice, said, "Excuse me I'm in the window seat."

Once she sat and buckled her seatbelt, she realized Edwin was the person she had bumped into in the terminal. She blushed, slightly embarrassed.

The other passengers finished boarding and the cabin doors were closed by the flight attendants.

For some inexplicable reason, Edwin glanced in Bindi's direction. She looked at him, and with a soft, sensual, voice, "I'm sorry for my behavior back there. It's not like me to lash out like that."

Bindi captivated Edwin's attention. Her shoulder-length sandy brown hair, pulled back into a ponytail, heightened her dazzling bright blue eyes. She had perfect, straight white teeth and a flawless complexion.

"My name is Edwin," as he reached across the empty middle seat to shake her hand.

"Bindi Maxwell." She shook his hand.

Edwin normally kept to himself, not speaking to anyone. "So where are you from?"

"Pella. It's a small town in Marion County, Iowa."

"So are you flying to Vegas for business or pleasure?"

"Mostly pleasure. I'm going to Vegas to attend my cousin's wedding. How about you?"

"Mostly business. I work for a company that brings people to Vegas on gambling junkets."

"How does that work exactly?"

"The company I work for arranges for people who meet certain qualifications to travel to Vegas for free."

"Free? How can they travel for free?"

"The casinos expect the junketeers to lose money. Based on the amount of time they play and the amount they bet, the casinos give them a room, meals, drinks and sometimes, show tickets."

"Do they always lose or do they sometimes win?"

"Some of them will win, most of them lose. My job is to make sure they have a great time so they don't feel bad about losing."

Bindi and Edwin carried on their conversation with each of them learning more about the other. Edwin asked, "If you live in Iowa, why were you flying out of Chicago?"

"I was in to Chicago for a job interview with United Airlines. It was more convenient for me to travel from there to Vegas to attend my cousin, Audrey's wedding."

"Are you applying to be a flight attendant?"

Bindi smiled, "No, I'm applying to work in United's marketing department. Their headquarters are in Chicago."

"Oh, well, I bet you would make a great flight attendant."

"Thank you, but I prefer to travel for pleasure rather than for work. Besides, if I do get the position, one of the perks is to be able to fly for free."

"Where are you staying?" Edwin asked.

"At the Flamingo Hotel. The wedding reception is going to be held at Caesars Palace. I couldn't afford to stay there. The Flamingo, I understand, is across the street. How often do you fly to Vegas?"

"Every other week. It's a bit grueling. But it pays well."

"Well, since you're the expert, can you recommend a restaurant I should go to tonight?"

A smirk came across Edwin's face. "Oh, what did you have in mind?" fishing for an invitation.

Bindi, was oblivious to his modest advance. "Nothing too expensive. Something close to the Flamingo. Unless you think the food at the Flamingo is good?"

Without hesitation, Edwin suggested, "Battista's Hole in the Wall is great for an excellent, inexpensive, Italian meal."

It seemed to take only a few minutes, but the plane had landed and taxied its way to the terminal. Edwin seized the moment. "Would you like to join me for dinner at Battista's tonight?"

Bindi blushed. "I'm not sure. After all, we just met. I don't know you."

Edwin persisted, "It's just dinner. Battista's is just around the corner from the Flamingo. Besides, I promise you'll enjoy it."

She pondered the invitation. "Hmm. This is my first time in Vegas. It would be nice to know someone who could show me around. My cousin will be busy attending to last-minute wedding details, and my other relatives aren't arriving until tomorrow. Okay. What time?"

"Seven. I'll meet you in front of the restaurant."

"See you at seven, then." With that they both exited the plane. Edwin's junketeers were already milling around waiting for him.

★ ★ ★

At seven o'clock, the June evening temperature remained hot. Bindi made her way over to Battista's. As Edwin had told her, it was a short walk, just around the corner from the Flamingo. She wore a light blue summer dress, and had let down her hair. Edwin was at the entrance waiting for her. He almost didn't recognize Bindi. She was an attractive woman, five foot five, slender, and had a certain aura about her.

Edwin wore dress slacks, and a light blue, short-sleeve-button down, dress shirt. They ordered their meal and made small talk waiting for their food to arrive.

The two carried on with their conversation, enjoying the fabulous food. "How's your lasagna?" Edwin asked.

"Excellent! And your shrimp Alfredo with the clam sauce?"

"Very good. Some more Chianti?"

"Yes, please. How is the travel business?"

Edwin lifted his glass of Chianti and spun the red liquid around the glass, "It's fun, but it's also a grind at the same time. I'm not sure how much longer I want to keep flying cross country twice a month."

Bindi's eyes glistened. "I hope I can travel all over soon. I'm hoping Untied will hire me. My friends think I'm not suited for living in Chicago. They think I'm some small town girl that should get married and stay in Pella. I have bigger aspirations."

"Oh, and what might those be?"

"I want to prove to my parents and everyone else that I can live on my own. I'm not objecting to someday getting married, but for now, I want to take care of myself."

Edwin quickly changed the subject. He didn't think talking about marriage with a complete stranger was proper. Yet, something about Bindi captivated him. "I think you can do anything you want."

Before Bindi had a chance to say another word, the waiter interrupted. "Will there be anything else, maybe some desert?"

"Not for me. This girl gotta watch her figure."

"No, just the check." Edwin said.

After they left Batista's, Edwin escorted Bindi back to the Flamingo. They sat at the piano bar for a few more hours, laughing and conversing as if they were long lost friends.

It was late when Bindi suggested they call it an evening. She and Edwin had made a connection. The two had similar values and expectations. Edwin appreciated Bindi's inner beauty. Unlike his experience with Valerie, Bindi never discussed money or gave any indication that material things or social stature were important to her. She was a down to earth, authentic person.

Both found it awkward to say goodnight. In a cumbersome manner Bindi asked Edwin, "Would you have time to go with me to my cousin's wedding reception?"

Without any hesitation, Edwin emphatically said, "Yes."

"Great. Can you meet me in the Flamingo's lobby at eight and we can walk over together?"

"Yes. Are you sure it will be okay for me to go with you? I mean, is your cousin expecting you to bring someone?"

"It will be fine." She gave Edwin a hug and quick peck on his cheek and left.

Bindi hummed as she made went back to her room. Giddy being with Edwin, despite just meeting him, it was as if she had known him for years.

★ ★ ★

Saturday night arrived. At eight the air outside started to cool down. A slight breeze swirled periodically. A short distance from the entrance of the Flamingo to Caesars Palace, Edwin arranged for a limo to drive him and Bindi. She felt nervous and excited at the same time, thrilled to arrive in style at Audrey's wedding.

Edwin wore a black tux and looked extremely distinguished.

Bindi, dressed in a dark blue with gold lace evening gown, looked stunning. If Edwin had not known she was from a small town in Iowa, he would have mistaken her for a New York Fashion model. "You look amazing,"

"Thank you," she responded.

Edwin and Bindi found the banquet room where the bride and groom hosted their wedding reception. The wedding ceremony had taken place earlier that afternoon. Bindi confirmed with Audrey that Edwin could attend the reception. As they entered the room, a band played while waitresses walked around serving the guest hors d'oeuvres.

She took Edwin's arm as they strolled across the floor to congratulate the bride and groom. Audrey, excited to see her, exclaimed, "You look beautiful."

"So do you. This is my date, Edwin."

"Congratulations," Edwin said, to the newlyweds. "Thank you for allowing Bindi to bring me with her to celebrate your wedding."

"I'm glad she met you." Audrey turned away from Edwin, looking to speak some more with Bindi.

Audrey took hold of both of Bindi's hands. "Have you seen Valerie yet?"

"No, not yet." She explained to Edwin that Valerie was a good friend of Audrey's. Valerie and Audrey both attended Northwestern University and graduated last year.

Edwin became unsettled by Bindi's announcement. "What?" *It couldn't be Valerie Taylor*, he thought. *Could it?*

Before Bindi had a chance to respond, she saw Valerie and Johnny Accardi. "There she is. Come on Edwin, I want to introduce you to Valerie Taylor."

Edwin was speechless. He went along with the flow. When Bindi started to introduce Valerie to him he said, "Yes, I know Valerie. We dated in college." Edwin did not go into any details.

Valerie smiled. She wore a striking red dress with a plunging neckline and low cut back. An expensive diamond necklace graced her neck. "Hello Edwin." She extended her hand to shake his. Edwin shook her hand without much acknowledgement.

Valerie then introduced Johnny Accardi to Edwin. "This is my finance, Johnny Accardi."

Johnny scrutinized Edwin. He had overheard his comment about dating Valerie in college. As the two shook hands, a chill went down Edwin's back and the hair on his neck rose.

"Are you related to the Accardi family in Chicago," Edwin asked wryly.

"Yes, I am. Do you know someone in my family?"

Edwin lied. "No, just heard of your family through a friend." Edwin knew full well that Joseph Carter once had connections with the Accardi family, and that Johnny was his Vegas insider.

Johnny had an advantage over Edwin. He knew all about Edwin without Edwin having a clue that he knew. Edwin did not appreciate the look Johnny flashed at him. He wanted to escape. "Bindi, do you want a drink from the bar?"

"Of course I do. Valerie, please excuse us, I'll catch up with you later." She took Edwin by the arm to mossy over there.

Edwin and Bindi were placed at the same table as Valerie and Johnny. The wedding seating forced them to sit together. Edwin felt awkward. He said very little and let the women talk between themselves. Johnny got drunk with the free booze.

After dinner, the newlyweds had their first dance. Once the couple finished, guests joined them on the dance floor. Johnny moved like a wild man on the dance floor and made several sexual advances toward other women. Valerie ignored Johnny, seeming more focused on Edwin and his relationship with Bindi.

"So how long have you two been dating?" Valerie asked Edwin.

"Oh, we just met on the plane yesterday."

"What about you, how long have you been with Johnny?"

Valerie lost her composure. A little time bomb went off inside her head. "You know damn well how long I've been dating Johnny."

"No, not really. As I recall, when you dumped me, you said, 'you met someone else.' You never mentioned his name. Bindi tells me you and Audrey were friends at Northwestern. Funny, you never introduced me to her when we dated."

"Well why would I want to introduce a loser like you to my friends? I intentionally kept you my little secret. You are so naïve. Had you amounted to anything, I would have been proud to show you off to them."

Bindi, oblivious to Valerie's comments, because she was engaged in conversation with another guest, did not seee Edwin's expression. Edwin, taken back, by Valerie's sudden hostility said, in a smug, sarcastic, voice "Seems like I touched a nerve. If you have issues, I have the tissues."

Valerie immediately pushed herself away from the table and left to find Johnny. Bindi overheard Edwin's nasty remark and punched him in the arm.

"Hey, what's that all about?" He looked at Bindi confused by her actions.

"Why are you being so cruel to Valerie?"

"It's a long story, and not one I want to get into right now. Do you want to dance?"

Bindi, more than happy to drop the subject, said, "I'd love too."

They made their way toward the dance floor, where Edwin displayed his smooth dance moves. Before the band finished the set, Johnny appeared from nowhere and grabbed Edwin's arm. "We need to talk, you and me."

Not wanting to make a scene, Edwin excused himself from Bindi and went with Johnny outside of the ballroom.

Johnny looked directly into Edwin's eyes. "I know who you are and who you work for."

Edwin glared back at him with cold, unblinking eyes, not backing down.

Johnny slurred his words as he spoke, "Carter, Joseph Carter. He's my partner."

"I thought Big Julie was Carter's partner." Edwin deliberately pretended he did not know Johnny's relationship with Carter.

"Look asshole, Carter is my casino partner. I take care of the markers you sign. I recognized your name when we were introduced." He appeared very agitated.

Edwin remained calm. He knew trying to talk rationally to Johnny was a waste of time. "What is it you want from me?"

"I want you to stay the hell away from Valerie."

"That's what you're so bent out of shape about? I'm telling you I have zero interest in her. She dumped me a long time ago. Besides, I'm interested in Bindi."

Johnny pushed Edwin aside and made his way back into the ballroom. Edwin waited a few minutes and then rejoined Bindi on the dance floor, where she was doing the Bump with Valerie.

Johnny stood at the bar, waiting to be served. He looked over and saw Valerie dancing with Bindi and Edwin. Infuriated, he dashed over and planted his fist directly on Edwin's face. Blood gushed from his nose as he bent over from the blow.

Valerie grabbed Johnny. "What the hell are you doing?"

"Come on Babe, let's get the fuck out of here," Johnny said, pulling Valerie away.

Bindi grabbed a napkin off a nearby table and handed it to Edwin. He held it to his nose hoping to stop the bleeding. Another person brought some ice for Edwin. He sat on a chair trying to collect his wits. Many of the other guests were wondering what happened. The small crowd that had gathered around him dissipated once they saw he was alright.

* * *

Late into the night, Edwin made sure that Bindi arrived safely back to her room. He escorted her to the door. "Do you want to come in?"

Edwin made an excuse that he had to attend to some junketeers back at the Dunes. "Can I see you tomorrow?"

Before leaving, Bindi leaned close to Edwin and gave him a long passionate kiss. Edwin did not resist. He enjoyed the moment.

"Call me tomorrow," she said, as she closed the door leaving Edwin in the hallway to ponder a missed opportunity. His nose still hurt. *Great, I'll bet I have a beauty of a shiner tomorrow*, he thought.

Edwin made his way back to the Dunes arriving at the craps table shortly before two a.m. He took his usual marker for ten thousand dollars. Still dressed in his tuxedo, he drew a little suspicion to himself. A few of the other players asked where he left his lovely bride. He assured them he was not married and held up his ring finger to dispel any doubts.

Gwenn stood at the other end of the table. She wore her redhead disguise. She was gorgeous, the type of woman that could turn heads. And turn heads she did.

Edwin made eye contact with her acknowledging her presence. She nodded back. Another gentleman in his mid-forties made an unsolicited advance toward Gwenn. She calmly stated as a matter of fact, "See that guy at the other end of the table? He's my date. You should see what he did to the other guy."

The man apologized and moved to another spot away from her. Within twenty minutes of play, Edwin, up a few hundred dollars, waited for Gwenn to finish rolling the dice before he colored up his chips. For good measure, he tossed her a black one-hundred-dollar chip. "For the beautiful shooter. May the lady continue to bring us luck at the table?" A few other players also tossed Gwenn chips as a gesture for her being a lucky shooter.

Both Gwenn and he cashed in their chips at the cashier's cage. Edwin's face was swollen, and his right eye had started to close shut. It had already turned shades of black, blue and purple. Once they moved away from the cage, she asked, "What the hell happened to you?"

"I ran into Johnny Accardi's fist at the wedding reception I attended with a girl I met on the flight."

"Oh." Gwenn did not say anything else. She left her comment open for Edwin to say something.

"Yeah, her name is Bindi Maxwell. We sat next to each other.

"So we talked. And she invited me to her cousin's wedding. I had no idea my former girlfriend, Valerie, would be there. And guess who Valerie is dating?"

"I have no clue."

"Johnny Accardi."

"Who the hell is Johnny Accardi?"

Edwin forgot that he failed to mention to Gwenn that Johnny was Carter's inside man. "Johnny Accardi is Carter's insider. He handles our markers. Johnny got drunk. He thought I was still interested in Valerie."

"Are you?" Gwenn interrupted.

"No. I told him so. He said he recognized my name from the markers. He warned me to stay away from her, so I went back inside and started to dance with Bindi. Valerie joined us. That's when Johnny decked me."

"Come on let's get some ice on that."

Gwenn took Edwin back to his room to make sure he put ice on his eye. Edwin quickly changed into his bedtime clothes and lay on the bed with ice wrapped in a towel covering his face. After she finished pampering him, she undressed and snuggled next to him. Edwin, fast asleep, didn't notice.

CHAPTER SEVENTEEN

Monday morning, at about eight a.m., the maid knocked on the door to the Las Vegas motel room, Room 353. After knocking three times she announced herself before opening the door. Something just did not seem right, even for Vegas. The stench in the room at the local motel was odious. Johnny Accardi's bloody body soaked the white linen bed sheets in crimson where he was found. Sunlight, peeked through the closed drapes and dimly lit the room. Only when she turned on the lights did the maid see the gory, horrific scene. She let out a loud scream and ran from the room.

The LVPD were immediately summoned. Upon their arrival they began their preliminary investigation. A chalk outline marked the position of the body. An officer took photos of the entire crime scene. Another officer spoke with the maid to see if she could provide other information. Additional officers canvassed the area searching for possible witnesses.

Police investigators at the crime scene were more than half done when Detectives Malone and Evans arrived. Detective Malone bent over Accardi's body while Detective Evans searched the room looking for evidence. A gunshot wound to the head as well as several others to his torso, indicated the cause of death.

Detective Malone investigated the crime scene with his partner Bill Evans. Several police officers as well as forensic experts were still on site. Yellow police crime scene tape stretched across the door-way to the room to keep passerby motel guests, onlookers, and busy-bodies from peering inside.

"What do we have here, officer?" Malone asked one of the uniformed cops.

"A maid found the body this morning. The medical examiners initial findings are that the victim was killed around three a.m. Sunday morning. We found his wallet on the nightstand. It had his credit cards and driver's license, but no cash. The victim's name is Johnny Accardi. He is from Chicago, Illinois. Several .45 caliber casings were found on the floor.

"The cause of death was a single gunshot wound to the head. Three other shots were fired into the victim's upper torso. According to the registration clerk on duty, the victim checked in with a young lady, probably a hooker."

"Any motive?"

"No sir."

"Okay, we'll get in touch with his next of kin and see what they know about our victim being in Vegas."

★ ★ ★

Detective Malone spoke briefly to Bill Evans to ascertain what he had found out from the victim's relatives back in the Midwest.

Detective Evans told Malone, "According to his father, Johnny was in Vegas with his girlfriend, Valerie Taylor, to attend a wedding. They're staying at Caesars Palace. This Johnny Accardi is connected and has juice with several local prominent people."

Malone knew exactly what Bill Evans meant without having to go into details. Malone said, "Let's pay a visit to Valerie Taylor at Caesars. Most likely she hasn't yet checked out."

Valerie, already up and ready to start the day, had not seen Johnny since their argument at the wedding reception. Detective Malone knocked on the door to the suite at Caesars and identified himself as well as his partner. Valerie opened the door. Detective Malone flashed his badge.

"Excuse me ma'am, but may we come in? We have a few questions about your boy friend, Johnny Accardi."

Valerie's face turned an alabaster shade of white as she suspected something awful had happened to Johnny. "Oh my God Detective, is Johnny alright?"

"No ma'am, I'm sorry to inform you he was murdered last night. His body was found this morning at a local downtown motel."

Valerie let out a scream of disbelief and began sobbing uncontrollably. "What? How?"

"Someone shot him at close range. I can't give you any more details because the case is still under investigation. When was the last time you saw Johnny?"

"I saw him late Saturday night. We had an argument because he thought I was interested in my ex-boyfriend."

"What's his name?"

"Edwin Goldberg. He was at my friend's wedding with her cousin, Bindi Maxwell. I didn't know he would be there."

"Do you have any witnesses who may have seen your argument?"

"Several of the wedding guests saw us. Johnny had too much to drink and flirted with a few of the wives. He also punched Edwin, without provocation."

"What do you mean, 'without provocation'?"

"I was dancing with Bindi and Edwin when Johnny came from nowhere and punched him in the face. He didn't say a word. Johnny took me out, and we argued."

"Anything else you can tell us as to why someone might want to kill Johnny?"

"I'd ask Edwin. He's still in love with me and made it known he wanted me back," Valerie lied.

Malone, skeptical of her story, merely said, "Okay, we'll check out Mr. Goldberg. Do you know where he is?"

"No, but I'm sure Bindi does. She's at the Flamingo."

"One more thing, Ms. Taylor, how come you didn't notice Johnny wasn't around all day yesterday?"

"To be honest Detective, I slept most of the day. I got up in mid-afternoon, went to sit by the pool and relax. It's not unusual for Johnny to be away taking care of business. I wasn't feeling well from the night before, so I ordered room service and went to bed early."

Malone raised an eyebrow before his eyes narrowed. "When are you planning to leave town?"

"Tonight. Is that a problem?"

"No, just provide us with your contact number in case we need to ask any more questions."

Malone looked at his partner. "Do you think she loved this guy? She seemed composed to point the finger at her ex-boyfriend."

"I think her entire story is fishy. How could she not notice he was missing for an entire day? It makes no sense."

Detectives Malone and Evans immediately went to the Flamingo and knocked on the door to Bindi's room. They identified themselves. "Ms. Maxwell, we have a few questions about Edwin Goldberg." Malone said.

Bindi opened the door to her room. "What's this about?"

"Johnny Accardi was murdered last night. Your friend, Valerie Taylor, suggested Mr. Goldberg may have been the murder."

"What? Edwin? Are you kidding me? I just met him a few days go. He seemed so nice."

"Let's not jump to conclusions ma'am. We don't know for sure if it was him? Do you know where Mr. Goldberg is?"

"He's staying at the Dunes. He told me he takes care of people on junkets."

Detective Evans stated, "We understand Johnny punched Edwin in the face at the wedding. Can you tell us what happened?"

"Yeah. Edwin was dancing with Valerie and me when Jonny came from nowhere and smacked him square between his eyes. He grabbed Valerie and left. I helped Edwin sit on a chair. Another guest got some ice. That was it."

"Did you happen to notice Johnny and Valerie arguing afterwards?"

"No. But Johnny confronted Edwin earlier. Johnny was wasted and was hitting on a lot of the ladies."

"When was the last time you saw Edwin?"

"He escorted me back to my room sometime after midnight. I invited him in, but he said he had to attend to the junketeers. He left."

"Alright, Ms. Maxwell, thank you for your cooperation. We'll let you know if we have any more questions."

Before Malone and Evans had a chance to leave, Bindi asked, "How's Valerie doing?"

Malone said, "Interesting you should ask. Based on our experience, she's handling it well."

Malone and Evans left to interrogate Edwin.

★ ★ ★

A loud knock on the door woke Edwin from a deep slumber. "Open up, Police," he heard from outside his room. Two police officers and Detective Malone greeted him as he opened the door.

"What's going on, officers?" he asked rubbing his eyes, and trying to focus. His left eye was slightly swollen and dark purple from Johnny's punch.

"Mr. Goldberg, we want to ask you a few questions about Saturday night."

"Certainly, how can I help you?"

"Would you mind coming down to the station with us? We don't want to make a scene or cause you any embarrassment."

"Of course, officers, but can you tell me what this is all about? Is one of my junketeers in any trouble?"

"No, it has nothing to do with your junketeers. How well do you know Johnny Accardi?"

"I don't know him at all. I just met him the other night at a wedding reception. He and my ex-girlfriend are dating. Why?"

"Someone murdered him late Saturday night."

The color from Edwin's face drained. His breathing slowed. He took a step backwards, and in a thunderous voice said, "And you think I did it?"

"Right now you're a person of interest."

The wrinkles on his forehead tightened. "Why?"

"For starters, we know he's the person that gave you that Shiner. Let's just say a potential witness said you had a motive."

Edwin cleared his throat and shook his head. His eyes had an unfocused gaze. "What? Who would say such a thing?"

Malone grew impatience with Edwin. "Get dressed. We can talk about this at the station."

Edwin got dressed and sat in the squad car with the officers.

He didn't say another word while being escorted.

When they arrived, Edwin was placed in a holding area for questioning. Detective Malone entered the room. "Mr. Goldberg, I just have a few questions for you."

"Am I being charged Detective?"

"No, not yet."

"Well can you tell me why I'm a person of interest in Mr. Accardi's death?"

"Do you know Valerie Taylor?"

"Yes sir, I know her."

"How do you know her?"

"I told you. She's my ex-girlfriend. Until last night, I had not seen nor heard from her for almost a year until we met at that wedding reception on Saturday night."

"Do you know the bride and groom?"

"No, I met them Saturday night for the first time. Bindi Maxwell invited me to attend the reception with her. I met her on the plane flight from Chicago. We struck up a conversation and met for dinner the night before. Is Bindi alright?"

"Yes, Ms. Maxwell is fine. We already spoke with her this morning. Where were you after you left Ms. Maxwell?"

"I came back to the Dunes and played craps with Gwenn Alexander. She handles the junketeers at Caesar's. The last thing I remember is her helping me back to my room and putting ice on my face."

"Will check with Ms. Alexander about your alibi."

"Detective, I'm still confused as to why you think I had something to do with Accardi's death?"

"Well, according to Ms. Taylor, she thought you were jealous of him because you are still in love with her and that was motive for you to kill him."

"What? That's absurd!" Edwin, beside himself, asked, "How could Valerie think he was jealous of me? How was Mr. Accardi killed?"

"Sorry, I can't tell you that. We are still conducting our investigation."

In a stern, authoritative voice, Edwin said, "Detective, either you arrest me or release me. Either way, I'm not answering any more questions without an attorney."

Malone smiled. He had nothing to hold Edwin. Besides, his experience and judgment made him feel that Edwin didn't murder Accardi. "You're free to go."

Malone spoke to Bill Evans and his Chief who watched the interrogation from behind a two-way mirror. The trio concurred that Edwin most likely wasn't the killer.

Immediately after being released, Edwin made his way to the Flamingo. He asked the clerk at the front desk to call Bindi's room and asked her to come down.

She made her way to the front desk and saw Edwin. He smiled when he saw her. "I'm glad you kept your word and called me," she said mockingly.

Edwin wrapped his arms around her and gave her a huge bear hug. Suspicious of Edwin after being questioned by the police, her body became limp. Edwin sensed something wasn't right. He asked, "Have you had breakfast yet?"

"No, not yet"

"Do you want to get something to eat at the coffee shop?" Edwin asked.

"Sure, why not?" She didn't say anything about the police, hoping he would broach the subject.

As the two made their way to the coffee shop to grab a bite to eat, Edwin asked, "Did you hear about Johnny?"

"Yeah, the police questioned me about his death. Do you know what happened?" Bindi looked worried.

"No, the police think I had something to do with it. They haven't told me anything. They mentioned they spoke to you earlier. Did they mention how he was murdered?"

"I heard he was shot in the head. But why would the police think you had something to do with it?" Bindi looked at Edwin. Her face slackened and brow furrowed, as her eyes darted about in concern as if she was searching for someplace to hide.

Edwin did not make light of the situation. He told Bindi straight up, "Valerie told the police that I was jealous of Johnny."

"Why would Valerie to that?"

"I have no idea. And to set the record straight, I have no interest in Valerie."

"I never thought you did."

Their meals arrived. Edwin told Bindi everything. "I want you to know I didn't kill Johnny. I think it might have been a jealous boyfriend or husband of one of the women Johnny hit on at the wedding. Did you know Johnny was a member of the Chicago Outfit, a crime family?"

"No."

"For all I know, it may have been a mob hit."

As Edwin talked, Bindi became less concerned and worried. She had a good heart and believed what Edwin told her.

When they finished their meals, Edwin said, "I need to get back to the Dunes. My group of junketeers and I leave on the five p.m. flight. Can I have your phone number? I want to see again."

Bindi liked Edwin. She felt a spark with him.

"Okay, but how do you think a long distant relationship will work out?"

"Don't worry, I'll figure something out." He gave Bindi a long passionate kiss. Deep down, he hoped to stay in touch with her. He felt less confident with all of the distractions and Johnny's untimely demise.

Back at the Dunes, Edwin made sure all of the junketeers were on the bus. Once they arrived in the terminal at McCarran Airport, Valerie approached him. "You bastard! Why did you kill him?" she yelled at Edwin in front of everyone. Edwin's face turned red with embarrassment.

Edwin lost control and shouted back, "Who the fuck do you think you are, you gold-digging whore, to accuse me of anything?"

Valerie, startled by Edwin's outburst, had never seen him show this much spine before. She stuttered, "I, I'm sorry." Without saying another word, she turned and ran toward the ladies' room.

Edwin scanned the crowd and said, "Show's over." He went about his business. None of the junketeers asked him any questions. They all seemed to act as if nothing had happened. As far as they were concerned, *What happens in Vegas stays in Vegas.* Besides, nothing really did happen. For all anyone knew it was just a lover's spat.

The next morning, Edwin called Joseph Carter. "Mr. Carter, I need to tell you that Johnny Accardi was murdered this weekend, and the police think I had something to do with it."

Carter remained clam. "Don't worry. I'll handled my end here. Try not to worry about it. I'll speak to everyone at the debriefing."

"Thank you, Mr. Carter. I'll see you later today."

Not trusting anyone and still suspicious of Carter, Edwin decided it was time to protect himself. He made an appointment with a prominent business attorney at Baker & McKenzie. Fortunately, Jeffrey Katz was available to see him that afternoon.

Katz, a new attorney at Baker & McKenzie, eager to take on a new client, agreed to meet Edwin on short notice. "How can I help you Mr. Goldberg?" Katz began.

"I'd like to set up a corporation to protect my assets."

"What type of assets do you have?"

"For now, cash. But I'm looking at purchasing a McDonald's franchise and a seat on the Chicago Board of Trade."

Katz sat back in his chair. "I'm puzzled by you Mr. Goldberg. How old are you, again?"

"I'm twenty-three. Why do you ask?"

"Nothing. It's just very unusual for someone your age to be thinking of setting up a corporation to hold business entities."

Edwin wasn't sure what Katz meant. "Well, I do have an MBA from Northwestern."

"Do you have a name for the business?"

"Yeah, I do. I decided to call it 'ERGENT'."

"What?"

"I'd like to call my business 'ERGENT.' It stands for Edwin Randolph Goldberg Enterprises. Is that a problem?"

"No. I'll get the paperwork prepared. Before I do, though, you'll need to sign a Fee Agreement and we need a twenty-five thousand-dollar retainer. My hourly rate is $400."

"I'll bring a cashier's check later this afternoon. When can I expect the documents to be ready?"

"Once your retainer is paid, I'll have everything ready within a week."

"Very good," Edwin said. He rose from his seat and shook Katz's hand. "See you this afternoon."

Edwin had spent many hours on the plane during the numerous trips back and forth to Vegas thinking about the best way to hide and protect his money. ERGENT would be the cornerstone of his fledgling empire. Once the initial corporate documents were in place, he opened a business bank account. His initial deposit was nine thousand dollars. Although he had more than two hundred thousand dollars in the safe deposit box, he didn't want to draw any unnecessary attention to himself with a larger opening deposit. He had planned to make additional smaller deposits over the next few weeks.

* * *

Edwin's friend from high school, Mark Lunram, worked for Allen Dorfman at Central States Southeast, Southwest Areas Pension Fund. Central States provided benefits for the teamsters. Edwin called Mark, an assistant to Dorfman, to meet for lunch. He hoped Mark had answers to some of his questions about Carter and his connections to Vegas.

Edwin chose to meet Mark at a restaurant downtown for privacy and to keep the meeting as inconspicuous as possible. At two in the afternoon, the place was quiet as most of the lunch crowd was gone. "Thanks, Mark, for taking the time to meet with me."

"How can I help you my friend?"

"I'm working for a travel company operating junkets to Vegas. Me and three other associates travel to Vegas every other weekend to make sure the junketeers have a great time. During the time I'm there I play craps."

Mark, fascinated with Edwin's position hosting junketeers in Vegas, because he loved the game of craps and especially enjoyed going to Vegas, said, "So what seems to be the issue? Sounds to me like you have an ideal job."

"I failed to mention one small detail,"

"Oh, what's that?"

"In addition to playing babysitter to junketeers, I'm taking markers at the craps table for ten-thousand dollars. The markers are never recorded and are made to disappear. We play for a few hours and cash in the chips regardless if we are winning or losing. Our only requirement is that we are not to lose more than five thousand.

"We give five thousand from each marker to our boss, Joseph Carter, and we keep the rest. Everything has gone smoothly for the past several months.

"Johnny Accardi was Carter's connection with the casino. Someone murdered Johnny this past weekend. No one seems to know why he was killed. I'm a person of interest. I'm not certain what will happen with the arrangement Carter had with the markers until Johnny's murder is solved."

Edwin paused when the waiter brought their meals. He did not want anyone to over hear his conversation. Mark looked at Edwin in utter astonishment. Before Edwin could utter another word, Mark said, "You're delusional. What? Are you living on a river in Egypt called denial?"

Edwin taken aback, asked, "How bad is my situation?"

Mark explained, "The Teamsters Pension Fund was instrumental in making hundreds of millions of dollars in loans to various Las Vegas casinos. Last year, Dorfman helped loan $62.7 million to Allen Glick at the Stardust. The casinos are owned and operated by syndicated crime families. You, my friend, are stealing from the Teamsters and the mafia."

Edwin's worst fears became reality in an instant. "Yeah, I already knew that. Any suggestions?"

"Yeah, get the hell out as fast as you can. If Johnny Accardi was Carter's inside man at the casinos, there's going to be hell to pay. I'm afraid more people are going to die. Accardi's murder sounds like a professional hit. It's a warning."

Edwin pushed his plate of food aside. He'd lost his appetite. "Any ideas how I can get out of this mess?"

"What have you been doing with the money?" Mark wanted to know.

"I kept all the cash in a safe deposit box. I still live in my studio apartment. I haven't bought anything expensive or flashy, unlike my colleagues."

"The only comfort I can give you, is that Edwin you've been smart not to flash any of the cash around. It might just keep you off the radar."

Mark tried to bring some levity to Edwin's situation. "Hey, Edwin, do you know how to do government math?"

"Government math?"

"Yeah, how much is two plus two?"

Edwin played along not knowing where Mark was going with his question, "Four."

"No. Government math is when you ask a government employee how much two plus two equals; they will respond, 'Whatever you need it to be.'" Edwin laughed.

Mark followed-up, "I lost my money in Vegas on my last trip did you find it?"

Edwin quipped back, "No, but is that my money in your wallet?"

"Touché."

Both men left the restaurant and went their separate ways. Edwin, although not happy with what Mark had to say, felt better knowing his situation.

CHAPTER EIGHTEEN

The crisp morning air made it a beautiful, clear, July day in Chicago. Edwin had just finished jogging when he listened to an urgent message on his answering machine. Joseph Carter asked all of the associates to meet him at the office for an emergency meeting. No other details were given.

When Edwin arrived at the office, Gwenn, Richard and Herbert were already present. They were talking amongst themselves when Edwin said hello to the group. "Hi everyone, do you guys know what's going on?"

They all looked at Edwin with blank stares. Gwenn spoke first.

"No, we were hoping you had some information. Have you spoken to Carter yet?"

"No, I received a message on my answering machine."

Herbert said, "Me too. No details, just a message to get to the office as fast as I could."

Richard did not know anything either. He said, "I got a similar message."

At that moment, Joseph Carter stepped into the room. "Greetings everyone," he said with a forlorn look. "I know you are all probably wondering why I called this meeting, so I will get right to the point. As you probably know, a member of the Outfit, Johnny Accardi, was murdered a few weeks ago.

"Johnny ensured your markers were never recorded. The police think Edwin had something to do it with it because his former girlfriend pointed the finger at him and the altercation between the two of them at a wedding. Edwin has assured me that he is innocent and had nothing to do with it. That has been confirmed by a colleague of mine.

"The Outfit, however, did not know about my deal with Johnny and your markers. One of the casino employees Johnny confided in about our agreement threatened to squeal unless they received hush money. That issue has been resolved."

As Carter delivered the somber news, one by one the associates grew fearful and nervous. Caught up in the news at hand, the associates found it difficult for their minds to remain in the present. Fearful thoughts began to take over and they felt sick to their stomachs. They were all aware that what they did wasn't quite kosher. They looked the other-way because the money was too good to ask any questions.

Richard asked, "How was the issue resolved?"

Carter's eye widened. In a calm, frank, voice he said, "That person's position has been eliminated. He is no longer with us. Need I give you the details?"

"No, sir."

Carter continued, "I can see the worried looks on your faces. For now, you can relax. I made arrangements for another person to take the fall for us if push comes to shove. A friend of mine who is a member of the Outfit will keep me posted of any developments. For now, they do not know about our operation. From this point forward, you will no longer be asking for markers from the casino. In fact, you are no longer going to play at the tables. If you do, you do so at your own risk and with your own money. Do I make myself clear?"

Before anyone had a chance to respond, Herbert asked, "What are we supposed to do?"

Carter laughed out loud. "Seriously? Are you really that dense? I'm still paying you to escort the junketeers. You still need to make sure they are all pampered. You'll just be taking a cut in pay until this thing blows over. I want to remind you that you cannot discuss this with anyone. No one can know.

"To make certain there is no suspicion towards us, I have told the other people involved to suspend your casino lines of credit and not issue you any markers until further notice. You will also be reassigned to different casinos. Make sure you provide each other with detailed notes about the casino hosts and what each patron prefers. Everything with the travel business goes on as if nothing has happened."

Carter then reassigned the casinos to the associates. Gwenn and Edwin switched, as did Herbert and Richard. Herbert and Richard made it clear to Edwin that they blamed him for the situation. Edwin did not care for the tone of their voice or their demeanor. Gwenn appeared to be more sympathetic and understanding. Even though Edwin declined her romantic advances, she persisted in building a relationship with him.

Shortly after the associates had left the office, Carter received a telephone call from one of the casino employees at the Dunes. "We have a problem," he started the conversation.

"What's the problem?"

"Johnny never picked up the markers signed by Edwin Goldberg from accounting. The day manager picked them up with the other markers for payment. I thought you should know."

"How many markers are we talking about?" Carter asked.

"Three, thirty grand. They were the markers for the last visit."

"Okay, I'll take care of it on this end. Hey, any idea who whacked Johnny?"

"No, the word on the street is that Johnny talked too much about a lot of different things to a lot of different people. I'll let you know if I hear anything."

"Thanks George. I appreciate the information."

$ $ $

Edwin did not have a lot of down time between trips to Vegas. Although each week became easier to book his junketeers trips, it took a lot of time to answer phone calls. Joseph Carter had done an amazing job promoting the junket business. Wealthy and non-wealthy people called wanting to schedule their free trips to Vegas.

Carter used a page from Big Julie's playbook: every guest was treated with respect and royalty. No want, desire, or need went unfulfilled. Every minute detail was monitored. Even when a guest lost, as they often did, they never complained. They knew that if they caused a commotion, there were five other people ready to take their spot. And they made certain that all markers were paid in full—no exceptions.

Carter had been pleased as punch with his associates. They all did magnificent jobs caring for the junketeers. The casinos were thrilled with the quality of people being brought to their establishments. As a result, they handsomely compensated Carter. Already a very wealthy man, Carter's net worth grew exponentially.

♥♥♥

A few weeks passed and Edwin, hopeful that his relationship with Bindi would blossom, called her a few times to chat. She appreciated his interest and the times they spoke. He always asked if she had heard anything from United Airlines. The answer, was always, no. With each day that passed, Bindi thought she wasn't going to get the position. Edwin kept encouraging her not to dwell on it and that things would work out. Bindi was grateful for his moral support.

★ ★ ★

Edwin called his college buddy, Barry Horowitz, who managed three stores for another owner. "Hi Barry, it's Edwin. Okay. Now that you've convinced me to invest in a McDonald's franchise I've saved enough to advantage of this excellent business opportunity. What's next?"

Barry expounded, "A McDonald's franchise cost twenty thousand dollars. To open a new store, it would cost another two hundred-thousand dollars or so to purchase the furniture, fixtures and equipment. An existing profitable store cost more—maybe four to five hundred-thousand dollars.

"McDonald's owned the real estate and built the building in ninety percent of their franchises. McDonald's Corp was in the real estate business. They bought the land, and if possible, did not notify the seller it was going to be a McDonald's. When the McDonald's opened, the value of the land and building shot up, and they could leverage it to buy more property and open more stores.

"McDonald's, shrewd business model was to, set their goal to own and operate twenty-five percent of the stores. The company's policy required each franchise be inspected once a month. Thereby, it allowed McDonald's to keep control of the quality, service and cleanliness.

"They charged the franchisee rent in the amount of eight percent of sales. In addition, the franchisee paid an additional three percent in advertising."

Barry told Edwin, "If you had a good store and it did one million dollars in gross sales, McDonald's got eighty thousand dollars and the franchisee would also pay another thirty thousand dollars to McDonald's for advertising. You, as the owner would keep any other profits."

For Edwin, McDonald's sounded an awful lot like Joseph Carter and how he operated his business. But, it was the perfect opportunity to legitimately have his cash working for him.

CHAPTER NINETEEN

The August day was like any other day in Pella, Iowa. The air hot and muggy at 4 p.m., as the sun set in the western sky. It painted the sky an orange, red, and grey picture as if watching waves on the ocean. Bindi sat on her front porch, admiring the spectacular panorama. Somewhere she had remembered a little ditty, *Red sky in the morning, sailors take warning. Red sky at night, sailors delight.* Her tranquility was disturbed by the telephone ringing. Quickly, she answered.

"Hello. Yes, this is Bindi Maxwell."

"Hi, Ms. Maxwell. This is Barbara Cunningham from United Airlines. I'm calling to offer you the position as a customer service and reservationist representative if you are interested in that position."

"Yes, ma'am." Although she hoped for the position as a marketing analyst she initially applied for, it would be a way to get her foot in the door.

"You're to report to the United Airlines headquarters in Chicago the following Monday."

"Thank you Ms. Cunningham. I'm looking forward to working for United."

"Here's the information you'll need. Do you have a pen and paper?"

Bindi wrote down all of the details. Ecstatic, she glowed with a new sense of confidence and self-worth. She had a lot to do to pack, and get ready to move to the Chicago area. After calming down from the exhilaration of being hired, she called Edwin.

"Hi Edwin, it's Bindi. How are you?"

"I'm doing great. What do I owe the pleasure of this call?"

"I'm so excited! I got the position at United. I start the following Monday. They're going to put me up in a hotel in Des Plaines for six weeks while I'm in training."

"Wow, that's awesome. Will you have time for us to get together while you are in training?"

"I'm not really sure. There will be twenty other people training with me. I'm going to drive out on Friday and get settled in. I'll call you when I arrive. Will you be in town?"

"No, unfortunately, I've got another junket trip this weekend. Give me a call Tuesday after training. I get in late Sunday night. I'm certain Monday will be a busy day for you."

"That sounds like a plan. Thank you for your moral support, Edwin. I'm grateful you were optimistic and kept me on track."

She hung up the phone and began to get organized. She had a lot to pack and get ready for her move to Chicago. The notion of a new job in a big city made it difficult for her to contain her emotions. A dream come true, she was especially happy to be moving near Edwin.

Edwin, not deterred with the recent events and suspension of taking a marker at the craps table still played craps with his own funds. Over the duration of his trips to Vegas he became proficient at winning. The very next trip to Vegas he took twenty-five thousand dollars of his own money. He decided to play at the Flamingo because he had never played there before.

The Flamingo, a bit run down from its former glory days when Benjamin "Bugsy" Siegel opened the joint, was still a great spot on the Strip to gamble. Edwin walked in through the main entrance and made his way toward the craps tables. Four of the six tables were open. He chose the table that had the least players.

Edwin laid five thousand dollars in hundred-dollar bills on the green felt and asked for change. The dealer pushed the cash in front of the box-man, who counted out the money so that the infamous 'eye in the sky' could see. Once the pit boss verified the amount, the dealer gave Edwin five thousand dollars in chips. He immediately placed the chips in the chip rail in front of him. His large-buy-in caught the eye of a few of the other players.

Edwin waited for the shooter to finish his roll. The stick person passed a new shooter the dice. Edwin made a five-hundred-dollar Don't Pass bet, much to the chagrin of the other players. Craps players were extremely superstitious. They believed that if a player bet on the Don't Pass, that player, bet with the house. Nothing could be farther from the truth. The other players did not understand the method behind Edwin's betting.

The shooter rolled an eight to start the game. Edwin made some place bets and bet one hundred dollars on each of the hard-way numbers. The next roll was a four and one, a five. Players who bet on the five were paid. The shooter rubbed his hand in a small circle on the felt before picking up the dice. He tapped the dice twice on the table and let them fly toward the opposite end. One die hit another player's chip and showed a three. The other die came back about half-way to the center of the fourteen-foot table and also showed a three. The stick person called, "Hard six." He then moved both dice back to the center of the table. Once the dealers had finished collecting the losing bets and paying the winning bets, the stick person pointed to the players who bet on the hard six one, at a time, and told the dealers how much to pay them. Edwin was paid nine hundred dollars for his hard six bet.

A few more rolls later, the shooter rolled a three and a four, totaling seven. The stick person called out, "Three and four, this shooter's out the door." A small groan was made by all of the players except Edwin. He won five hundred dollars for his Don't Pass bet.

Edwin continued to play and made certain bets based on hunches or gut feeling. On one particular roll, he bet one hundred dollars on a horn bet. The horn bet included the two, three, eleven and twelve. It was a one-roll bet—win or lose. Fortunately for Edwin, the next roll of the dice was a twelve. Edwin won six hundred and seventy-five dollars.

The average player made five-dollar or ten-dollar bets. People of more affluent means generally wagered twenty-five dollars on each bet. The extremely wealthy players wagered one hundred dollars or more. Based on his play, the pit boss considered Edwin to be a high roller.

By coincidence, Gwenn also happened to be at the Flamingo and saw Edwin at the craps table. She wedged herself between players next to him. Fixated on the action, Edwin did not notice she was standing next to him until she made a snide comment. "Hey, what does a girl need to do to get some attention?" She wore a beautiful red evening gown and looked stunning. Startled, Edwin smiled and said, "Hi honey, where have you been?"

Gwenn played along, "I just finished shopping and hoped you won some money so I can get a pair of shoes I found at the store."

Edwin did not miss a beat, "Of course I won some money." As if on cue, Edwin colored up his chips. He'd won more than five thousand dollars in less than an hour. "Let's go buy you that pair of shoes," he said as he took his chips, placing his hand in Gwenn's as if they were lovers. They went to the cashier's cage. Gwenn snuggled next to Edwin, holding his arm as she gave him a tender kiss on his cheek. He blushed enjoying the moment.

Gwenn's eyes grew wide as saucers when she noticed how much money the cashier had counted out in front of Edwin. "Looks like you had a profitable night," she said, clinging to his side.

"Yes, I did."

"How much did you win?"

"I'm up about five grand."

"I'm going to hold you to buying me that pair of shoes."

The couple strolled to the exit and decided to go to the MGM across the street. The MGM, a lavish megaresort, opened in December 1973. The inside consisted of red plush, gilt, mahogany and crystal. Billed as the largest casino in Vegas, larger even than Caesars, it had ten craps tables, ninety-four blackjack tables and nine roulette tables, not to mention hundreds of slot machines. The 26th Floor hosted the Metro Club for high rollers. It cost one thousand dollars just to get inside. The

Grand Arcade, the world's largest shopping area, contained twenty-four stores that offered almost everything imaginable.

Gwenn and Edwin stopped into one of the stores. Gwenn showed him the shoes she liked. She tried them on and immediately fell in love with them. They fit perfectly. The clerk complimented Gwenn on how beautiful she looked and how gorgeous the shoes were.

Without hesitation, Edwin asked, "How much?"

The clerk said, "Two hundred fifty dollars."

Edwin did not blink. He said, "We'll take them."

As Edwin paid for the shoes, another sales clerk carefully placed them in their proper box and put the box in an eye catching bag. Gwenn gave Edwin a big hug and kissed him. Edwin enjoyed the attention.

As they strolled around the MGM shopping area, Edwin asked Gwenn, "What's with the couple's charade?"

"Nothing, I just like being with you and appreciate your generosity."

Gwenn had a room at the Dunes. Edwin stayed at the Riviera. Neither of them felt like taking a taxi to their respective hotels. With a Freudian slip, Gwenn suggested they get a room at the MGM and spend the night together. Edwin thought about Bindi. Although he had spoken to her a few days earlier, they had not seen each other since Vegas. Being in the moment, Edwin thought, *Why not*. Without realizing it, his thoughts came out in words through his lips.

Pleasantly surprised, Gwenn turned to face him and gave him a long passionate kiss. Edwin became aroused. Within a matter of a few moments of deciding to spend the night together, they had checked-in and had gotten a suite. Before Edwin had a moment to catch his breath, Gwenn ripped off his clothes. They spent the next several hours in fervent love-making.

The next morning, Edwin and Gwenn departed from the MGM. Each had a big smile on their face. The two said nothing to each other. No words were necessary. They both understood this was a one-night stand.

CHAPTER TWENTY

The sounds of clanging of tokens dropping into metal trays beneath one-armed bandits, combined with the ringing of bells and chimes, made the casino come alive like a carnival. At two o'clock in the morning, Edwin made his way past the blackjack table to the café when Norman Johnson spotted him. "Hey, Edwin, take a seat and play a few hands with us. This dealer is beating us out of our dough," Norman said.

Edwin took the open seat at third base and bought in for five hundred dollars. It wasn't surprising that three of his junketeers were playing blackjack at two a.m. "Hi fellas; how's the trip so far?" he said, as he made a twenty-five-dollar bet. The dealer dealt each player their hands.

Norman responded, "Not so good. I'm losing my shirt."

"Well maybe we can change your luck."

The dealer showed a four as his up card. Every player stood pat and did not take another card. The dealer flipped up his down card. It was a ten. He took a card from the top of the deck, a Queen of Hearts. The dealer busted. A small cheer went up from the table.

On four of the next five hands, the dealer busted. The junketeers high fived each other and gave Edwin a pat on the back. Shortly thereafter, Edwin colored up and left the group. "Thanks, guys, but I gotta go. I need to get some food."

Most of them were wasted from the free booze. Those that weren't, were so tired they could barely keep their heads off the felt. These were true gambling degenerates. Only Norman seemed awake enough to notice Edwin's departure. He did not say anything, happy to be winning a few hands. The distraction of the cocktail waitress bringing another round of drinks helped Edwin make his escape.

He finally made it to the café and took a seat at an open booth. The waitress brought him a cup of coffee and asked, "The usual—two eggs over easy, bacon and an English muffin?"

"Yes," Edwin replied, thankful for the brief moment of solitude.

"Hi Mr. Goldberg, may I join you?" the voice said. Edwin did not recognize the man's voice. He looked up to see Howard standing next to the bench on the other side of the booth.

"Sure, how can I help you?"

Howard, out of uniform, slid in on the red leather cushioned seat. Edwin almost did not recognize the craps dealer in street clothes. "Did you know Johnny Accardi?"

Edwin froze, an unmistakable look of fear etched across his face. Howard had unknowing struck a nerve. "Are you okay, Mr. Goldberg? I didn't mean to cause you any concern."

Edwin twitched a bit and said, "Why are you asking me about Accardi?"

"Well, it's just such a shame he got whacked, I mean with him being your representative and all."

Edwin had no idea what Howard babbled about. "What do you mean my 'representative'?"

"He's the person who took care of all those markers you signed and never paid."

"I don't know what you're talking about. What is it you want?"

"I want a piece of the action."

Edwin took a sip from his coffee mug. He waited for the waitress to finish bringing his food before he responded. "You know I don't sign for markers. I buy-in for cash."

"Yeah, that's the rumor going around. Don't get me wrong Mr. Goldberg, I'm very appreciative of the large tips you give us at the table, but I know you were skimming the casinos for cash. You must have another idea for taking money from this joint."

Edwin sighed. Howard obviously knew about the scam. "Not really. But I'm opened to suggestions." Edwin was being sarcastic with Howard. He took another bite of food.

"Here's my idea. When I'm dealing, you sign the marker as you always do, but instead of me giving you your normal ten thousand in chips, I add another yellow chip underneath the stack. After you're done playing, you color up and pay off the marker. You keep the rest. The eye in the sky is not sophisticated enough to see how much I'm giving you, and there's no way for the floor to communicate with security how much the marker is for."

Edwin's forehead crinkled and his nose turn upward. He rubbed his chin as he thought about what Howard had just proposed. The yellow chip was five-thousand dollars. "How much do you want?"

"A grand from each session you play. I noticed you only play one session each night. You give me three grand each trip you're out here with the junketeers. We never have to see each other. I have a safe deposit box at the bank on Charleston near downtown. I'll add your name as an authorized signer. You'll have your own key. You make sure you put the cash in the box before you leave."

"Are you playing me, Howard?"

"No sir. I need to make extra dough to get out of this town."

"What about the boxman and pit boss. Won't they be watching to make sure you're not giving me too much. I'm certain other dealers have thought of a similar scam, if the not the exact one?"

"Not to worry about the boxman. I'm giving him a piece of the action. As for the pit boss, I'll make sure he's not watching when I pass you the chips. Besides, he relies on the boxman to take care of that."

Edwin mulled the idea over. He was too tired to debate with Howard on the risks. "Okay, you got a deal."

Howard slid a safe deposit key in Edwin's hand as he shook it. "Thank you sir. I'll see you tomorrow night. My shift starts at ten p.m."

Edwin sat, contemplating the arrangement he just made. The way he figured, if he could get Gwenn to play opposite of how he played liked they did before, they could walk away with almost five thousand each night. Giving Howard his share would leave roughly two thousand dollars for him and Gwenn each. Almost six thousand dollars each trip.

Edwin had stashed over two hundred thousand dollars away over the past seven months. He had enough to purchase a seat on the Board of Trade to begin trading and buy a McDonald's franchise. His decision what to do had been made. His lessons with Bill Beckwith had been very informative. Bill enlightened Edwin that the elite traders cleared over five hundred grand every year; all legal. No one to worry about, no shady deals. He felt ready to move on from the travel business. Things were getting too dicey. He did not trust Carter. The Las Vegas police were still investigating Johnny Accardi's death, and rumor had it the feds were tightening down on the families, especially those involved with the Stardust Casino.

CHAPTER TWENTY-ONE

AUGUST, 1975

On a hot muggy Sunday afternoon in the Windy City, Bindi had the day off from training. Edwin, not travelling, remained in town. They decided to watch a ball game at Wrigley Field, affectionately referred to by local patrons as the "Friendly Confines." The Houston Astros were in town for a four-game series. Bindi had never been to Wrigley Field. Edwin always took his baseball glove to a game.

The malty aroma of beer, cigar smoke, and peanut shells wafted through the left bleachers. The air was permeated with a distinct stench from fans who sat on the bleacher seats in the hot sun. Many of them did not wear shirts.

Wrigley Field, known for its Boston ivy that covered the outfield brick walls, had a unique charm and charisma that made watching a game a happening. The Cubs, unfortunately, played so badly they even offended Charlie Brown and Linus. Hence, the Cub fans were called *Loveable Losers* and their fans' favorite expression was, *Wait till next year.*

Then, in the fourth inning, the Cubs' center fielder, Rick Monday, connected on a fast ball and hit a deep towering drive toward left field. Back, back, it drifted over the left field wall into the bleachers and headed directly toward Edwin. A bunch of people tried to catch the ball. Bindi ducked and covered her head as a scuffle to catch the orb ensued.

Edwin was usually on the wrong side of close when it came to catching a ball, either during batting practice or during the game. This time, however, it was different. Edwin heard a pop. He squeezed his mitt to make sure that if the ball was inside, it stayed there. He pulled his mitt toward his body to protect it. Once the crowd around him dispersed, he opened the glove. There it sat in the pocket. He'd caught the home run. Edwin turned and handed the ball to Bindi, excited to receive the souvenir.

Even though it was a beautiful day at the ballpark, the Cubs, unfortunately, lost to the Astros, 8 to 4.

After the game, Edwin took Bindi out for dinner at a local eatery. Although they had only spent a few days together in Vegas and met again more than six weeks later, each felt as if they had known each other for a long time. They felt comfortable being together.

For some reason he had the notion that if a woman was hot, she must have a boyfriend. So while they waited for their order and discussed the game, he asked, "Bindi, you're beautiful and smart, how come you don't have a boyfriend?"

Initially, Bindi, taken aback by Edwin's question, did not respond. After a pause, she answered, "I had a boyfriend in high school. We dated most of our senior year. He went to Alabama on a football scholarship. I went to the University of Iowa for my undergraduate degree in marketing. At first we kept in touch, but after a few months he stopped calling. And that was that. I focused on grades and worked to pay for college. Besides, I'm very comfortable and secure with myself. I don't need a man to make me happy."

Edwin smiled. "I'm lucky I met you."

Bindi's eyes widened as her lips turned upward. "Awe, that's so sweet. I'm lucky I bumped into you too."

"Yeah, literally," Edwin said, as a smirk crossed his face.

They ate quietly enjoying their time together. When they were done eating, Edwin escorted Bindi to her car. She had parked near the ballpark and met Edwin at the gate. As they strolled down the street, they held hands and talked about getting together the next evening.

"How about a movie? Have you seen *Jaws*, *The Stepford Wives*, or *One Flew Over the Cuckoo's Nest*?" Edwin asked.

"No, I haven't had a chance to see any of those movies. That sounds good."

"Excellent. Do you want to drive over to Old Orchard Shopping Center? *One Flew Over the Cuckoo's Nest* is playing at seven thirty. I'll catch a cab and meet you there."

"Okay. We have a plan. I'll meet you at the entrance to the theatre."

Upon arriving at Bindi's car, Edwin hugged her and gently brushed the hair away from her face with his hand. Electricity travelled through Bindi's body. He locked his eyes onto hers and moved closer. Edwin's lips met Bindi's. The warmth of his mouth sent a flow of excitement through her body. She wrapped her arms around his neck and lost herself in the passionate embrace. And just like that, the kiss was over. Bindi became aware of her surroundings. "Uh . . . I should go. It's getting late and I need to get up early."

Bindi got into her car and drove off. Edwin stood watching her tail lights disappear into the blackness of the night. Like a thief in the night, Bindi had stolen his heart. He never knew what hit him.

The next morning, Edwin stopped in at the local florist and ordered two dozen gorgeous red roses to be delivered to Bindi's residence. Bindi arrived home at approximately 4:30 p.m. The flowers arrived in an exquisite glass vase about fifteen minutes later.

She cried tears of joy, overwhelmed that Edwin cared enough about her to take the time and effort to show his appreciation by sending flowers. She placed the vase on her dining room table. They immediately brightened her spirits and broke the monotony of her daily routine. She called Edwin to thank him. "Edwin, the roses are gorgeous. Thank you so much."

A smile crossed Edwin's face and his eyes lit up. "I'm glad you like them. Are we still meeting tonight?"

"Yes, we are. I'll meet you at the theater around sevenish."

The movie, a drama, gave Bindi and Edwin a lot to discuss as they sat enjoying a late night dinner at a local café. Bindi was curious why Edwin took a cab to the theatre. "Edwin, I'm surprised you took a cab tonight. Is your car in the shop?"

Edwin's lip turned up slightly. "No, I don't own a car."

"What? How to do you get around?"

"I take the 'L'. Living downtown makes it easy to either walk or take public transportation."

A blank look crossed her face. "I'm confused. You make a lot of money, but you don't own a car, why not?"

"Because I'm saving my money for other things."

"Huh. I guess it makes sense with your traveling so much," she finally said.

Engrossed in their conversation, already after midnight, Bindi finally looked at her watch and said, "It's getting late, and we both need to get up early."

Edwin walked Bindi to her vehicle and hugged her tightly. She moved her face close to his and let their mouths touch. It was a long kiss with a lot of tongue they each enjoyed. She stepped back and put both her hands on Edwin's chest, "I gotta go," she said as she got into her car.

Edwin walked back into the all night-café to use the payphone to call a cab. He knew he would have hell to pay at five o'clock, but the way he felt when he was with Bindi, made it worth it.

CHAPTER TWENTY-TWO

The next weekend, Edwin returned to Vegas. It was mid-afternoon when detective Malone knocked on Edwin's suite door. Edwin, relaxed, after he made sure all of his guests' requests had been taken care of that morning. Tickets waited at the Will Call window for those who wanted to see a show. Dinner reservations were made at various eating establishments for others. And other requests would be fulfilled discreetly. Edwin, not expecting anyone, called, "Who is it?"

"Detective Malone, mind if I come in?"

Edwin cautiously opened the door and invited the detective inside. "How can I help you Detective?"

"I heard you were back in town and wanted to give you an update on Johnny Accardi's case."

"Oh," Edwin said. He noticed the Detective held a large manila envelope.

"Yeah, we found more evidence at the crime scene. We also have surveillance tapes from various casinos. As far as we can tell, you're not off the hook. Incriminating evidences links you to the murder. You must have really pissed off Valerie Taylor to make her point the finger at you."

"Not really. She's the one who broke off our relationship. I hadn't seen her for over a year. It was a mere coincidence that Ms. Maxwell asked me to attend the wedding with her. What did you want to tell me, Detective?"

Malone opened the envelope and held out copies of the markers Edwin had signed right before Johnny's death. "Do you recognize these?"

"Of course I do. These are markers I signed at the Dunes. How did you get them?"

The Detective pointed to the initials J.A. scribbled on the "Approved by" line of the markers. "These are Johnny's initials. The pit boss gave copies of them to us. Apparently these markers were never repaid. Thirty thousand dollars in unpaid markers is a lot of motive for you to kill Johnny."

Edwin's nose and forehead scrunched up. His eyes narrowed. He scratched his head and asked, "Why would the casino give you these markers without asking me to make good on them? I have enough money to cover these."

"According to one of the pit bosses, he received an anonymous call telling him you had no intention paying these." Edwin didn't comment. He waited before speaking.

Malone broke the silence and said, "This is a small town, and word gets around quickly. If you skip out on paying your debt, bad things can happen."

Edwin's heart began to race. He glared at Malone. "You still did not answer my question, Detective Malone. Why did the pit boss give you copies of these markers instead of asking me to pay them?"

"I don't know. Why don't you ask him?"

"Oh, I can assure you that I will. What is his name?"

"James McCracken," the detective said.

"Thank you detective. Any other questions I can answer for you?"

"No Mr. Goldberg. Have a nice day. Thanks for the cooperation."

"This is the evidence you have to incriminate me in Johnny's murder? Three unpaid markers? Seriously, Detective, if I didn't know better, I'd think you were harassing me. What about the other evidence you said was found at the crime scene?"

"What about it? You know I can't divulge any information to you in an ongoing investigation."

As soon as the detective left, Edwin called Carter. "Joe, we have an issue with my markers."

Joe interrupted Edwin before he could say another word, "Not over the phone. Let's discuss it when you're back at the office."

The phone line went dead. Edwin stood holding the receiver. Frustrated by the turn of events, he could feel palpitations as his heart fluttered. His face reddened as his mind raced in a million different directions.

Undaunted, Edwin went to the Dunes to confront James McCracken. Edwin strolled through the casino asking various employees where he could find the man. He finally located him at the craps pit area. McCracken saw Edwin first. "Well, look who showed up. If it isn't the deadbeat junket host. You have a lot of nerve showing your face around here."

Edwin pulled out three stacks of cash and said, "Here are three stacks of 'high society.' Stick it where the sun don't shine, Phil." He put the cash on an empty craps table. "High society" slang for a pile of cash worth ten-thousand dollars. "Now give me back my markers. And I want them stamped 'Paid-in-Full'."

McCracken, a large man who did not take heat from anyone, was well connected with the families. "My name is James, not Phil. Wait here. I'll get you your markers."

A few moments later McCracken returned and handed the markers to Edwin. They were stamped "Paid-in-Full." Edwin took the markers and said, "You will always be Phil McCracken to me."

McCracken retorted back, "Why's that?"

Edwin said, "Because if you say it out loud you'll understand, dumb-shit." He turned away from McCracken and began walking away.

McCracken said, "Phil McCracken," out loud.

"Hey asshole, that's not funny," he heard McCracken call out.

Edwin knew that McCracken would not dare touch him in front of witnesses in the casino.

* * *

The evidence gathered by the Las Vegas police did not amount to anything much. They still had not found the murder weapon.

They were able to lift five sets of finger-prints from the crime scene. Only one set remained unidentified.

The few witnesses who saw Johnny go into the room with the female gave different descriptions of what she looked like. Detective Evans and Malone were getting frustrated. They were getting a lot of heat from their Captain. Every lead they had led to a dead-end.

Someone had to have seen something. "What are we over-looking?" Malone said out loud as he intensely studied the evidence pinned to the crime investigation bulletin board.

Evans interrupted Malone's train of thought. "Finally, we have a break in the case."

Malone glanced at Malone, "What do you got?"

"The unidentified set of finger prints showed up in the FBI data base. It belongs to Aaron Taylor. Taylor had to register his finger prints with the Federal Government when he owned his seat at the Chicago Board of Trade."

"Where is Mr. Taylor now?"

"He lives in Morton Grove, Illinois."

Malone shook his head back and forth. He thought, *Can solving this case get any worse*? Because Taylor resided in Illinois, they were going to need to enlist the cooperation of that city's local police department.

* * *

Aaron Taylor was not home when the police rang the door bell to his dwelling in the Chicago suburb of Morton Grove. His wife, Margaret, answered the door and invited the officers and detectives in. She had no idea why they were there. One of the uniformed officers showed her a warrant that allowed the police to search the premises. A short time later, another officer called out, "Over here in the home office."

The spacious abode had a separate home office located toward the rear of the ground floor where Aaron worked at nights and on weekends. The officer showed the detective an open desk drawer from which he had removed several file folders. Sitting at the bottom of the drawer was a Colt "Combat Commander" .45ACP M1911 pistol. Another detective, wearing gloves, put the weapon into a plastic evidence bag for testing.

The third detective on the scene asked Margaret where her husband was. "He's at work at the Chicago Board of Trade. Why? What's going on?"

"Were investigating a homicide ma'am."

Margaret's mouth opened wide and her eyes widened. "Homicide? Whose?"

"The victim's name was Johnny Accardi. We have reason to believe your husband was involved in the crime."

"That's impossible. Why would my husband kill our daughter's boyfriend? When was Johnny murdered?"

"I'm surprised your daughter didn't tell you. He was killed when they were in Vegas."

"You're making a big mistake Detective. My husband was here with me the entire weekend that my daughter and Johnny went to Vegas."

"Sorry, ma'am. We're only doing our job. We got a call from the Las Vegas Police Department, and a judge issued the warrant to search your home."

The officers went through the rest of the home looking for anything that might link Aaron Taylor to Johnny Accardi's murder. They did not find any.

Immediately after the police left, Margaret called Aaron. "Hi honey, the police were here. They found a gun in your desk drawer and said something about Johnny's murder investigation. What's going on?"

Aaron remained calm. He said, "Not to worry. It's probably a misunderstanding. I'll talk to the police and get it straightened out."

"Did you know about Johnny's murder?"

"Yeah. I did. Valerie told me about when she got back."

"Why didn't you tell me? Why didn't she tell me?"

"I don't know dear. You'll have to ask her. I thought she'd told you that's why I didn't mention it."

"I don't believe you. You're hiding something." Before Aaron could respond, she hung up on him.

Aaron Taylor left his office and immediately drove home. He wanted to clear his name. He knew he had nothing to do with Johnny's murder.

CHAPTER TWENTY-THREE

The pleasant warmth of the September day faded as the cool night air drifted over the town of Morton Grove, Illinois. Two detectives greeted Aaron Taylor, who waited for him as he drove his Silver Mercedes Benz 450 SL into the drive-way. "Can I help you, officers?" he asked pretending that he did not know why they waited for him.

"Sir, we would like you to come to the station to answer questions about Jonny Accardi."

"Sure thing, officers. I just want to tell my wife that you are taking me to the station for questioning."

"Yes, sir."

The two officers followed him into his home. "Honey, I'm going to the police station with these officers. They have some questions about Johnny's murder. I'll be back as soon as I can."

Margaret was in a foul mood. Upset that neither her daughter or husband told her about her daughter's murder. "Whatever," was all she said.

Meanwhile, Detective Malone looked over the file folder. None of the airline manifests showed Aaron Taylor traveling to Las Vegas from Chicago during the weekend Johnny Accardi was killed. It made no sense. Detective Bell called Malone. "I got the ballistics' report on Taylor's gun. It's not a match."

"What? Did you say it's not a match?"

"Affirmative. Looks like we're back too square one."

Bell made his way into the interrogation room where Aaron Taylor sat. "Mr. Taylor, can you explain to me how your finger prints ended up in the hotel room where Johnny Accardi was murdered?"

"No sir, I have no clue; especially since I wasn't even in Vegas that weekend. I was here with my wife. We went out for dinner that Saturday evening at Mr. Ricky's in Old Orchard. You can check my credit card statement. If you ask me, I think Edwin Goldberg plugged Johnny."

"Why would you think that?"

"Because he's jealous and wanted my daughter back. He told me so."

"When did he tell you this?"

"At the Board of Trade. I introduced him to my boss. He wanted to learn how to trade options. Edwin approached me and said he wanted to make a lot of money to win my daughter back." Aaron Taylor fabricated the story. He saw an opportunity to implicate Edwin and bring the bastard down. He looked for any reason to cause friction between him and Beckwith.

Bell shook his head. Something stunk about the whole case.

Aaron asked Bell, "By the way, where did they find my finger prints?"

Bell looked him straight in the eyes. Aaron's face appeared cold and callous. Bell said, "On a silver cigar case, of all places."

"Huh." Aaron thought it best not to say another word.

The detective showed a photo of the cigar case to Taylor. "Do you recognize this?"

"Yes, of course I do. It looks similar to my cigar case." Taylor's cigar case had three tubes and interior cedar lining, the perfect size to fit in a suit jacket pocket. The initial's 'AT' were engraved on the front of the case.

"Any idea how your cigar case ended up with Johnny Accardi on the night he got murdered?"

"No. I don't. Do you have any other questions, detective?" Taylor's eye twitched. His nose curled up and his fist tightened ever so slightly.

"Not for now." Bell turned away from Taylor. Half looking over his shoulder he said, "Okay, you're free to go Mr. Taylor."

§ § §

Malone sat at his desk, despondent with the turn of events. How did Aaron Taylor's cigar case get into the room where Accardi was shot? It made no sense. Aaron Taylor was not in Las Vegas. An idea to solve the mystery presented itself as he flipped through the file. He phoned Valerie Taylor. "Hello, Ms. Taylor? Detective Malone from the Las Vegas Police Department, do you mind if I ask you a few questions about the night Johnny Accardi was murdered?"

"Hi Detective. No, I don't mind so long as you promise to stop harassing my family."

"Sure thing. We're just doing our job, ma'am. Do you have any idea how your father's silver cigar case ended up in the room where Johnny was found?"

Valerie paused to ponder the question. She thought for a moment. "Did Johnny still have his suit jacket with him?"

Malone did a cursory review of the file in front of him, "Yes, it was in the room."

"Well then, it makes perfect sense to me."

"Care to enlighten me Ms. Taylor."

"It's simple Detective, before we left for Vegas I took my father's cigar case from his office. Johnny mentioned he enjoyed my father's cigars. I thought it would be a nice gesture to bring him a few to enjoy while we were in Vegas. I didn't know how to pack the cigars so they wouldn't get damaged. I took the case with the three cigars and stuck it in his coat pocket as a surprise. Johnny smoked one of the cigars at the reception. In fact, Edwin commented on the case. Johnny probably forgot he had it with him when he met up with the hooker. He was extremely wasted."

"Sounds plausible. Thanks for clarifying it for me."

"Any luck with the investigation?"

"No ma'am. Looks like we hit another dead end."

A wicked smirk graced her face. Her eyes narrowed. "I still think Edwin did it."

"Yes ma'am. I understand. We're keeping all possibilities open. I'll let you know if we find anything else."

Valerie placed the handle of the phone on the cradle.

Detective Malone, satisfied with Valerie's explanation, made a note for the record. The evidence implicating Edwin in the crime was sketchy at best. Nothing gave the District Attorney enough to indict him and certainly not enough to get a conviction.

There must be someone we haven't considered yet Malone, thought. They'd ruled out the murder being a mob hit. Deep down Malone didn't believe Edwin had anything to do with the crime. If anything, it looked as if the prostitute might be the person who whacked Johnny for his money. But that made no sense either. He yawned. The case would have to wait until the next day. Malone had other cases to solve. He left early that night to spend some time with his family.

CHAPTER TWENTY-FOUR

"You disgust me. This conversation is over," Gwenn said to Herbert. He had asked Gwenn on a date. She was fully aware of his fetish for fucking hookers in Vegas. He had boasted frequently about his conquests.

"What, I'm not good enough for you? I bet you like banging Edwin."

"Leave him out of this." She walked away before the conversation got more heated.

Herbert, wound tighter than a drum, did not know what he should do. He worried the hooker he hired to be with Edwin the night of Johnny Accardi's murder would point the finger at him. He just didn't know how to get back in touch with her. The number she gave him had been disconnected.

Everything had gone wrong that night, it seemed to Herbert—unbeknownst to him Johnny had approached the lady of easy virtue after he left Valerie. Flashing a roll of Benjamins had caused the hooker to lose focus. Johnny offered her twice what Herbert had given her. Seeing all of that cash she thought, *how would Herbert find out she went with a different man?*

As instructed by Herbert, the lady of pleasure brought the mark back to her hotel room. She wore a blond wig to hide her true identity. Johnny, wasted, passed out within ten minutes of getting to the room.

Herbert watched as the two had entered the room where the indecent act would take place. Fixated on Gwenn's romantic interest in Edwin, he secretly adored Gwenn and wanted her for himself. He was pissed that she had rebuffed him every time he made an advance toward her. Tonight he would put an end to Edwin's life. High on cocaine he was not thinking rationally.

Herbert mistook Johnny for Edwin, an obvious case of mistaken identity. Herbert could not distinguish Edwin from Johnny in the darkness. It never crossed his mind that his favorite lady of the night would pick-up the wrong man.

Johnny's date left the room with a smile on her face. She had taken over five-thousand dollars off of the passed-out Johnny. Easy money. She tossed the blond wig into a plastic bag, put it into her oversized purse and walked out of the hotel into the blackness of the night.

Herbert seized the moment. Quietly, he opened the door that she left ajar where Johnny remained. Though dark, he did not turn on the lights because the glow from the clock radio made his target visible. He pulled the gun from his jacket pocket and fired once at the man's head. He heard a thud. He quickly fired three more rounds into the figure. The sound of the gunshot was muffled by a pillow he'd placed over the barrel. Anyone hearing it would have thought a car backfired. Herbert, giddily removed what he considered to be the only obstacle between him and Gwenn.

He replayed the events of that night in his mind over and over again. The next morning, when Edwin did not show up he thought he'd succeeded in his endeavor. Only when he saw Edwin at the airport terminal with his junketeers did he wonder who he had killed.

At the airport terminal, Herbert sat deep in thought and wondered how could he plant the murder weapon in Edwin's possession? Richard then broke his train of thought.

Richard asked, "Hey man, you alright? You look like you'd just seen a ghost."

"Yeah, just thinking about the score we made."

"Did you see Edwin's face? Looks like someone pummeled him good. I wonder what he did to deserve getting walloped."

"No, I haven't seen him. But I'm sure he deserved it."

"Deserved what?" Gwenn interrupted overhearing the conversation.

Richard answered, "Getting his face brutalized. Have you seen it?"

"Yeah, who do you think helped him get some ice on it? For your information, Johnny Accardi hit him."

A scowl came across Herbert's face. He left Richard and Gwenn before he said anything else. "Excuse me," he mumbled. He quickly made his way toward the restrooms.

Richard looked at Gwenn, "What's eating him?"

"I have no idea. But he seems to be upset with Edwin for some reason."

"Why? What did Edwin ever do to him?"

"As far as I know, nothing. But I think it has to do with me. Herbert keeps asking me out, and I keep turning him down." Gwenn turned to Richard and looked directly at him, "Why would Herbert think I'd want to be with someone like him who screws hookers?"

Richard started to open his mouth. Before he had a chance to say something, Gwenn realized her mistake. "Don't answer that," she said quickly trying to retrace her steps.

Richard did not say another word. He turned and left Gwenn. The plane started boarding, and they both had to attend to their respective guests.

CHAPTER TWENTY-FIVE

Jonny's uncle, Tazio, spoke with Valerie briefly at Johnny's funeral. Nearly two months after Johnny's untimely demise, Valerie requested another audience with Tazio Accardi. She agreed to meet with him at a Jim & Pete's Italian Restaurant, a local favorite since 1941, near River Forest.

Three body-guards sat in the booth in front of where Valerie and Tazio sat. Another four men sat in the booth behind them. Two additional men sat at the table directly next to theirs. Tzaio and Valerie were well protected. Tazio, wasn't expecting trouble, but took precautions anyway because he didn't know what trouble Johnny had gotten himself into that ended up get him killed.

"My nephew never listened to me," he started the conversation. "I told him to keep a low profile. But, instead, he had to flash his money and be the big shot. How long did you know him?"

"I met Johnny last June. We were introduced by a mutual friend." Tears welled up in her eyes as she spoke. Tazio handed her his handkerchief to wipe the water droplets from her face.

"I understand you were with Johnny the night he got shot. Any idea who whacked him?"

Valerie regained her composure and said, "No Mr. Accardi. We had a fight that night at the wedding. Johnny got drunk and was hitting on several other women. My former boyfriend also attended the wedding. Johnny became jealous. We argued about him and then Johnny left. According to the police, Johnny checked into another hotel with a female escort."

Tazio interrupted, "You mean a hooker."

"Maybe, I don't know. He never came back to our suite at Caesars Palace and I didn't know what happened to him until the police showed up at our room two days later."

"Why didn't you call the police if Johnny went missing for two days?"

"Because, Johnny often left me alone for a day or two when he took care of business. I never asked him what he did or where he went."

"You're a smart young lady. About your former boyfriend, what's his name?"

"Edwin Goldberg. Why do you ask?"

Tzaio took a swig from his glass of Chianti to wash down his food. He looked around the restaurant. At 2:30 p.m., the eating establishment was empty apart from themselves and his men. "Valerie, is there anything else you might want to tell me about Johnny, or anything you think I should know? Did Edwin kill Johnny?"

"Edwin said he wanted me back. He told me he made a lot of money in the junket business. Also, I want you to know I had no interest in Edwin and that I loved your nephew. I had hoped we would get married someday."

Tazio raised an eyebrow. "Interesting. Do you know why your father, was in Vegas that weekend?"

"What are you talking about? My father wasn't in Vegas that weekend. If he were, I certainly didn't know about it. What makes you think my father was in Vegas that weekend?"

Valerie was coy. She wondered if Detective Malone had mentioned the cigar case to Tazio.

"Apparently your father flew out to Vegas, and Johnny made arrangements for him to stay at the Dunes. My confidant there gave me this information when he heard about Johnny's body being found."

"I'm confused. I don't know why my father would have been in Vegas. He never said anything to me about it. Besides, I already explained to Detective Malone about my father's cigar case being found at the crime scene. Are you sure it was that same weekend?"

"Okay. How are you holding up? Is the condo working out for you?"

Tazio changed the subject. He knew that Aaron Taylor was not in Vegas that weekend. He wanted to see how Valerie would respond to his accusation.

Tazio Accardi liked Valerie. He thought Johnny had made a wise decision to be with her. Tazio made sure Valerie could stay in Johnny's condo for as long as she wanted. He took care of the expenses. Arrangements were made for Johnny's father to remove all of Johnny's personal possessions from the residence. For all practical purposes, it was as if Johnny had never lived there.

"Yes, the condo is wonderful. Johnny's father gave me his Corvette. The family has been generous and supportive. I want you to know that I traded it for a Mercedes. It was too painful when I drove the Vette because it reminded me of Johnny." Valerie's face turned red. She cried, wiping away the tears with her hand.

Tazio believed family came first. Because Valerie was Johnny's girl-friend, he considered her to be family. "You let me know if you need any money. I'll help you for a few more months until you get back on your feet again."

"Thank you, you're very kind. I'm alright with cash for now."

Valerie conveniently forgot to mention that when she opened the safe in the condo she found more than one hundred-thousand-dollars inside. She took the cash but left Johnny's jewelry and other important documents for his father to find. Johnny's father did not ask any questions about anything else that might have been inside before he had a chance to open it. He still mourned the loss of his son.

"If you'll excuse me, Mr. Accardi, I've got some other matters to attend to. Thank you for meeting me and for lunch."

"You're quite welcome, Ms. Taylor. Luigi will follow you to make sure you get home safe."

Valerie left the restaurant and got into her car. Luigi followed behind her. She had visions of Luigi pulling out a pistol and plugging her in the head. Fortunately, once she arrived home, Luigi honked and waved goodbye. She took a deep breath and sighed in relief that she arrived home in one piece.

♠ ♠ ♠

The knock on the door woke Edwin from a deep slumber. Before answering, he called out, "Who is it?" He did not expect anyone at his apartment this early in the morning.

"Luigi, I'm here on behalf of Tazio Accardi." Standing six-two, weighing about two hundred fifty pounds, and muscular, he was a foreboding image of a man. At age forty, he could out do men half his age.

Edwin's throat tightened when he looked through the peep-hole, "Just a minute."

He opened the door. Luigi stood waiting to be invited in. He wore a black suit, white shirt and a black tie. His shoes were highly polished. He said, "May I come inside?"

"Sure, come on in. How can I help you?"

"It's been brought to my boss's attention that you work for Mr. Joseph Carter helping with his junket business. It has also been brought to his attention that you were in an altercation with Johnny before he was killed. I've been sent here to get some information for Mr. Accardi."

"Such as?"

"Such as, for starters, how much do you get paid to bring the junketeers to Vegas?"

"Five-thousand a month." He moved over to his desk and pulled open a drawer.

Luigi started to reach for his gun. Edwin saw the movement and slowly backed away from the desk. "Hey, relax. I'm getting my pay stubs for you." Edwin pulled out several pay stubs from the drawer. "Here, these are my pay stubs from Global Enterprises."

Luigi took the check stubs from Edwin. "May I take these to show Mr. Accardi?"

"Of course."

"Next question; did you have anything to do with Johnny's death?"

"No sir, I did not. I met Johnny at a wedding reception. He was dating my ex-girlfriend, Valerie Taylor. He got upset and sucker-punched me. We got into it for a few seconds, but that's as far as it went. I then escorted my date back to her hotel room before heading back to my own hotel. That was the only time I had any involvement with Johnny. I had a black eye for several weeks."

"So far, your story checks out with what we know. What kind of a car do you drive?"

"I don't own a car. Why does everyone think I own a car?"

"Really? I find that hard to believe. The other associates for Mr. Carter all drive brand new expensive cars. They all live lavishly. What are you doing with all your money?"

Edwin didn't want to say too much about his financial situation, so he made up a story. "I have student loans to pay, I have rent, after taxes, there's not really a lot left over."

Luigi, though a thug, was highly intelligent. He didn't buy Edwin's story, but he chose not to press the issue.

"Okay, thank you for your cooperation. One last question, though: did you happen to see Valerie's father in Vegas the weekend Johnny was killed?"

"Aaron Taylor? In Vegas? No. I didn't know he was there."

"Have a good day, Mr. Goldberg."

Luigi left Edwin's apartment. Edwin sat down on his couch contemplating what to do next.

Luigi went to his boss's office to report what he learned about Edwin. Tazio Accardi's office, sparsely decorated, looked bare. He kept things simple. He never liked to show off.

"Hey boss, this Goldberg fella, he seems to be an odd ball compared to the other associates working for Carter. He lives in a studio apartment, doesn't own a car, and doesn't spend any money. He said he only earns five thousand a month in the junket business. I can't find anything to remotely suggest he has any money. If he does, he's very careful not to show it."

Tazio listened to Luigi's report, fascinated with Edwin. Edwin reminded him of someone else—himself. "Do you think he had anything to do with Johnny's death?"

"No boss. I don't think so."

"Have you spoken to Joseph Carter yet?"

"Not yet sir. Apparently he's out of town for now."

Tazio smiled. "How convenient for him. Okay, stay on it and see what else we can find out about Joseph Carter. And one more thing, I want a face-to-face meeting with this Edwin Goldberg."

Three days passed after Luigi spoke with Edwin. The morning air, felt damp as the fog slowly lifted and the sun began to shine through. On his morning jog, Edwin failed to notice when a black sedan pulled alongside of him. The rear door opened, and a man dressed in all black exited the vehicle and stopped him. "My boss would like a word with you Mr. Goldberg," the mystery man uttered.

Edwin realized it behooved him to cooperate and got into the car without making a fuss. A man sat in the back seat. He wore an overcoat over his suit and a dark grey fedora. "Mr. Goldberg, my name is Tazio Accardi, I understand you knew my nephew, Johnny, God rest his soul. Any idea who killed him?"

"No sir," Edwin answered showing deference to the elderly man. He knew enough not to upset him.

"What happened between you and my nephew the night he was murdered?"

Edwin repeated his story and explained what he had told everyone else. He finished telling Tazio everything he knew about the case and that Valerie's allegation that he wanted her back was not true. Then, in a flash, he had an idea.

"Mr. Accardi," he began, "With all due respect, if your business acquaintances had nothing to do with Johnny's death, and the last person to have seen him was a prostitute, maybe you could offer a reward for anyone who provides you information leading to the arrest and conviction of Johnny's killer."

Tazio sat quietly mulling over Edwin's suggestion. "Why would I do that?"

"Well, sir, if it were me, I would see who came forward. Someone has information about your nephew, but might be afraid to go to the police. As a grieving uncle, it makes perfect sense to want to find the killer and make it profitable for the lady who was with him that night to earn some extra money by being a good citizen."

Accardi told the driver to stop the car. "You have a point, young man. I want you to place the announcement about a reward in Vegas and take care of it. Just keep my name out of it. Make up some story about Johnny's parents offering the reward. I'll make sure my brother is told about it. I think you have your own motive to find out who the killer is as much as I do."

Tazio opened the door and told Edwin, "Get out."

Edwin wasted no time getting back to his apartment. His mind raced at warp speed to conjure up a reward worthy of the mystery woman coming forward. *Twenty-five thousand dollars should be enough*, he thought.

Edwin called Detective Malone and told him his idea. The detective approved, and said he would get the newspapers and TV networks to make the announcement. Before he ended the conversation, Malone needed to get something off his chest. He believed this to be the appropriate time to tell Edwin exactly how he felt. "You know you're no better than the whores in this town. They smile and pretend they're happy to see you.

They cater to your desires and make you feel good while they take your money. To them, you're just another mark; a sucker. Inside, underneath the smile, they hate you."

Edwin interrupted, "I have no idea what you're talking about."

"Sure you do. The casinos provide the dazzle for those junketeers you bring. You lure them in with free rooms, free booze, free food and whatever else they crave. Then the casinos take all of their money and you laugh behind their back. You don't even need to figure how to get them back because you have a waiting list of other gullible victims. The casinos just bleed them dry. You know as well as I do that no one leaves Vegas a winner."

"Are you finished Detective?"

"Yeah, I'm done."

"Just remember, if it weren't for the casinos and the junketeers who patronize them, you'd probably be out of job. Keep me posted if anybody calls about the reward money."

And with that, the conversation ended.

Tazio Accardi rarely showed any emotion. But when Luigi showed him a photo of Joseph Carter, he slammed his fist on the table. Regaining his composure, he looked at Luigi and said, "So Mr. Joseph Carter is a ghost." He crumbled up the photo and threw it off to the side.

"What do you mean he's 'a ghost'?"

"Because Joseph Carter is Paul Bazzoli. Bazzoli supposedly died in 1962. Damn him."

Luigi remained quiet. He knew better than to say anything when Tazio was this upset.

"What about the junket business he's operating—Global Enterprises? Did you find anything?" Tazio asked.

"No boss. When we went to the place, the office was empty."

CHAPTER TWENTY-SIX

Empty. The entire office sat empty except for the cubicle partitions. Even the desk and chairs were gone. Nothing remained. Edwin raced over to Carter's office and pushed open the door. His vacant office; cleaned out as if it never existed.

Edwin felt a sinking feeling in the pit of his stomach. Shortly after he arrived at the office, Gwenn, Richard and Herbert showed up. One word could sum up all of their emotions—stunned.

"What the hell?" Richard blurted out.

Gwenn stood at the front door speechless.

Herbert went to his cubicle. His personal items hanging on the interior walls were gone. He crumpled to the ground, bent his knee, put his head down and wept.

Edwin asked everyone, "So do any of you have any idea what we should do now?"

No one spoke. "Well I do. Meet me back here tomorrow afternoon. And bring your list of junketeers with you."

Edwin did not wait around. He had things to do and people to see. Gwenn followed him out of the building. "Hold up there 'Bandit', what are you up to now?"

Holding both of her shoulders and looking straight into her eyes. "Do you trust me?"

"Yes, of course."

"Good. Then let's talk tomorrow night. I'll stop by your place at about eight and tell you the plan." He released his grip and walked away. Gwenn just stood in the same place, dazed and confused. She did not know what to do next.

* * *

Edwin first stopped at the bank and then immediately went to Jeffrey Katz's office. Katz's receptionist asked, "Do you have an appointment?"

"No ma'am, but, I'm a client of his. If Mr. Katz is available, I'd like to speak with him."

The receptionist, a middle-aged woman, eyed Edwin suspiciously. Edwin, not the typical client of Baker & McKenzie, was younger than the other clients, who were mostly corporations and high end executives.

She picked up the phone and dialed Jeffrey Katz's extension. "There's a Mr. Edwin Goldberg here to see you, sir. He says it's important that he meet with you. All right, I'll tell him." She hung up the receiver, smiled at Edwin and said, "Please have a seat. Mr. Katz will be out in a moment."

Edwin, too anxious and nervous to sit, paced around the empty waiting area, sometimes stopping to look out the large window at Lake Michigan. Only five minutes elapsed, but it seemed like an eternity to him.

Jeffrey Katz came around the corner and greeted Edwin. "Hello, Edwin." The two men shook hands. Edwin said, "I know I don't have an appointment, but I need to get started on a new project right away."

"Come on back. Let's see what I can do for you."

Edwin explained the dilemma he had with Carter vanishing into thin air. Not too concerned about Carter, especially knowing that he made waves with the mob, Edwin spelled out his plan to Katz. "I want you to find an office to lease downtown for my business, ERGENT. Also, start the negotiations with McDonald's to purchase a franchise, and start the paperwork for me to buy a seat on the Chicago Board of Trade."

Katz wrote down detailed notes of Edwin's requests. He put his pen down on the yellow legal pad. "When would you like me to start on all of this?" he said, mocking Edwin.

Edwin, in no mood to play games, replied "Yesterday." He pulled out a cashier's check made out to Baker & McKenzie in the amount of twenty-five thousand dollars, and handed it to Katz. "Here is another retainer."

Katz looked at the check. His eyes widened, his jaw dropped. He rose from his seat from behind his desk and said, "I'll start on this immediately. Stop by Ms. Burk's desk on the way out and she'll get you a receipt."

After he left Katz's office, Edwin immediately went back to his studio and called Big Julie. "Hello, Big Julie?"

"Yes?" came his reply.

"This is Edwin Goldberg from Chicago. I met you in Las Vegas with Joseph Carter. I'm one of his associates that help with the junketeers"

"Oh yeah, how is Joe?" Julie asked.

"Gone. He vanished. When I arrived at our office with my colleagues, the place was vacant. That's why I'm calling you. Do you know anything about him disappearing?"

"No son, I don't."

"Wow. Well, okay. Can I ask you another question?"

"Sure, how can I help you?"

"If Joe is gone and left without a trace, do you mind if I continue running the junket business from Chicago? After all, my co-workers and I did just about everything but recruit the junketeers. We still have all of our contacts and list of people who want to go to Vegas."

After a long pause, Edwin broke the silence, "Hello, Big Julie, are you still there?"

"Yes, yes, I'm still here. Okay. Yeah, why not? I don't see any downside to you bringing people to Vegas. Besides, it's a free country."

Edwin heaved a sigh of relief. "Thank you sir. I appreciate this. I just need to know how we can get paid by the casinos like you and Joe did."

"I'll get in touch with my contact and tell him you're my new partner. I'll have him call you and work out the details."

"Excellent. If you don't mind me asking, about how much can we expect each month?"

Big Julie laughed. "How much did Joe pay you?"

"We each got five thousand a month as a salary."

"What? Joe paid you five grand each, is that what you're telling me?"

"Yeah, that's exactly what I'm telling you."

"Hoy vey. Joe must be in some deep shit to leave everything behind. He only got a total of ten thousand each month from the casinos. That's about all you can expect. Are you still interested?"

"Yes I am," Edwin replied. He had one other ace up his sleeve.

"Okay. I'll make the necessary arrangements. Expect a call from a Mr. George Abramson. Oh, and by the way, I get a percentage of Joe's take?"

"What? I'm confused. How does that work exactly?"

"Joe and I are partners, or, at least we were, until now. For each person you brought to Vegas, the casino paid me a small percentage. Nothing comes from you. The casinos make sure we each received our share. I still want to be compensated by the casinos. Any problem with that?"

"No sir. None at all."

"Good. Then we have an understanding."

Edwin hung up the receiver. He needed help and cooperation from his fellow workers if they were going to continue the junket business.

★ ★ ★

The next day, Edwin arranged to meet the other associates at the office. The rain had stopped, but a light drizzle, almost a mist, still fell outside. The weather, damp and dreary, made it a bleak day. Edwin arrived at the Global Enterprise office. Waiting outside the door were Gwenn, Richard and Herbert. Gwenn spoke first. "Looks like we're locked out," she said as she turned the door knob to show Edwin.

"No matter," Edwin replied. "I'm in the process of leasing new office space. I spoke to Big Julie, and he's agreed to let us continue the junket operation from Chicago. There's a catch though."

Richard interrupted, "What's the catch?"

"Big Julie told me that Carter only got ten thousand each month in total for the junket business. So you need to decide if you still want to be part of the team."

"How much you gonna pay us?" Herbert asked.

Edwin sensed Herbert's skepticism. "I'll still pay you five thousand each month. Just like Carter."

Gwenn nodded her head indicating she wanted in. Richard spoke in a whisper to Herbert. The conversation did not last long. Richard said, "I'm on board."

Herbert snarled at Edwin. "Good luck, I'm out of here." Herbert bolted toward the elevator. He did not want to be near Edwin. He hated him.

"What's his problem?" Gwenn asked Richard.

"I don't know."

"What a jerk. Good riddance, who needs him anyways?" Gwenn said, directing her comment toward Edwin.

"Okay, give me a few days and I'll call you with our new location. In the meantime, keep calling our junketeers and act as if nothing has changed. Richard, do me a favor and see if you can get Herbert's list of people."

Richard smiled. "I already have it. I kept a copy when Carter had us change casinos."

"Okay then, I'll call you later in the week."

Edwin, Richard and Gwenn left the office building for the final time. Once on the street, Richard left promptly. It gave Gwenn a chance to confirm with Edwin that he still planned to meet her that evening.

"See you later tonight. I tell you all of my ideas." Edwin told her.

She smiled and left.

Later that evening, Gwenn greeted Edwin at the entrance to her home. She anxiously awaited hearing about Edwin's plan.

Edwin sat on the black leather sofa with Gwenn and began telling her about his new company.

"ERGENT stands for Edwin Randolph Goldberg Enterprises."

"Cute," Gwenn said.

"I put all the money that I made during the last year into the business. I hired an attorney. I met with him earlier this morning. I asked him to lease an office for me under ERGENT. The office is where we'll operate the junket business. He's in the process of negotiating the purchase of a McDonald's franchise and getting the paper worked filled out for me to buy a seat on the Chicago Board of Trade. I need someone I can trust to help me with operating the businesses."

Gwenn sat quietly listening to Edwin. The blank stare on her face indicated Gwenn's confusion. She did not comprehend what he just told her. "What does this have to do with me?"

"Because I want you to be my partner."

"But I don't want to invest any money into your business. I'm trying to figure out how I'm going to support myself now that Carter is gone."

Edwin blushed. "Do you really think I'm asking you for any money? That's not what I had in mind. I want you to run the businesses for me. I need someone I can trust while I'm at the Board of Trade during the week. I'm going to be a floor trader. I can't be doing the junket business, and I thought you could run it. I don't trust Richard. Herbert is gone."

Gwenn got up from the sofa and poured herself a glass of wine. "Do you want some?" she asked, tilting the bottle in his direction.

"No, I'm fine."

Edwin sat patiently waiting for Gwenn to say something. She took three sips of the wine and put her glass on a coaster on the coffee table directly in front of Edwin. "Okay, I'm in so long as I can have the title, 'Executive Vice President.' What's my salary and other perks for the position?" She looked at Edwin and flashed him a sinful smile that lit up her face. It left no doubt in Edwin's mind what the wily temptress wanted.

"Does ten thousand a month, plus health benefits, four weeks of vacation, and a car allowance sound fair to you?"

"Yes, I accept. Should we consummate our agreement in my bedroom?"

Edwin thought about the invitation for a brief moment. "No, I don't think we should be romantically involved. I want to keep this strictly professional. Besides, I have a girlfriend."

Gwenn clearly disappointed and upset at being rebuffed by him, knew Edwin was right. She reluctantly agreed, "Yeah, if we're going to be business partners, we should keep our personal lives separate. Hey, who's the girlfriend?"

"Bindi Maxwell. The girl I met in Vegas when Johnny got murdered."

"Huh. I hope it works out for you."

"Thanks."

Edwin rose from the sofa, and gave Gwenn a bear hug and quick kiss on the cheek. "I'd better go," he said.

"Yeah, you probably should."

"I'll call you once the attorney finds office space for us."

Gwenn watched as Edwin left her home. An unexplained feeling of exuberance overwhelmed her. She sensed she was going to be a part of something great.

CHAPTER TWENTY-SEVEN

It didn't take long before Alison Mills called the Las Vegas police number to provide information about Johnny Accardi's murder. Dressed in business attire, she strutted into the police station. "Is Detective Malone available?"

The Sergeant at the front desk looked at her with condescending eyes. "Who should I tell him is asking?"

"I'm here about the reward for that murdered guy they found in the hotel."

"Hold on Ms. I'll get him."

The Sergeant picked up the phone and dialed Malone's extension. "There's a lady here asking for you. Says she's got information about Accardi's case. Okay. I'll tell her." He put the receiver down and told Alison, "He'll be right up ma'am."

Detective Malone approached her. "I'm Detective Malone, can I help you?"

"Actually Detective, I'm here to help you—for the reward money of course."

"Of course. Follow me."

Malone escorted her back to the interrogation room and had her take a seat in front of a desk. Detective Evans joined them within a few minutes.

Detective Evans sat directly across from Alison. "So what information do you have for us Ms. Mills?"

"I was with Johnny Accardi the night he was murdered."

"Oh really? How can we be sure you're not here just for the reward?"

She scowled at him. "Of course I am. Do you want to know what happened or not?"

"Okay, tell us what happened."

"A man hired me too pick-up a guy named Edwin at a wedding reception at Caesars Palace. When I got to the party, another good looking guy approached me. He was drunk but offered me a grand to spend some time with him, especially when he heard I was looking for Edwin. We went to a hotel room. Within five minute he's passed out. So I left."

"Who hired you?"

"He told me his name was Herbert."

"Do you know his last name?"

"No, I don't."

Detective Evans looked at Alison. The brow on his forehead wrinkled. "The witnesses who saw the woman with Johnny gave different descriptions of what she looked like. Can you explain the discrepancies?"

"Sure, I wore a blond wig when I met Johnny and I took it off and put it in my purse when I left. Here." Alison removed a blond wig from her purse and handed it to Detective Evans.

Detective Malone was not amused. "So the guy who hired you, how much did he pay you?"

"Five hundred dollars."

"Why did he want you to pick-up Edwin? Did he give you a last name or a reason?"

"He told me it was a prank. That his friend didn't date much and he wanted to get him some action. Herbert's one of my regulars. We hooked up twice a month."

Detective Evans interjected "Let me see if I got this straight. You're a hooker and some dude pays you five hundred dollars to go to Caesars and make a play for some guy named Edwin. Instead, you're approached by Johnny Accardi, who gives you a grand to spend time with him, and you never even meet with Edwin. Is that it?"

"Yeah."

"So why'd you come forward now? Why'd you wait so long?"

"Simple. I want the twenty-five-thousand-dollar reward that's being offered. I already told you that. Also, when I found out it was Johnny Accardi and he had ties to the Mafia, I became fearful for my safety."

Detective Malone asked the most important question of the entire interview. "Can you identify the man who hired you?"

"Sure thing. If I saw a photo of him, I would recognize him. Sure."

Malone excused himself from the room. "I'll be back in a few minutes."

He returned with a sketch artist. Based on Alison's description, he drew a facsimile of the person that hired her. Mills described the man in detail. The sketch artist emerged from the interrogation room with an exact likeness of Herbert Shoemaker. Detective Evans took the sketch and told another officer to get it on the wire. Copies were handed out to other law enforcement agencies.

Detective Malone had a hunch. He called Edwin, "Hi Edwin, Detective Malone. When are you coming back to Vegas?"

"Well, hello, Detective. I wasn't planning on being there for a few weeks. Why?"

"Your scheme paid off. The hooker who was with Johnny Accardi the night he was murdered came forward and gave us some information. Of course, she wants the reward money. We have a sketch of the person who hired her."

Edwin, hopeful that the police would apprehend the culprit, asked, "Can you fax me a copy?"

"Yes, but I prefer not to. Too many eyes if you catch my drift?"

"Yeah, I can be there tomorrow if you want. I'll catch the red-eye tonight."

"We might have a picture of our killer. We just don't have a name. I'm hoping you might be able to identify him."

"Me? Why do you think I would know him?"

"Because, the hooker said she was hired to meet some guy named Edwin at a wedding reception at Caesars."

Edwin gasped. "You're joking? Aren't you?"

"No, Mr. Goldberg. It seems someone wanted to kill you and they killed Johnny by mistake. Any idea who may want you dead?"

"No Detective. I don't. I'll be out on the first flight tomorrow morning." Edwin visibly shaken up by the news, placed the receiver on the telephone's cradle and sat down.

★ ★ ★

The United flight from Chicago to McCarran Airport took longer than usual. Edwin fidgeted most of the flight. He dwelled on the thought of someone wanting him dead. Many thoughts went through his mind. None of them made any sense. He couldn't think of a single person who might want him dead. Not even Joseph Carter had a reason to knock him off.

His mind drifted in and out of different scenarios. He felt relieved when the plane finally landed. The ride to the police department seemed to take forever.

Malone greeted Edwin. "Good morning Mr. Goldberg. Did you have a nice flight?"

"Not really. I can't stop thinking about who would want me dead. Can I see the artist's sketch?"

Malone showed Edwin the drawing. "Oh my God," Edwin blurted out. "That's Herbert Shoemaker. He worked with me at Global Enterprises in the junkets business."

"Are you sure?" Malone pressed.

"Yes, I'm positive. But why would he want to kill me? I hardly spent any time with him." Edwin's knees buckled as he sat down in the chair next to him.

"I'll be right back," Malone told him. "Are you okay, do you need some water?"

"I'm fine. I'll wait."

Malone left and immediately called the FBI and local law enforcement for the Chicago area.

* * *

A team of six officers surrounded Herbert's condo in downtown Chicago. Two officers went around to the back entrance, while two officers stayed out front. Two other officers went to the twentieth floor. They pounded on Herbert's door. "Police, open up!" they shouted. The officers had their weapons drawn and ready to fire if needed. Herbert opened the door slowly and came out with his hands up. He looked disheveled. The officers quickly handcuffed him and read him his rights. Herbert did not resist. Herbert muttered over and over as he was escorted, "I killed him with *Kindness*."

Herbert had not shaven nor showered for five days. A pungent odor from his body inundated the air. Wearing a short-sleeve-button down shirt and blue jeans he sat in the interrogation room, dazed. He did not utter another word. The smell of booze reeked from his breath.

While Herbert remained in custody, two detectives from the precinct obtained a search warrant. They looked through his apartment. A detective found a pistol in Herbert's dresser. Ballistics quickly matched the gun as the murder weapon.

The local law enforcement called Detective Malone. "We have Herbert Shoemaker in custody. We found the murder weapon in his apartment. Let us know when the paper work to transfer him to your custody has been processed. In the meantime, we'll get him cleaned up. He's a mess."

Malone asked, "Did he say anything when arrested?"

"No sir. To be honest, he appeared to be in shock. And, he had been drinking heavily. His breath reeked of alcohol. He just repeated over and over, 'I killed him with *Kindness*.' Any idea what that's all about?"

"Hmm, no. Well okay. I'll make arrangements to get him back here even if I have to pick him up myself. You should keep a close watch over him. If word gets out to Johnny's uncle, we may have a security issue."

Malone told Edwin the news about Herbert's arrest and being in custody of the local police. "How long are you in town for?"

"I'm catching the next flight back home now that I feel safe. Did Herbert say why he wanted to kill me?"

Malone shook his head. "No, according to the officer I spoke with, he appeared to be in shock and drunk. They didn't paint a pretty picture of how he looked. He didn't resist arrest or anything. Just went with them without incident. Only, the officer did mention that Herbert uttered 'I killed him with *Kindness*.' Do you know why he said that?"

Edwin knew exactly what it meant, but he decided not to tell the detective and said, "No, no idea, sir."

* * *

Herbert arrived in Las Vegas within a few days. Back in Vegas, Alison Mills identified Herbert in a police line-up as the person who hired her to bring Edwin back to her hotel room.

Detective Malone sat in the interrogation room with Herbert. He read him his rights again. "Do you want an attorney?"

"No. I'll waive my right to an attorney. I know I have no chance of getting acquitted. The evidence is air tight. I'll confess for a lesser sentence."

"I can't make any promises, but I'll see what I can do," Malone said.

"Detective, cut the bullshit. You and I both know my confession doesn't matter. As soon as Johnny's uncle finds out, I'm a dead man walking."

"Why did you kill Johnny Accardi?" he began.

"I didn't know it was Johnny. I thought I shot Edwin."

"Okay, why did you want to kill Edwin?"

"Because he stood in my way of being with Gwenn. If she wasn't with him she'd be with me."

"I still don't follow you," Malone said. He began to wonder if Herbert was putting on an act for an insanity plea.

"I hated Edwin. He didn't care for Gwenn, but I did. Every time I tried to ask her out, he interfered in one way or another. I thought if he was out of the way she'd given me a chance."

Malone leaned forward. He shook his head. "Okay, I need you to write out everything and then sign and date it." He pushed a pad of paper and pen toward Herbert.

He wrote out a lengthy confession detailing why he hated Edwin. How he hired Alison to lure him to the hotel room. How he shot Johnny who'd he mistaken for Edwin. Every gory detail was put on paper.

Edwin had closure. Valerie Taylor did not. Upset that her meal ticket to a life of luxury had been snuffed out because of mistaken identity; she vowed to make Edwin suffer.

CHAPTER TWENTY-EIGHT

Before Edwin's first day on the trading floor, Bill Beckwith, his mentor, told him, "Keep your hands to your sides and your mouth shut. As you know, traders use both voice and hand gestures to make their intentions to buy or sell known. I don't want anyone thinking you're making a trade with them. These bastards would steal from their own mothers if they could."

Bill pointed to the electronic board with prices flashing that surrounded the outer edge of the floor area. Pointing in the direction of the corn pit, Bill said, "Son, the action will be fast and furious. There will be no time for me to explain what's transpiring. I'll explain everything afterwards. Do you understand?"

"Yes, sir."

Before Beckwith allowed Edwin to be on the floor, Edwin had to pass a series of tests regarding the hand signals used. Hand signals were the sign language of the futures traders. They represented a unique communication system that effectively permitted basic information to be communicated on the trading floor. These signals let traders and other floor employees know the price of the bid and ask, how many contracts, the expiration months and the types orders and the status of the orders.

Edwin himself had spent several evenings practicing these gestures until he felt comfortable. The hand signals enabled rapid interaction between the pits and order desks from a distance as far away as forty yards within the pit area itself. The deafening noise level created by the sizeable number of people on the floor made hand signals more practical to communicate than by voice. Hand signals would permit Edwin and other traders to remain anonymous so that large orders did not sit on a desk subject to inadvertent disclosure.

Edwin reviewed the various signals in his mind to refresh his memory. Palms facing toward a trader indicated a "Buy" order. Palms facing away from the trader indicated a "Sell" order. As Beckwith had explained it, "You can remember this by thinking that when you're buying, you're bringing something in toward you, palms face you. When you're selling, the palms face away from you you're pushing something away from you."

By extending the hand in front of and away from the body a trader showed price. The numbers one through five were designated by holding the fingers straight up. Six through nine were designated by holding them sideways. A clenched fist meant Zero. Price signals only indicated the last digit of a Bid (buy) or Offer (sell).

Traders indicated quantity, the number of contracts being bid or offered, by touching the face. If a trader touched his chin, it meant he wanted to sell between one and nine contracts. Multiples of ten contracts, such as fifty contracts, were done by touching the forehead. Contracts in multiples of hundreds were indicated by a fist touching the forehead.

The huge trading floor of the Chicago Board of Trade could house a 737 aircraft. It contained a series of raised octagonal platforms or "pits" with steps up the outside and down the inside that allowed hundreds of traders to see and hear each other during trading hours.

Edwin stood next to Bill Beckwith on the bottom row of the octagonal podium in the corn pit. They each wore a purple jacket to indicate they were independent floor traders. The frenzy of thousands of arms waiving, hoarse-voiced traders yelling, and runners and clerks abounded throughout the gargantuan area. Attired in the bright blue, red, gold or other colored jackets, runners and clerks rushed in and out of revolving doors for quick breaks. The different colored jackets differentiated the various brokerage houses.

As Edwin watched, hundreds of traders gestured wildly, pointed and executed a series of peculiar hand motions. He kept his hands in his pockets. The activity gave an illusion of total chaos, unless you understood the underlying method to the madness. During the trading session, a number of men and women scurried about, puffing profusely on cigarettes that generated a billowing cloud of smoke. It seemed almost humorous watching the other floor employees wade through the surging smoke cloud.

During the final sixty seconds before the closing bell rang, an earsplitting wail of shouting, begging and pleading erupted as traders hoped to consummate a last-minute buy or sell. The last few seconds produced absolute bedlam. Traders jockeyed for position, shoving, pushing, and flinging their arms as they yelled out final orders. The final bell rang. Instantly, the clamor stopped. Traders started to disperse. Some disgustedly tossed handfuls of unplaced order slips into the air but did not watch as they floated down to the floor like confetti in a ticker-tape parade.

Edwin welcomed the silence in the elevator going up to Bill's office. It gave him a moment to delve into his inner thoughts. When they reached Bill's private office, Bill sat down in his office chair and motioned Edwin to sit in one of the chairs facing his desk.

"What did you see?"

"It appeared that you were buying and selling at the same time."

"Exactly. You're very observant."

"I don't understand, sir. Why would you be buying and selling at the same time?"

"It's called arbitrage. Do you know what arbitrage means?"

"No sir, I don't." Edwin's eyes widened. His eyebrows were furrowed as he leaned slightly forward in his chair.

"Arbitrage is the simultaneous purchase and sale of the same or an equivalent commodity to profit from price discrepancies. As a floor trader, I can exploit the price differences quickly using hand signals. Before hand signals it was impossible to communicate fast enough to take advantage of the price differences. I buy and sell until prices are back in equilibrium and it is no longer profitable."

"Sounds to me like it's a legal way to front run?"

Bill pointed his hand with his index finger extended toward Edwin motioning it slightly up and down. His lips turned upward as the smile on his face widened. "I like you. You're very perceptive."

"What does this mean?" Bill began hand signals for Edwin to interpret.

Edwin called out "Buy five contracts of March corn at 2.60. Sell five contracts of corn at 2.65 per bushel."

"How much did you make if you made this trade?"

Too slow to calculate what he would have made had the trade been done, Edwin winced.

Bill could see the wheels in Edwin's head turning. Already a long day, rather than wait for Edwin to figure out the answer, Bill said, "Let me walk you through it. Take notes. You're going to need to know this frontwards, backwards and inside out. Memorize it like you would the multiplications table. A one-cent move in a corn contract equals $50. Remember, there are 5,000 bushels per contract. You had a five-cent move. For each contract, you made $250; five cents times 5,000 equals $250." Bill walked over to a white board mounted on his office wall. "Here," he told Edwin and he began to quickly write the pricing scenarios down for him. "With five contracts you made $1,250. Two hundred fifty dollars per contract times five contracts equals one thousand two hundred fifty dollars, 5 contracts X $250/contract = $1,250 for the trade." Edwin whipped out a notebook and began to take copious notes.

Trading corn occurred from 9:30 a.m. until 1:15 p.m. A daily price limit of 20 cents per bushel existed above or below the previous day's settlement price.

Edwin's head was spinning, because of so much information for him to absorb. Bill sensed Edwin was overwhelmed. "Tell you what you should do. Go home, study, practice and keep your spreads tight."

"What do you mean keep my spreads tight?"

"Let's operate on the K.I.S.S. method—keep it simple, silly. Make your spread at two cents per trade. Keep your trades at five contracts until you get more proficient at this. Remember, $2.60 per bushel times 5,000 bushels per contract equals $13,000 per contract. Trading one to two contracts for each trade means you have up to $26,000 worth of funds tied up."

Edwin interrupted. "But we trade on margin. Margin is 4.5% of the face value or $2,925. So my exposure is a lot less."

Bill grimaced. "It's that kind of thinking that got Aaron Taylor in trouble. There will be a day when no matter what you do, a trade will go against you. Or, worse, you are in the middle of a rally when a sudden reversal, a change in direction price, and there is a break; a rapid and sharp price decline. You're caught, unable to offset your positions. Bam! You're toast. You never want to be a position of a margin call. Never. Am I clear?"

Edwin nodded in the affirmative. "Very clear. No margin."

"Aaron Taylor made megabucks trading in the soybean pit. He was arrogant. Then one morning he made some trades thinking he was going to make 'fuck you" money. He leveraged everything. The price started to tick upward. Instead of liquidating his contracts and taking a modest profit, he waited.

"Within the blink of an eye, the market turned down causing a real frenzy. It broke down so fast and so quickly that the daily limit hit within two minutes and closed the market.

"Aaron lost everything to settle his margin call. After that, he was never the same person. His confidence shattered, he became a shell of a person. I remember that day vividly. I was wishing I was in the pit trading, until a friend reminded me, 'It is better to be on the outside wishing you were on the inside, rather than being on the inside wishing you were on the outside.'

"Think of it this way; if you made a trade with a two-cent move that equals $100 per contract, times two contracts, that equals $200 per trade. You can make five trades within an hour. Five trades each day at $200 per trade equal $1,000 per day. Five days each week equals $5,000 per week. Working fifty weeks per year is the equivalent of making $250,000 per year. Are you making over a quarter million dollars a year now?"

"No."

"If you can wrap your head around this, then you can be a very lucrative floor trader. If you can't, then you're just another gambler in the biggest casino. I'll see you tomorrow at 7:30 a.m. You'll trade live with real money."

Edwin had to step back a moment to comprehend the magnitude of what Bill just said. He rose from his chair and said, "I'll see you tomorrow." He walked out the door, his head in a fog.

The books Edwin read and study discussed different types of trades from a simple buy or sell to complicated Inter-market and Inter-commodity spreads and straddles. They explained the difference between a Buy Stop Order and a Sell Stop Order to a Stop Order and Good to Cancelled Order. None of this mattered to a floor trader. A floor trader was more intense than day trader. Every position was liquidated within minutes. A Day Trader took a position in a commodity and then offset it prior to the close of trading on the same day.

Edwin, an independent trader, had another advantage to make a profitable trade. Bill Beckwith made certain that Edwin became acquainted with his brokers. Brokers were the actual people who entered trades for the public. The broker stood next to the independent trader and literally handed him the trade. It was a rigged system, all perfectly legal.

At 6:00 a.m., the alarm clock blared out the song *One of These Nights* by the Eagles, as Edwin hit the snooze button on the radio clock. Five minutes later he turned off the alarm and took a hot shower. He still had a throbbing headache. After his shower, he popped two aspirin into his mouth, gulped down half a glass of water, and got dressed.

By the time he arrived at Bill Beckwith's office, his headache was forgotten and he was ready to face the onslaught of the corn pit.

"Are you ready to make some money?" Bill asked.

"Yes I am."

Bill went through the procedure of how orders were written and what Edwin had to do to trade in his own account. Edwin's stomach was tied up in knots. He had to excuse himself twice to use the men's room. Bill laughed, no doubt, remembering his first day of trading. He told him, "Anyone who claimed they did not get nervous was a liar. Even the traders who had been trading for a long time still got a sick feeling every day."

Bill handed Edwin an Order form that he could easily fill in to formalize and record his trades. The form was mostly filled in with his name, account/broker number, buy/sell, and number of contracts, month and other pertinent information such as the price. Every little detail was explained to Edwin to make certain he completed the form correctly so that it could be processed by the clearinghouse. If an order did not match, there would be no credit for the trade.

Corn closed the day before at $2.63 per bushel. Bill and Edwin had reviewed the charts. Based on their analysis they believed the market would open higher. They agreed that if the market opened at $2.80 or above, they would sell. If the market opened at $2.68 or lower, they would buy.

At precisely 9:30 a.m., an explosion of sound engulfed the corn pit. The price of corn opened at $2.67. Edwin called out "Buying one, March at $2.67." Another trader in the pit wearing a green jacket called back and gave the hand signals to him indicating "Sold." Edwin recorded the trade on his card noting the other broker's number.

Within two minutes, the price of corn was trading at $2.70. Edwin quickly called out, "Selling one March at $2.70 and made the hand signals to indicate as such." A broker next to Edwin sporting a gold jacket called back "Buying one March at $2.70" and gave the appropriate hand signal. Edwin acknowledged the trade and wrote the information on a separate card. The broker gave him a wink. He flipped to the next card to write the next order.

Within fifteen minutes, corn was trading at $2.80 per bushel. Edwin called out "Selling one March at $2.80," and gave the proper hand gestures. From a few feet away, the trader donning a bright red jacket called back, "Buying one March at $2.80." Edwin recorded the trade.

The price of corn moved higher. Bill nudged Edwin to get his attention and yelled in his ear, be patient. Wait. The price was at $2.84 when a broker nudged Edwin, and called out "Selling one hundred March at $2.83" and made the proper hand signal. Edwin heard "Buying one hundred March at $2.82," an indicator that the price could reverse direction. It did. The price of corn dropped from $2.84 to $2.80. Edwin breathed a slight sigh of relief. He was even for his last trade so far. Edwin jumped into the fray and yelled, "Buying one March at $2.78." A trader wearing a green jacket cried back, "Selling one March at $2.78." The proper hand signals were exchanged between the two, and Edwin entered the trade into his book.

Edwin felt exhilarated and exhausted at the same time. He left the pit area and time-stamped the four trades he made and turned them into the clearinghouse. After receiving his confirmation slips, he left too fatigued to continue.

The silhouette of Aaron Taylor watched from the observation deck. He paid special attention to Edwin. Once Edwin left the pit, Aaron immediately went to the floor to fulfill his responsibilities to Bill. He had the duty to take Bill's order cards and make sure they were properly time-stamped and given to the clearing house to be processed. Because Bill focused his attention on Edwin to make sure he did not get in over his head the first day, he did not notice that Aaron was not immediately available.

Just past noon, Bill found Edwin and motioned for him to follow him to his office. Edwin followed him like a lost puppy dog.

"Let me see your confirmation slips," Bill said, reaching his hand forward toward Edwin. Edwin handed the slips to Bill who made notes on the four trades. His notes showed a buy for one March contracts at $2.67 and sold for $2.70; another buy for $2.78 and a sell at $2.80. "Hmm," Bill said. He raised his head and narrowed his eyes to look at Edwin. "Smart. I see you sold at $2.80 and then bought at $2.78. Most novices are afraid to sell first and buy second."

Edwin traded one contract with a net of five cents profit. His profit for the day was $250. Bill's eye brightened as his lips turned upward. "Well done, young man," he said as he handed the slips back to Edwin.

"Thank you."

"Get out of here and get some rest. I'll see you at the Y tonight."

Edwin nodded in acknowledgment. He left, weary from the morning's activities, content with his first day of trading.

It did not take long for Edwin to realize that being in the pit on the floor as a trader had significant advantages over the general public. He had a new appreciation for being an insider; it felt like Vegas. Bill explained to him that a novice trader should only trade one or two contracts at a time. Once he had more experience he could trade more contracts. He recalled Bill's words; *"Don't get greedy. Be patient."*

CHAPTER TWENTY-NINE

The brisk evening air swirled with a gust of wind every now and then. Edwin held Bindi's hand as they walked along the shore of Lake Michigan near Oak Street. The waves rumbled as they broke over the rocks. The smell of fish wafted through the air. Twilight had begun but the city lights obstructed the glimmering stars.

Bindi had completed her training with United Airlines and was now working as a customer representative. Edwin listened attentively as Bindi talked about her day. When she finished, she turned her head slightly. "How was your day?"

The gaze in her eyes revealed she was genuinely interested to hear about Edwin's first day as a floor trader.

"Profitable." He didn't want to bore her with the details of what transpired or even attempt to explain what he did. For most people, it would be incomprehensible.

As they strolled along the walk way, Edwin turned and stood in front of Bindi. His heart raced. He embraced her shoulders, looked directly into her eyes and leaned closer. Bindi gazed into his hazel eyes and noticed they were more green than brown. She tilted her head and moved closer. Their lips touched. Bindi threw her arms around Edwin's neck as she lost control in his minty breath. He was lost in the fragrance of her perfume. The romance was abruptly broken as some teenage boys passed by and one called out, "Hey, get a room."

Bindi gently squeezed Edwin's hand as they continued walking. "Do you want to come over to my place?" he offered.

"I thought you'd never ask."

Edwin's apartment was small, but tidy. "This is it, my humble abode." He opened the door.

Bindi scanned the apartment. Her eyes widened. "Wow, this is a lot smaller than I imagined."

Edwin immediately sensed the disappointment in Bindi's voice. "Yeah, it's not much. I lived here during college. Come on in and make yourself at home. Would you like something to drink?"

Bindi sat down on the couch. "No, I'm good. How come you never moved into a larger place?"

Edwin sat beside her. He held his hands together and stared toward the wall. He did not make eye contact or look in her direction. Edwin embarrassed, said, "I saved all of my money. I didn't need much. Between work, traveling to Vegas and working out at the 'Y' I didn't spend a lot of time here. It was a place for me to rest my head at night."

"Oh, well it's cozy."

Edwin wanted to escape from the dreariness of the space. He felt his energy being sucked out. Abruptly he said, "Let's get out of here and have some fun."

Bindi hurriedly rose from the couch, anxious to get out of the dreary place. "I'm with you. Where to?"

"Are you in the mood for Chinese food?"

"Yeah, that sounds good."

"Excellent, I know a great little place around the corner."

They bolted from Edwin's dismal place and headed toward the restaurant. At eight o'clock, the place was half full with patrons. They were promptly seated. Edwin ordered a glass of plum wine for each of them. "Now that you're done with training, where were you thinking of moving?" he asked as they perused their menus.

"I was thinking of getting an apartment near work. I haven't had much time to go apartment hunting. Do you have any suggestions?"

Edwin smirked. His eyes glistened as his mouth curled upward. "Yeah, how about we move in together? I need to find a bigger place."

Bindi's pulse increased. Her heart pounded. As much as she liked Edwin, she did not know him well enough to make a major commitment to him just yet. *Oh shit,* she thought.

"Um, huh, well we only just started dating. It seems so soon."

Edwin was not deterred, "Hey, I'll tell you what, let's look at two bedroom places and we'll be roommates. If our relationship moves from platonic too romantic, great; if not, let's see what happens."

Bindi sat quietly. The special spark between them grew more intense each time they were together. A tingling sensation ran through her body. She pondered the idea. Edwin sat patiently waiting for a response.

"Okay. But we need to have an understanding on expenses and how the costs are going to be split. I don't want you to pay for everything."

Edwin leaned across the table and gave Bindi a soft kiss, "You make me happy. I'll call a realtor and we can look this weekend."

"Sounds like a plan to me." Bindi's eyes gleamed. She felt assured of her decision. Something about Edwin made her feel safe and secure. She also felt alive when she was with him. He had an indescribable way of making her feel good. "Just out of curiosity, how much do you make?"

The expression on Edwin's face was priceless. He looked like the cat who'd just swallowed the canary. "More than one hundred twenty thousand."

Bindi's jaw dropped. Her mouth gaped open. Her eyes widened as she gasped, "How much?"

"More than one hundred twenty grand a year."

She clumsily picked up her glass of wine and took a sip. "You're telling me you make over a hundred grand a year, and you're living in that dump?"

"Yeah, how did you think I saved enough to buy a seat on the Board of Trade and purchase a McDonald's franchise?"

"I'm impressed. You certainly have a lot of discipline." She paused, processing his last statement. "Wait a minute. You're buying a McDonald's franchise? I didn't know that."

"Well, I'm in the middle of buying it. My attorney is reviewing the documents. It should be finalized in the next few weeks."

Bindi sat mesmerized by Edwin's revelations. She had no idea he made so much money.

"Look, I want someone to like me for me, not just my money. So for now, can we please change the subject?"

"Sure. Bye the way, I make thirty grand a year in case you were wondering."

"The thought never crossed my mind." He smiled.

She smiled back.

The food arrived and the two sat enjoying their meal. Bindi, giddy at the thought of apartment hunting with Edwin during the weekend enjoyed the moment. With their combined incomes, they could live wherever their hearts desired. The conversation revolved around locations that they should consider moving, and purchasing furniture. "Where did you have in mind look for a place," Bindi asked.

"I think downtown is best for us. Somewhere close to where we work. What do you think?"

"Yeah, I agree. It will make it easier for you to commute to the Board of Trade and its close to my office. What about furniture? I don't have any. United put me up in a furnished apartment."

"Uh," Edwin stuttered. "Yeah, we should buy new stuff. My furniture has seen better days. I want to start fresh."

A wide smile crept across her face. "I like the way you think. A fresh start for both of us."

After dinner, Edwin walked Bindi to her car. Her aura glowed around her. He tenderly kissed her lips. The warmth of her mouth sent a cheerful fuzzy feeling radiating through his body. After a few minutes, Bindi said, "I'd better go. I'll see you Saturday."

She gently pushed him aside so that she could open her car door. He watched as she drove off.

Saturday could not arrive fast enough. Edwin had arranged to meet Bindi and the realtor at the first apartment, they'd chosen. Both of them agreed that the unit located on LaSalle Drive was too small for them. The realtor showed them a number of other units in the area, but none were to their liking. Frustrated at not finding exactly what they wanted, Edwin asked, "Are there any condos for sale?"

The gasp from Bindi indicated she wasn't in favor of purchasing a place to live. "Excuse me, may I have a moment to talk with my boyfriend alone?" she said to the realtor.

"What are you doing? Renting is one thing, buying is another."

"It won't hurt to look. Let's see if we can find something. I can afford to purchase a condo. We can still split the mortgage and other expenses. It will be no different than if we rented. I'll even put it in both our names. Besides, we can offer rent with an option to purchase."

Reluctantly, Bindi said, "Okay."

After an exhaustive search between 400 and 1660 North LaSalle, they finally found a condo they both agreed upon. It was 1,325 square feet, two master bedrooms and two full baths, with all of the amenities Bindi wanted. Edwin made an offer for the full price of $135,000. He planned to put 20% down, which was $27,000. The mortgage would be for $108,000. Interest rates fluctuated between 8.75% and 9%. The monthly payment, including taxes and interest was $1,010. Edwin had no problem being approved for the mortgage. Bindi felt comfortable paying $600 for her half of the expenses.

The seller accepted their offer. Edwin and Bindi celebrated the purchase with an expensive diner at Morton's Steak House. Although Bindi's decision to buy a home with Edwin came as a complete surprise, she nonetheless felt confident. They spent the evening talking and laughing about the anticipated move.

"I can't believe we just bought a home together," she said.

"Are you always this impulsive?"

"Only when I'm with you. You seem to bring the worst out in me," she said with a smirk.

"Yeah, I do, don't I."

"I think I'd better wait to tell my parents until we actually move-in. I'm not sure how they'll feel about my living with a guy, especially one I just met."

"Have you told them about me yet?" A quizzical expression crossed his face.

"Sorta. I told them I met someone and we were dating. How about you? Have you told your parents about me?"

"No. I haven't spoken to my parents for several months. They don't approve of my working in the travel industry. My dad never has any confidence in my ability to succeed. He's always chiding me."

"Interesting."

"What's interesting?"

"Nothing. It just seems odd that you're making more than a hundred grand and your parents don't think you're successful. It doesn't make sense to me."

"I haven't told them how much I make. They only know that I still live in my studio apartment and don't own a car."

"Well, I believe in you." She leaned over the table and gave him a kiss.

Edwin held-up his glass of wine. He waited for her to raise her glass. "To us and new beginnings."

She repeated, "To us and new beginnings."

They clinked their glasses together before drinking. They smiled at each other with tender eyes.

CHAPTER THIRTY

OCTOBER, 1975

The next four weeks flashed by in a wink of an eye for Edwin. Trading in the corn pit on the floor of the Chicago Board of Trade became second nature for him. He followed the advice of Bill who strongly suggested that all of his contracts be closed out before noon.

Bill explained, "During the last half-hour, trading in the pit becomes too volatile. Too many traders have been financially wiped out because of rapid and sharp price declines or price rallies where prices had sharp increases."

He described moments that the daily limit was triggered and trading suspended. This prevented the trader from liquidating a position and being subject to a margin call.

Edwin maintained a strict discipline trading his account. He only traded a maximum of five contracts at one time, and he closed out his position after he had a five-hundred-dollar positive gain. During the past four weeks of trading, Edwin made an average of twenty-five hundred dollars per day. He made about twelve thousand five hundred dollars per week. Despite his financial success, Edwin still lived a frugal lifestyle. Other then the purchase of the condo with Bindi, not much had changed.

Always guarded and wanting to maintain his privacy, Edwin never shared his Purchase and Sale Statements with anyone other than Bill. The P & S statement sent by the commission house to a customer showed the prices at which contracts were bought or sold, the gross profit or loss, the commission charges, the net profit or loss on each transaction, and the balance. Edwin kept his trading account separate from ERGENT.

With the help of Barry Horowitz, Edwin succeeded purchasing two McDonald's franchises. He became partners with Barry. Barry would be paid a handsome salary to manage both stores. The profits, if any, would be split equally.

Meanwhile, Gwenn and Richard had traveled to Vegas ten times since Carter left. Only a handful of clients asked about Carter. They were told Carter left for Europe to take care of some personal issues. No details were provided.

The scam with Eddie the dealer had gone smoothly. Still, Gwenn got an uneasy feeling in the pit of her stomach. One afternoon, she approached Edwin. "Can I speak with you?" she asked.

"Sure. What's on your mind?"

"I don't like traveling to Vegas with the junketeers. It's wearing on me."

"I can sympathize with that. What do you suggest?"

Gwenn leaned forward, placing her elbows on Edwin's desk, resting her chin on her hands. He was glad she wasn't wearing a low-cut blouse, because her position would have revealed her firm rounded breasts. The sweater she wore hid any cleavage. Edwin sat back in his chair as she spoke.

"What if I handle all the calls for the junketeers, and Richard travels with them on the trips? I can also oversee and review all the McDonald's reports and help with any other businesses you might want to acquire." Gwenn looked directly into Edwin's eyes, smiling broadly.

"That's fine with me. But I need you to go on a few more trips and let Richard ease into handling all of the junketeers."

"Thank you." Gwenn lifted her head from her hands and stood up. She walked out of Edwin's office straight into Richard's.

"Hi Richard, we have a change in plans."

Richard looked up from his reports, "Oh?"

"Yeah, after the next two trips, I'm going to take over the daily routine of calling the junketeers and making their arrangements. You'll just need to babysit them in Vegas. I won't be traveling after that."

"Okay by me."

Gwenn, surprised that Richard did not put up more of an argument, sensed something wasn't right.

* * *

On the next trip to Vegas, Gwenn asked her father to travel as one of the junketeers. Being suspicious of Richard, she needed her father's help to see what shenanigans he might be up to. "Hey dad, can you go to Vegas this weekend with me?"

"Sure, but why?"

"I need you to go as one of our junketeers and keep an eye on Richard, your host. He's in charge of making sure all of our guests are having a great time. Something's bothering me about him."

"Okay. Anything I can do to help my daughter. Besides, who wouldn't want a free trip to Vegas?"

♣♥♦♠

At three o'clock in the morning, only a handful of players were at the craps table. Richard stood next to Gwenn's father, Keith. Richard asked for a marker for ten thousand dollars. The dealer, Ken, pushed a stack of chips in various denominations to Richard.

Keith noticed that Richard was scamming the casino in the way the dealer pushed the chips to him. Normally, the dealer split the stack of chips into piles by denominations to show them on the felt so that the eye in the sky can see. Ken did not do this. He just shoved one tall stack of chips to Richard.

Keith saw a five-thousand-dollar chip hidden on the bottom of the stack, obscured from the eye in the sky. The box person either ignored the extra chip or did not see it. Either way, Keith realized something shady was going on.

Richard played very conservatively. He made what some would deem small wagers compared to his buy-in. After an hour of play, Richard colored up. Only Keith noticed that Richard had pocketed the five-thousand-dollar chip. He paid off his marker and had about five hundred dollars in remaining chips.

Keith watched and waited a full minute before he colored up and left the craps table. He stood behind Richard at the cashier's cage as Richard's chips were exchanged for five thousand five hundred dollars in legal tender. "Looks like you had a good night," Keith said.

Richard, startled by the comment, gazed over in Keith's direction. He immediately recognized him as one of his junketeers and said, "Yeah, I got lucky. How did you fare?"

"Not too bad, I'm down about a grand."

"Are they treating you alright here? If not, you let me know. That's what I'm here for; to make sure you have a fun-filled trip."

"Everything's great. Thank you. It's been a blast so far. How long have you been doing this?"

"Oh, a little over a year. I love this town."

Keith didn't want to stay around much longer; he was not used to staying up all night. "I'd better get some sleep. I haven't done this in a long time. See you around."

Richard finished stuffing the wad of cash in his front pants pocket. "Yeah, see you around. Let me know if you need anything." The two men went their separate ways.

Gwenn met her father for breakfast late that morning. Keith gave a detailed report of everything he saw Richard doing at the craps table. After breakfast, she immediately called Eddie.

"Eddie, we need to talk. Where can we meet in private?"

"How about the Denny's on Charleston Boulevard?"

"Perfect, I'll see you there in twenty minutes."

Gwenn left the Sands and headed over to Denny's. Eddie had already arrived and sat waiting for her in one of the booths.

Gwenn ordered a cup of coffee. Eddie, who had not eaten yet, ordered a full meal. She began, "Do you know a dealer named Ken at the Riviera?"

Eddie took a sip from his orange juice and said, "No, why?"

"I think he and Richard might be doing their own scam with an extra chip like we are."

"What makes you think that?"

"Because one of my junketeers saw him last night getting an extra five-thousand-dollar chip from Ken."

Eddie's eyes became sullen. His lips turned downward. Gwenn could tell this news upset him.

He looked around before he spoke. "I saved enough to blow this popsicle-stand and get out of town. I suggest you do the same. The word on the street is that the feds are cracking down on the families. It's too dangerous to keep stealing like we've been doing. I'm done. I'm giving notice and heading back east."

Gwenn swirled the spoon in her coffee cup, pondering what Eddie just told her. "Thanks for the advice." She tossed a twenty-dollar bill on the table. "Breakfast is on me." She left knowing this would be her last trip to Vegas if she wanted to keep out of jail or stay alive.

She couldn't get to the Riviera fast enough to find Richard. She found him sitting at the bar schmoozing with a beautiful lady. "Pardon the interruption can I have a word with you?" She then shot a glance at the woman. "Don't worry honey, I won't keep him long, and then he's all yours."

Richard, in an annoyed tone, said, "Hey, what are you doing?"

"Eddie won't be at the table tonight. He said he made enough to go back east."

"No big deal. We can tell Edwin when we get back home. It's his issue, not mine."

Gwenn smiled. Richard fell for the trap. "Works for me. Have fun with your lady friend."

Richard went back to talking with the woman as Gwenn left. "What was that all about?" the woman asked.

"She's my business associate. Just an issue with one of our junketeers. It's handled. You want to see my suite?"

"Sure, let's have some fun."

★ ★ ★

That night, Gwenn dressed up in her redhead disguise. She stood at the craps table with her father, pretending to be interested in the dealer, Ken. Richard stood next to Gwenn. He didn't recognize her, although she looked vaguely familiar. "Do I know you?"

"I don't think so."

Richard shook his shoulders and asked for a ten-thousand-dollar marker. Gwenn watched as Ken gave him fifteen thousand dollars in chips. The box-man did not say a word. She assumed he was in on the scam. Richard noticed Keith standing next to Gwenn. "Hey, how's it going tonight? Any better than last night?"

"The dice are hot. Must be lady luck standing next to me."

Richard laughed. He waited for the shooter to seven out before making any bets. He put five hundred dollars on the Don't Pass line.

Keith got a bit perturbed with Richard. "Hey man, I just told you the dice are hot. You want to lose?"

Richard shot back, "You play the way you want and I'll play the way I want."

"Fine by me."

Gwenn recognized the shooter at the opposite end of the table. She was the same woman who had been sitting at the bar with Richard earlier that afternoon. Gwenn noticed that she had a lot of black, hundred-dollar chips on the rail in front of her. She made a five-hundred-dollar Pass Line bet. She picked up the dice and tossed them toward the end where Richard and Gwenn stood. A six and one appeared. The stick person called out, "Seven, front line winner, pay the Line, take the Don'ts."

Keith picked up his winnings from the Pass Line. He'd bet one hundred dollars. He glanced over at Richard, "I told you, the dice are hot."

Richard ignored the comment. He put another five-hundred-dollar chip on the Don't Pass line. The stick person passed the dice to the lady shooter. She picked them up and hurled them. They spun around before settling down. A three and five appeared. The stick person called out, "Eight, mark the point."

The lady shooter rolled for about fifteen minutes before she rolled a seven out. The players at the table gave her a round of applause for a good roll. Richard won his bet on the Don't Pass line. Keith lost his Pass Line bet, but made enough on the other numbers to make a profit.

Gwenn nudged her father. "Hey, I'm tired. Buy me a drink at the bar."

Keith recognized the signal telling him it was time to leave. "Sure thing sweetie."

Richard was too involved with the action and didn't notice Gwenn and the gentleman next to her had left. His focus had been on his lady friend at the opposite end of the table. Besides, he found Keith to be a nuisance.

The two made their way to the cashier's cage and cashed in their chips. Gwenn turned to her father. "Not a word till we get back to the Sands."

Once they arrived at the Sands, Gwenn explained to her father what Richard did. She knew it would be a matter of time before Richard got caught. He was too arrogant and sloppy.

* * *

Edwin arrived back at the office in the early afternoon. He had another profitable day trading at the exchange. The gloomy weather cast an ominous pall over the day. Gwenn came into his office and closed the door for privacy. She wanted to make sure her conversation with Edwin would not be overheard by anyone else.

"How was the trip?" Edwin began.

"Enlightening."

"Oh. How so?"

"Eddie quit. He told me he was going to leave Vegas because he was afraid of the families getting wise to our scheme. Apparently, the feds are cracking down on them. He warned us to do the same. Richard hooked up with another dealer at the Riviera who snuck him an extra five-thousand-dollar chip when he bought in. I saw him betting like we did with an unknown woman as his partner."

"Thanks, Gwenn. I have an idea on how to handle the matter. Hey, Gwenn, no more Vegas or junketeers for you to deal with. I'm going to delegate the entire operation to Richard."

"You sure you can trust him? He's a sleaze-ball."

"Yes, trust me on this."

Gwenn left without saying anything else.

Shortly afterwards, Edwin asked Richard to meet with him. Richard, surprised, asked "What's up boss?"

"How would you like to have the junket business for yourself? Gwenn told me she's tired of traveling and wants to focus more on the business acquisitions I'm considering buying."

"What's the catch?"

"No catch. I'm making a small fortune as a floor trader and I'm looking to invest in other businesses. My buddy Barry is taking care of the McDonald's franchises for me, and I want to expand."

Richard, cautious about the offer, asked "How did you make all your money? We both started working for Carter with nothing and made the same."

"Simple." Edwin said. His eyes widened and he smiled. "I saved all of my money. I didn't buy new clothes, a Rolex watch or a fancy car. I'm still living in my studio apartment for now. What did you spend your money on?"

"Huh, I see your point. How much do you want for the junket business?"

"Nothing. It's yours. Just find another space to conduct your business. I'll make sure Gwenn provides you with the name of

every junketeer we have on file, and I'll call George at the Riviera to tell him you're taking over the operations. He'll make
the arrangements with the other casinos to make certain you're
compensated."

Richard, giddy at being handed a small gold mine, thanked
him profusely. He knew how much the casinos raked-in from
the junketeers they brought in to be fleeced. "Wow, I'll find a
new location by the end of the week. Again, thank you. I'll say
'hi' to Big Julie for you when I see him."

Richard kept his word. He had leased an office in one of the
high rises on Randolph Street. Edwin had Gwenn sent out letters to all the junketeers informing them that Richard Esposito
was the new owner of Vegas Escapades and would handle their
trips to sin city.

Edwin, being shrewd, realized he needed to eliminate any
evidence that tied him to the junket business. He instructed
Gwenn to shred every document relating to Vegas and destroy
all the junketeers' contact information. He wanted his ties to
Vegas to be left in the past.

CHAPTER THIRTY-ONE

Aaron Taylor, a disgruntled employee working for Bill Beckwith, remained suspicious of Edwin. He thought *How did he save enough money to buy a seat on the Exchange?* There were many days when Aaron watched Bill and Edwin celebrate their profitable days over an expensive lunch at a restaurant near the Board of Trade. Although, invited as Bill's guest, he felt awkward. Aaron could not be upset with Edwin because his daughter, Valerie, was living a life of luxury. But he knew it wouldn't last. In the meantime, Edwin's connections at the "Y" and being a part of Woit's Warriors had provided him with tremendous business opportunities. Edwin became extremely wealthy, almost overnight.

Desperate to bring Edwin down, Aaron anonymously reported Edwin to the Internal Revenue Service for tax evasion. Based on the tip, the IRS investigated Edwin for tax fraud. He was subjected to a full audit.

The IRS agent did not intimidate Edwin. He had nothing to hide. Edwin paid one of the CPA's who worked out at the "Y" to prepare and file his 1974 Federal Tax Return.

The agent looked at the return and then at Edwin. "Mr. Goldberg, your return indicates you made $35,000 in wages last year. I see from your W-2 that you were employed by Global Enterprises. Do you have your pay stubs to verify this information?"

Edwin handed the agent all of his pay stubs for 1974. "As you can see, I also reported $50,000 in winnings from the craps tables in Vegas. I wanted to make sure I paid taxes on those winnings."

The IRS agent smirked. He raised an eyebrow. "You're a real angel."

Because Edwin lived frugally, the IRS audit found Edwin did nothing wrong or illegal.

The IRS agent asked, "I understand you just bought a condo, a seat at the Chicago Board of Trade and not one, but two McDonald's franchises. Care to explain where all of this money came from?"

"Sure, so far in 1975, I won $100,000 at the craps tables in Vegas, in addition to my salary from Global Enterprises. As you can see from my P & S Statements I'm doing extremely well as a floor trader. I've made my estimated quarterly tax payments as instructed by my CPA."

Bill Beckwith advised Edwin to report all his gains from trading commodities. He followed Bill's advice. People who were raised in Chicago were aware that Al Capone went to prison for tax evasion. Edwin made enough that paying taxes did not bother him or dampen his modest life style.

"Okay, thank you for your cooperation. My report will show that you reported all of your income and all taxes were paid. Sorry to have wasted your time. You're free to go, Mr. Goldberg."

Edwin and his CPA left the IRS office. He'd thwarted Aaron Taylor's attempt to repudiate his reputation once again.

Stubborn and undaunted, Taylor, without informing his daughter, asked for a meeting with Tazio Accardi. Tazio granted Aaron's request to meet with him. Aaron met with Tazio at his office.

"Thank you for meeting with me Mr. Accardi. I know you're a busy man."

"How can I help you?"

"As you know, my daughter, Valerie, dated Edwin Goldberg before she met your nephew. Edwin didn't have a pot to piss in when he graduated from college. Now, the young man has a lot of money. I think he stole from the casinos on his junket trips. Maybe you could review the surveillance tapes and see if there's some truth to what I'm saying."

Tazio didn't show any expression. He sat quietly until Aaron finished. "You know, Mr. Taylor, Edwin suggested offering a reward that helped catch Johnny's killer. But, I'll look into the matter. Thank you for bringing this to my attention."

Aaron left Tazio Accardi's office. He realized by the tone in Accardi's voice that he'd just made a huge mistake. The knot in his stomach tightened as he drove back to work.

After Aaron left, Tazio told Luigi, "Ask Mr. Goldwin to come see me. I want to talk with him."

Luigi drove straight to Edwin's office. He politely asked Edwin to accompany him to talk with Mr. Accardi.

Edwin did not balk at the invitation. "Can I ask what this is about?"

Luigi respected him. "Yeah, something about you stealing from our casinos in Vegas."

He swallowed hard. His first thought was that Richard got caught. He remembered he had the paid markers in his desk drawer. For some inexplicit reason he had kept them. "Oh, okay. Can I get something from my desk drawer to show to Mr. Accardi?"

"Of course."

Once they arrived at Accardi's office, Luigi escorted Edwin into Tazio's office. "Have a seat," Tazio said, gesturing to a chair in front of his desk.

Edwin did not speak. He sat quietly in the chair and waited for Tazio to say something, but he remained motionless. Finally, he said, "Rumor has it you were stealing from our casino on your junket trips. Care to explain yourself?"

Edwin sat calmly in the chair. His hands were folded in his lap, the briefcase he brought with him on the floor next to his chair. He looked directly into Tazio Accardi's black, lifeless eyes and said, "I never stole a dime from the casino. But I did help Mr. Carter and your nephew, Johnny."

Tazio no longer remained expressionless. His brow furrowed and both eyebrows raised.

Edwin continued, "I took out a marker for ten thousand dollars at the craps table. The markers were approved by Johnny. I never paid the markers before I left the table. I gave the money to Carter. Johnny took care of the markers. I don't know what Carter did with the money after that. If I may, I have three markers in my briefcase I'd like to show you."

Tazio held his fingertips together as if praying. His fingers touched his bottom lip and he nodded in an affirmative motion Luigi moved his coat jacket slightly in case Edwin had a gun. Edwin opened the briefcase and took out the three markers he paid to James McCracken and put them on the desk in front of Tazio.

He picked up the markers and examined them. When he finished, he put them back on his desk.

Edwin said, "I paid these markers at the casino. As you can see they're stamped Paid-in-Full. Those are Johnny's initials. I'm sorry about your nephew, but I don't know what happened to the money."

Tazio rubbed his chin. "Lucky for you that Mr. Carter disappeared."

Edwin played ignorant, "How so?"

"Because he's not available to corroborate your story, now, is he?"

"No sir, he's gone. When my colleagues and I arrived at the office a few weeks back, it was empty. That's when I started working as a floor trader."

"What happened to the junket business?"

Edwin smiled ever so slightly. "I ran it for two months, but it remained unprofitable. My co-worker, Gwenn, and I were tired of traveling to Vegas. So we let Richard Esposito take it over completely. As far as I know, he's still operating it."

Tazio, satisfied with Edwin's explanation, said, "Okay, thank you for clearing this up. Luigi will take you back to your office."

"Glad I was able to help." Edwin rose from the chair and left with Luigi.

★ ★ ★

When Luigi returned to Accardi's office, he had a conversation with Tazio.

Tazio started the conversation. "Do you believe, Mr. Goldberg?"

"Yeah boss, I do. There is nothing to indicate that he's done anything. Hell, the IRS just audited him, and our inside man said that he reported all of his gambling winnings and paid the taxes on it."

"Gambling winnings? How much did Mr. Goldberg win?"

"Gee boss, I'm not sure. Let me dig around and see if I can find out."

"This Aaron Taylor, he's made a fool out of Johnny, and now me. Johnny spent a lot of man hours investigating Edwin Goldberg. The investigators he hired, found nothing to incriminate him. A waste of money and time. Now he's being a snitch. I don't like snitches. What benefit would it serve him to rat on Goldberg? It makes no sense. I don't like the man. Make arrangements to eliminate the problem."

"Understood, boss." Luigi left Tazio to take care of the matter.

The next day, Taylor went to have lunch, at his favorite delicatessen, Mr. Ricky's, on Skokie Boulevard, near Gross Pointe Road. Mr. Ricky's, a local eatery, was a favorite place of the residents.

Aaron had just finished lunch and walked to his car when a black sedan hurled past him. Four shots fired in his direction hit their target. Aaron Taylor immediately dropped to the street, dead before he hit the ground. The black sedan sped off as blood oozed from his body. There were no witnesses.

The local police did a cursory investigation. The report stated that it was a mob hit. The lieutenant in charge of the case and the chief agreed not to spend too much time and manpower in solving the murder. No one cared, other than his wife and daughter, that Aaron Taylor was gone.

* * *

Luigi made several phone calls to the casinos in Vegas and a few more to people in the Chicago area. He immediately reported his findings to Tazio. "Boss, Goldberg won more than a hundred grand this year according to our sources."

"What? A hundred grand. How?"

"Apparently he had very good luck at the craps tables."

"Hmm, okay. Mr. Goldberg is a very smart man. Him and Bazzoli were taking money from us with the markers. Bazzoli used this method back in the day."

"Bazzoli? Who's Bazzoli?"

"Joseph Carter is Paul Bazzoli. He must have faked his death. He hasn't been seen nor heard from for more than ten years. Damn him! With Johnny dead, Carter missing, there's nothing to pin anything on Goldberg. Tell our Vegas men to keep a close watch on this Richard Esposito fella."

"You got it, boss. Oh, boss, I can tell you that Esposito has been living a very lavish lifestyle. More so than Goldberg."

Accardi didn't say anything. He swirled the scotch in his glass, and lit a cigar. He sat back with a sigh. *Goldberg is one smart man*, he thought. The cigar smoke rose upward as he took several puffs.

CHAPTER THIRTY-TWO

Richard had one of those days where nothing went right. It started with the red-eye flight from O'Hare International being delayed three hours and the plane sitting on the tarmac with a bunch of rowdy Junketeers. Richard kept the unruly crowd quiet by buying several rounds of drinks for everyone. The passengers were content for the first hour until all of the booze was gone.

When the plane finally arrived, Richard checked his guests into their rooms and suites. Some of them became belligerent upon learning their rooms would not be ready until the late afternoon. As a gesture of goodwill, Richard arranged for the inconvenienced guests to be given one-hundred-dollar gambling vouchers.

An inauspicious moonlit night cast a foreboding spell of gloom when strong winds blasted through downtown Vegas. One of the heaviest rainstorms in history was followed by hurricane winds. None of the guests could leave the casinos that night. It made the casino owners very happy to have their clientele trapped.

Richard watched lightning strike outside his window once, and then again. It lit up the night. He thought he saw the image of a face in the dark clouds. He rubbed his eyes several times. The lighting show lasted for about an hour.

Even though totally exhausted, Richard made time to make his way to the craps table. At four o'clock in the morning, the table was full. Richard managed to wiggle his way into a tight spot at the table. He signed for a ten-thousand-dollar marker.

Ken, one of the dealers that shift, slipped a five-thousand-dollar chip under his stack and pushed it to him.

At the opposite end of the table, Sally, Richard's new partner in crime, gave him a signal to acknowledge that she saw him. They made their bets so that Sally bet the Pass Line and Richard bet on the Don't Pass Line. Richard always made $20 wagers on twelve on the Come-out roll.

After thirty minutes of play, the table turned cold and most of the players departed to their rooms or suites to get some sleep. Those that were too wound up to sleep made their way to the café for an early morning meal.

Ken finished his shift and headed to the employees' area to clock out.

"Ken, a moment of your time, please," a thunderous voice called out.

Ken looked around. Two men dressed in black suits, black shirts and black neckties stood in front of the exit.

"Sure, how can I help you gentleman?"

"We need you to follow us."

The two men positioned themselves to keep Ken between them. One man gently grabbed his arm as they marched him out of the employees' area. He had no clue where they were taking him. The sick feeling in the bottom of his stomach made him nauseous. He knew he was in deep shit.

Richard went to the cashier's cage to redeem his chips for cash. Before he had a chance to put his chips for the cashier to change into greenbacks, the same two men that took Ken away greeted him in the same manner. Sally watched from a safe distance, pretending to play a slot machine. When she saw the men roughly escort Richard from the room, she didn't stick around to find out what happened next. She promptly left the casino floor.

Sally, fortunate to escape from the casino without being grabbed, hid her chips deep inside the lining of her purse in case anyone accosted her. Still dark at five o'clock in the morning, she made her way home and quickly locked the door to her apartment. She didn't bother to turn on the lights.

Ken and Richard were both tied to chairs with rope. The chairs sat on a large sheet of plastic; much like a painter's tarp. Rocco, the man with the deep voice, smacked each of them in the face twice before saying anything. "Gentleman, do I have your attention? Look at me!" he demanded.

Ken wet his pants. His body shook with fear. Richard, ever the cocky bastard, remained calm. "What do you want?"

"What do I want? I want to know who else is helping you steal from us. Did you really think you could take our money and get away with it?"

The backroom in a Vegas casino wasn't a place you wanted to find yourself. Nothing good ever happened to the people who were taken there. A person considered himself lucky if he escaped with a few broken bones and a stern warning.

Ken stammered. "I don't know about anyone else. Richard approached me and told me to put a five-thousand-dollar chip in his stack when he took out a marker. I got a piece of the action. I don't know anything else." Tears streamed down his face.

"That's more like it," Rocco said.

"You bastard!" Richard yelled at Ken. "They're going to kill both of us for sure now, you idiot!"

Smack. The thud of Rocco's hand crashing into the right side of Richard's face caused him to tip over in his chair. The other fellow, a muscular type, called Franco, effortlessly picked him back up in an upright position. Rocco's other hand caught Richard square in his nose. It began to bleed profusely.

Ken passed out from seeing Richard have the snot beat out of him. "Get him out of here," Rocco barked at Franco.

Franco dragged Ken's body to the back alley and dumped him. He quickly went back inside.

Rocco looked at Richard and said, "I'm going to ask you once more, who else is in your group?"

"I don't know, I swear."

"You swear."

Richard still smug. "Yeah, I swear, every damn day."

Rocco lost his patience with him. He pulled out a Smith and Wesson revolver with a silencer attached and squeezed the trigger twice. The suppressor muffled the sound of the bullet being discharged from the barrel, but it still made the sound of a heavy book being smacked on a wood table. With all of the noise in the casino, none of the patrons would have heard it or paid any attention.

Rocco had put two bullets in Richard's head. Drenched in a pool of blood, Richard's body lay on the plastic. Rocco unbound the body from the chair and rolled it up in the plastic by the time Franco returned.

"Grab an end and let's get him out of here," he said to Franco.

Franco did not ask any questions. He obeyed Rocco's order and helped him place the body in the trunk of the sedan. They drove away from Vegas toward California. About thirty minutes out, Rocco pulled over to the side of the road. It was still dark as the sky was overcast with threatening rain clouds and intermittent showers.

Rocco and Franco carried Richard's limp body about a hundred yards off the highway. They took a shovel and buried him a shallow grave. Richard's corpse filled one of the infamous holes in the desert.

The two men hurriedly made their way back to the vehicle and sped back to town.

At the same time Richard gasped his last breath, an inmate in the Nevada State Prison confronted Herbert. The homemade blade tore through his orange jumpsuit before he knew what had happened. His body crumbled, but the inmate prevented him from falling to the ground. His eyes widened as the inmate turned and twisted the cold steel in his underbelly. A stream of blood emerged from the corner of his mouth. Another inmate placed his hand over his mouth to keep him from making a sound.

Two more knife-thrust struck Herbert's belly and chest. The two inmates departed, leaving him in a heap on the cold, concrete prison floor. Herbert had cashed in his last chips.

* * *

Luigi whispered something into Tazio Accardi's ear. Tazio did not smile or show any signs of emotion upon hearing that Herbert was dead. "Thank you," he said to Luigi.

Luigi also said, "Richard Esposito won't be stealing from us anymore. Our sources told me they took care of the situation. The dealer involved was made an example to deter anybody else from getting ideas."

Tazio looked at Luigi acknowledging the information he had received. He continued with his daily activities as if nothing had happened.

CHAPTER THIRTY-THREE

Fumes from the fresh coat of white paint permeated the air as Bindi and Edwin opened the front door to their new condo. Bindi's face lit up as she saw the updated interior. *Impeccable*, Edwin thought as he admired the workmanship of the newly installed hardwood oak floor.

"Do you like our new home?" he asked.

"It's beautiful. I can't wait until the furniture is delivered later today."

Edwin opened a window to let the crisp outside air overpower the paint fumes. The temperature felt unusually warm for October. A cool breeze filtered through the home.

Bindi inspected the stainless steel stove and refrigerator. She could hardly believe she and Edwin had purchased the home to live in. She thought back to how she first bumped into Edwin at O'Hare airport and the chance encounter sitting next to each other on the flight to Vegas. Tears that welled up in her eyes did not go unnoticed by Edwin.

"What's wrong?"

"Nothing, just tears of joy."

She wiped the droplets from her cheek and turned to Edwin. Softly she whispered, "Thank you so much." She moved closer and gave him a passionate kiss as she wrapped her arms around his neck and held him tight.

"Come on, let's go see the rest of the place," as she grabbed Edwin's hand and wandered through the bedrooms and other rooms. The echo of their footsteps resonated throughout the home. *A few area rugs will take care of the noise*, she thought.

The couple moved into the condo with relative ease. Neither Edwin nor Bindi had much to move. He had sold all of his furniture in the studio. What few dishes, clothes and personal items he owned fit neatly into a small van rented from U-Haul. Similarly, she did not have much to move; just her clothes and some personal items. Edwin finished unloading the van by ten in the morning.

The Ethan Allen furniture delivery truck arrived at two o'clock. After the three men properly placed the furniture where Bindi directed them, she inspected everything.

Edwin had returned from his workout with the Woit Warriors. She hugged him and rested her head on his shoulders. "Can we go shopping for some pictures and other knickknacks to decorate?"

"Sure."

Edwin and Bindi strolled through the stores along Michigan Avenue. Marshall Field's was her favorite place to shop. By six o'clock, Edwin, tired and ready to relax back home, made arrangements for several things to be delivered the following week.

Once they arrived home, Bindi, too excited to sit and relax, bounced from one room to the next, finding places for the items they purchased. She persuaded Edwin to help her hang some of the artwork. He lovingly obliged her wish to get things unpacked and put away.

Late that night, Edwin sat on the large recliner. Bindi sat on his lap, hugged him and kissed him affectionately. *So much for a platonic relationship,* she thought. "Take me to bed," she said. "I want to make love with you."

Edwin didn't say a word. He carried her into his bedroom and gently placed her on the bed. He removed her tight-fitting jeans and then his. The ensuing romp left both of them satisfied and exhausted. Later, as Bindi blissfully cradled Edwin to her body she felt a deep sensation of serenity. Although she'd only been with Edwin for a short while, it felt like they'd been together forever.

In the morning, Edwin woke to the sizzling of bacon in a frying pan, the aroma of fresh brewed coffee and eggs frying. "Good morning," she said as he stood next to her. She gave him a quick kiss on the lips. "Did you want toast or an English muffin with your Breakfast?"

"English muffin."

"Go ahead, sit down at the table and I'll bring the food over. It's almost done," she said smiling. She nudged him, ever so slightly toward the table.

Edwin sat down. The Sunday paper awaited him along with a glass of freshly squeezed orange juice. Bindi served the food and sat down to enjoy the meal. Her face glowed with happiness.

Edwin stared at Bindi, his fork held loosely in his hand. His eyes were bright and his smile indicated intense joy.

"What? Is something wrong?" she asked.

"Nothing at all. I think you're awesome, and I'm a very lucky man to have met you."

Bindi blushed. "You're so sweet."

Edwin did not say anything else as he ate his food.

They spent the rest of the day unpacking and setting up their new household. Periodically, Edwin would check on the score of the Bears game. It was a dismal performance by the "Monsters of Midway." They lost the game to Detroit 27 to 7. Edwin was glad he hadn't wasted much time watching the debacle.

Late in the afternoon, Edwin was hungry. He looked at Bindi. "Have you had a Lou Malnati's pizza?"

"No, why do you ask?"

"I have a craving for one. Feel like going for a drive?"

"Where to?"

"Lincolnwood. It's just a short drive. I promise it's worth the trip."

"Okay. Let's go, I'm hungry."

Twenty minutes later they were seated in a booth at Lou Malnati's. They ordered the Chicago style deep-dish pizza with pepperoni and mushroom. Bindi's mouth watered as she watched the waiter bring a pizza pie to a nearby table.

When their order finally arrived, she gushed over the delicious pizza. "They don't have anything like this in Iowa," she said, in between bites. It was the perfect ending to a beautiful weekend.

CHAPTER THIRTY-FOUR

Valerie Taylor wept uncontrollably the day her father was laid to rest in Graceland Cemetery on Clark Street. A large crowd attended the funeral, including Bill Beckwith and Tazio Accardi. Accardi didn't want to draw any suspicion to him by not attending. Edwin chose not to attend worried that Valerie would cause a scene.

Edwin learned about Aaron Taylor's untimely demise from Bill when he arrived to the floor of the Board of Trade. "Please extend my condolences to Valerie for me," Edwin told Bill.

Neither Bill nor Edwin did much trading that day. Both were distracted by the news of Aaron's death, but for different reasons.

The prime colors of autumn leaves turning to hues of orange, yellow and red occurred the first two weeks in October. The crescendo of colors glistened in the trees as the sun-filled day of the fickle weather cooperated for Aaron Taylor's final moment above ground. His grave site, near a large oak tree, had a special bench for visitors to sit.

Tazio Accardi paid his respects to Valerie and her mother as they watched the last few shovels of dirt cover the grave. "I'm deeply sorry for your loss. Let me know if I can help you in any way." Valerie had no idea Tazio gave the order to have her father eliminated. The police, baffled by the random drive-by shooting, could do little to apprehend the culprits.

After a few more mourners expressed their sympathy to the grieving widow and her daughter, Bill Beckwith, said, "My prayers are with you." He whispered into Valerie's mother's ear so that no one else could hear. She nodded, shook his hand, and said, "Thank you."

Valerie looked at Bill with a blank stare on her face. "I'm sorry for your loss. Your father was a good man," he said to her. He departed immediately thereafter.

"What was that all about?"

"Nothing. Bill told me he's going to send me a check for one hundred thousand dollars to help me. He knew your father didn't have any life insurance."

"Oh." Valerie said nothing else.

Long after the funeral concluded, Edwin called Valerie from his office. "Hey Valerie," He was cut-off in mid-sentence.

"What the fuck do you want?"

"To tell you I was sorry about your dad."

Valerie calmed down. "How come you weren't at the funeral?"

"I didn't feel comfortable going. I wasn't sure how you'd feel about me being there, and I didn't want to upset you. I can't imagine how you must feel. How is your mother doing?"

"My mom is holding up. I don't think it's fully set in that my dad is gone."

"Yeah, well, again, I'm sorry for your loss. I should get going."

"Okay. Thanks for calling. I appreciate you thinking of me."

Edwin hung up the receiver and left the office. He looked forward to spending time with Bindi in their new home.

Valerie's narcissism misconstrued Edwin's condolence call. The crazy bitch got it in her mind that Edwin still loved her and wanted to be with her. She planned to take advantage of the opportunity the next day.

Gwenn objected when Valerie walked into the outer office and demanded to see Edwin.

"He's not here." Gwenn said. "He's probably at the Board of Trade, finishing up for the day."

"I'll wait. Is that his office?" Valerie pointed in the direction of Edwin's private office.

"Yes, but you can't go in there," Gwenn insisted.

Valerie blithely ignoring Gwenn's warning marched into Edwin's office and closed the door behind her. Gwenn didn't make much an effort to stop her. Gwenn knew that Valerie's father had been buried the day before and showed her some empathy.

Standing in front of the closed door, Gwenn said, "Fine, I'll tell Edwin you're waiting for him when he arrives."

Edwin arrived fifteen minutes later. Gwenn intercepted him before he went to his office. "Valerie Taylor is waiting for you in your office."

Edwin looked puzzled. "Oh. Did she say what she wanted?"

"No. She didn't say anything other than she wanted to see you."

Edwin walked into his office to find Valerie sitting in his chair. *Get Together* by the Youngbloods played softly on the radio in the background. He noticed her jeans and blouse lumped in a pile on the floor next to his desk. Valerie stood up. She wore only her fur coat. She flung it open, revealing her naked body.

"Remember these?"

"What the fuck are you doing? Get dressed. I'm not interested in you. I'm in love with Bindi."

Valerie abruptly closed her coat and picked up her clothing. "When did this happen?" Tears streamed down her cheeks.

"We've been seeing each other since she got the position at United. We moved in together this past weekend."

Valerie wiped the droplets from her face. Edwin moved closer and handed her a tissue.

Suddenly, without any warning, the office door was pushed open. "Am I interrupting anything?" Gwenn said.

Edwin blushed. "No, Valerie was just leaving."

"Good. Can I see you for a moment?"

"Sure, I'll let you gather yourself. Excuse me," Edwin said.

He followed Gwenn into the corridor and closed the door behind him.

"Thanks, for the save. That was awkward."

"You think? I don't like that wench. She's evil."

Within a minute, Valerie opened the office door, waved good-bye to Edwin and said, "Ciao darling. I'll call you tomorrow."

Gwenn's mouth opened. Before she could say anything, Edwin held up a finger to her lips. "Not now."

Once Valerie left, Gwenn glared at Edwin. "What's that all about?"

"Nothing. For some reason she thinks I'm still in love with her. I told her Bindi and I moved in together this weekend."

Gwenn looked at Edwin with adoration. "Fine, just don't let Valerie's issues become my issues. I need to go over the terms for the Shapiro Roofing Company acquisition. I think you'll find them favorable."

Gwenn handed Edwin a file folder full of documents. He flipped through them and gave them a cursory review. "I'll read these over tonight and give you my feedback tomorrow."

★ ★ ★

Valerie sat motionless in the quiet solitude of her mind remembering the love she lost with Johnny and what she once had with Edwin. Caught up in her own raw emotions, she did not grieve for her father.

She failed to get married while attending Northwestern. It was Valerie's reason for attending college—to meet a man, and get married. Four months had passed, and she still lived in Johnny's apartment. She thought, *Why shouldn't I?* After all, Tazio Accardi continued to pay for it. Tazio told her she could stay in the condo for six months. Time was running out. Yet, Valerie did not seem too concerned about her future.

Two months after Johnny was killed, Valerie received a large envelope from an anonymous source. When she opened the package she found fifty-thousand dollars and a note from Joseph Carter. The note read, "From Johnny. This was his share." She also had another $100,000 in cash from Johnny's safe.

* * *

That evening, after Edwin rebuffed her advances, she decided to go clubbing and have some fun. It was one o'clock in the morning when she brought a man named Douglas back to her place. Drunk and high on cocaine, she banged his brains out. When she awoke the next morning, Douglas was gone. She didn't even know his last name, nor did she care.

Valerie continued her frolicking and picking up men for the next two weeks. The doorman at the Condo had seen enough. He made a telephone call to Tazio Accardi and reported what Valerie had been doing the past few weeks. "Mr. Accardi, I'm sorry to bother you, but I think you should know that Ms. Taylor is whoring around. She's brought a different man home each night for the past few weeks."

"Thank you George. I appreciate the information. Have a nice day."

Accardi summoned Luigi. "I have another assignment for you."

"Sure thing boss, what do you want me to do."

"It seems Ms. Taylor has been abusing our generosity. She's made the mistake of taking our kindness for being soft."

"Understood boss. I'll make the necessary arrangements."

"Thank you." Accardi went about his daily routine.

CHAPTER THIRTY-FIVE

Edwin made a lot of money trading at the Board of Trade. He appreciated that Bill Beckwith had taken him under his wing and given him guidance to become a successful trader. Notwithstanding his success, Edwin had bigger aspirations to become a successful business person. One evening after finishing a grueling workout with Dick Woit, while sitting in the steam room, he approached Sid Turner to ask for his help.

Sid Turner, a lawyer who gave up practicing law many years earlier, had become a powerful businessman with many different business interests and passions. He had a reputation of making "fuck you," money, or making over fifty million dollars per year.

Sid, surprised when Edwin approached him, asked, "What can I do for you, young man?"

"Well, sir—"

Sid, an impatient man, cut Edwin off in mid-sentence. "Wells are for wishing, state your case."

Startled by Sid's brusqueness, Edwin stuttered a bit before he regained his composure. "I'm not interested in making 'fuck you' money like yourself, I just want to make 'piss off' money."

Edwin's directness got Sid's attention. "Do you know how I made my money?"

"No sir, I don't. Will you share your story?"

"Yes, I will, since you're the first person who has asked."

The steam hissed and the temperature got hotter. Edwin did not even notice. Only he and Sid remained in the enclosed area as they perspired profusely. Sid said, "When I was a lawyer, I represented small business owners, not all businesses could afford my fee. The ones that couldn't, usually a start-up venture with little or no capital, I asked for a ten-percent ownership. Most of the start-up companies became successful. That ten-percent ownership is now worth ten times what I would have made if I had taken an hourly fee instead. And it's perpetual. They pay me year after year after year. So my advice to you is to help high quality start-up companies with a small investment for ten-percent ownership. You never want to invest a lot in a small company or a start-up because of the risk. Ten percent, that is the magic number."

Edwin sat pondering Sid's advice. *Ten percent* he thought. "Would you consider being an advisor for my company, ERGENT, for a ten-percent equity interest?"

"You're bold. Most people don't feel comfortable talking to me because of how rich I am."

"Sir, I was told in here, it doesn't matter how much money you have. We all put our pants on one leg at a time. How else am I going to learn if I don't ask?"

"Fair enough. What did you have in mind?"

"If I have an investment opportunity, I want you or someone from your firm to review it and tell me if I should make the deal. Also, if you're going to make an investment in a business, I want an opportunity to buy-in for ten-percent also."

Sid did not say anything. He sat contemplating Edwin's proposal. He was aware of Edwin's trading savvy, having watched Edwin grow from when Bill first brought him to the group. He knew Edwin had the mental discipline and toughness to endure Woit's verbal tongue lashings, and that he used sound judgment as it pertained to being financially prudent and fiscally responsible. He rubbed his face with the extra towel that was draped over his head. "Is your trading profits part of ERGENT?"

"No, I keep that separate. That is my revenue source for my investment money."

"What else are you bringing to the table?"

"I have a fifty-percent ownership in two McDonald's franchises, and I'm considering purchasing a roofing company.

But after our conversation, I am rethinking my position in the matter."

"Okay. Bring me your research and due diligence report on the roofing company. If I like the deal, we each purchase a ten-percent equity interest in the company. And yes, I will work with you for a ten-percent stake in ERGENT."

"Thank you." Edwin rose up from his seat on the beach in the steam room and shook Sid's sweaty hand. He left the sweat box and headed to take a cold shower. His face was beet-red.

The next morning, Edwin reviewed the report about Shapiro Roofing. The numbers looked good. The roofing company made a decent profit. The only reason the owner offered Edwin an opportunity to invest in the company was because he wanted to take some money out to travel with his wife. Edwin looked forward to Sid's recommendation. He summoned a courier to deliver the dossier to Sid's office before heading to the exchange to trade.

At two o'clock that afternoon, a large envelope was laid on Edwin's desk. It contained the documents from Sid formalizing their agreement. Edwin read each word of each sentence very carefully. Once he was satisfied that the agreement fully encompassed his understanding with Sid, he called his attorney to schedule an appointment to review the agreement before he signed it. Edwin wanted the attorney to scrutinize the document before noon the next day.

Unable to focus the next morning, he decided not to trade that day. It turned out to be a wise decision. His attorney called at ten o'clock. "Edwin, the document looks fine. I don't see any issues with you signing it. Are you certain you want to give up ten-percent of ERGENT?"

Without hesitation, Edwin responded, "Yes."

"Okay, come on over and we'll get this done."

Edwin made a beeline to the attorney's office to sign the document. He wanted the deal consummated as quickly as possible. He understood the tremendous opportunity that presented itself and did not want to delay the matter.

Shortly after leaving his attorney's office, Edwin received a telephone call from Sid Turner. "Hello, young man. I've countersigned our agreement. Congratulations. Also, my staff has given the go-ahead on the Shapiro Roofing Company. They'll prepare the necessary paperwork and I'll make certain your attorney receives a copy. We can do the deal simultaneously."

"Thank you, sir. I appreciate your trust and willingness to work with me."

"Son, you're not working with me, you're working *for* me. I own ten percent of your business. Have a nice day."

Edwin held the receiver in his hand as Sid hung up, still excited because of the upside potential of Sid letting him ride his coattails on other deals. Edwin suddenly realized that he needed to save a lot more money to have available when other deals were presented.

CHAPTER THIRTY-SIX

Valerie Taylor became an inconvenient nuisance to many people. She'd blown through the one hundred and fifty thousand dollars in a matter of months. Tazio Accardi had grown tired of footing the bill for the condo where she lived. He was more disturbed about her lifestyle and whoring around than ever. Despite his many attempts to persuade her to find work and make something of her life, she chose to go clubbing nearly every evening.

On a cold, silent night, a man sat quietly waiting in Valerie's residence. A silencer muffled the sound of the gun used to put two bullets in her chest. A plastic tarp had been placed on the floor. Valerie, extremely intoxicated at that moment, did not even notice her murder at all. Her limp, lifeless body was wrapped in the plastic and put into the back of a van. The carpeting and padding were completely removed and replaced. The smallest details were carefully examined to ensure there was no evidence or residual trace of blood to indicate anything bad happened. The entire process had been completed within a matter of hours.

Several days passed before Valerie's mother notified the police that her daughter was missing. The police went to her apartment to find no one there. A thorough search turned up nothing out of the ordinary, and the report they filed indicated no evidence of foul play.

The police followed up their investigation at Edwin's office.

"Ma'am, I'm Officer Jackson, and this is my partner Officer Martin. Do you know a Valerie Taylor?"

"Yes, why do you ask?"

"She's been reported missing and we're just looking for information as to her whereabouts."

"Oh, well I haven't seen her since she visited Edwin about three weeks ago."

"Do you know why she wanted to see Mr. Goldberg?"

"Yeah. The bitch thought he still loved her. He told her about his relationship with another woman."

Jackson raised his head and looked up from his notepad.

"From the sound of it, you didn't like her much. What happened next?"

Gwenn didn't comment other than to say, "Nothing. She left."

"Is Mr. Goldberg available? We'd like to ask him a few questions?"

"Sure. Right this way." Gwenn took the officers to Edwin's office.

"Edwin, these officers have a few questions for you?"

Edwin looked perplexed. His eyes widened and his forehead crinkled.

"Mr. Goldberg, we are investigating the disappearance of Valerie Taylor. When was the last time you saw her?"

Not again, Edwin thought. He kept his cool even though his mind was racing. "Three weeks ago. She came to my office and wanted to know if I still loved her. I told her 'no' and she left. I haven't seen her since."

"Any idea where she may have gone, or if she had any enemies?"

"No, sir. I have a girlfriend and we're very happy in our relationship. I don't know where Valerie lives or even if she works. Sorry, I can't help you, officers."

Officer Martin finished scribbling in his note pad and said, "Is there anything you can tell us that might help us with our investigation?"

"No. As I said, she came to my office several weeks earlier. Once I told her that Bindi and I were living together, and that

I didn't have any interest in her, she left. Albeit, embarrassed. Before that, it had been months since I saw her."

"Thank you for your cooperation." Officers Martin and Jackson left, apparently satisfied with Edwin's explanation. They had nothing else to go on.

More than three weeks passed, and still Valerie remained missing. Tazio Accardi contacted the detectives assigned to the case. "Detective, any new developments in Valerie Taylor's case?" he asked, fully knowing the answer.

"No, what's your interest?"

"She is living at my deceased nephew, Johnny's, condo. I would like to have her possessions removed so that I can either sell the place or rent it out."

"Hmm, I see. I'll contact Valerie's mother and have her make arrangements to remove Valerie's stuff. Can you give her a week to make the arrangements?"

"Certainly, I'll have the doorman, George, let me know when they have removed the girl's stuff. Thank you."

Tazio hung up the phone, his face expressionless.

Detective Stuart reviewed the case file once again to see if he had missed anything. He then went to speak to Officer Martin. "Martin, did you and Jackson interview the doorman, George about the Taylor matter?"

"Yeah, he was off duty at seven o'clock. Receipts from Valerie's credit cards indicated she was at a nightclub until two in the morning. We spoke to some of the patrons at the club that night. As far as we can tell, she went home alone."

"Do you know if she drove herself home?"

"No, we're not even sure if she drove to the club. Her car is still parked at her condo. The last person to see her was the bartender. He didn't provide us with much information. Just that she paid her tab, and left alone."

"And there's no evidence of foul play at the club or at her home?" Detective Stuart closed the folder he held in his hand.

"No, sir. We had the crime lab boys' scour the area. Police officers canvassed the area between her home and the club.

They examined every nook and cranny in her home. They found nothing to indicate a crime had been committed. If her mother hadn't reported her missing, no one would have known Valerie Taylor even existed."

"What about where she works? Did you contact her employer?"

"She didn't work. She had no job. You know she lived with Johnny Accardi before he was murdered. Recently, her father was gunned down. It appeared to be a mob hit."

Stuart persisted. "Tazio Accardi just asked about our investigation. Something about wanting to clean out his nephew's condo where the Taylor girl is residing. Do you know anything about this?"

"No, sir. Nothing in our investigation showed any evidence of foul play. The girl just vanished."

"Okay, thanks." Detective Stuart flipped the case file onto his desk and left the precinct. He had nothing to go on. Based on the information gathered, it looked like Valerie Taylor got mix up with the wrong people. There was absolutely nothing to incriminate Tazio Accardi or any evidence of foul play. If anything, the detective considered the possibility that she chose to disappear and did not want to be found.

CHAPTER THIRTY-SEVEN

DECEMBER 1975

A winter's day brought a chill to the Chicago area. The outside temperature on the thermometer read minus six. The wind chill factor made it feel like twenty below. Edwin sat in his office, pondering what had transpired since he graduated from Northwestern only a year and a half before. For him, it felt like a lifetime. As the wind howled outside, Edwin stayed warm and cozy inside. He had made his decision to call Big Julie.

"Hello Big Julie. This is Edwin Goldberg."

Big Julie said, "Yes, I remember you. What can I do for you?"

"I remembered that you're in the jewelry business. I want to purchase an engagement ring. Can you help?"

Big Julie, delighted to hear from Edwin, said, "Of course, I can help you. But why are you calling me when there are so many diamond merchants in Chicago?"

"Because I don't trust them. Most of them are thieves—a ganev, if you know what I mean."

"Yes, I understand. What did you have in mind?"

"Actually, I was wondering if I can meet you in New York tomorrow? I'm planning to fly out in the morning and fly back the same day. Are you available to meet me?"

"Tomorrow? Sure why not."

Big Julie gave Edwin his office's address and worked out the details for their meeting. The next morning, Edwin took the first flight from Chicago to New York. Once there, he took a cab from the Kennedy Airport to Big Julie's office.

Big Julie smiled when Edwin came through the door. His eyes saw dollar signs on Edwin's face. He greeted him with a firm handshake and a big hug. "So, what are you looking for?"

"I want a round, one-carat diamond mounted in a four prong tiffany setting. The diamond should be at least an f color, internally flawless and be ideal cut. None of the drek or chazerei."

Big Julie fully understood. "Drek" in Yiddish meant "shit" and "chazerei" meant "garbage." Edwin knew about diamonds. His uncle had been in the diamond business and taught Edwin how to grade diamonds before his untimely death.

Big Julie surmised, why Edwin did not trust the Chicago merchants. Big Julie's reputation with the junketeers would be tarnished, if not destroyed, if Big Julie tried to swindle Edwin.

He looked at Edwin, his eyebrow cocked. "Son, you don't want to put that quality of a stone on your wife's finger. That is considered to be an investment-grade diamond. I recommend maybe a VS1 or VS2 that is a G/F color."

Big Julie had passed Edwin's first test. People that are in the jewelry business understood the difference between a high-quality diamond for an engagement ring and an investment-grade diamond that belonged in a safe deposit box.

"Okay, that sounds perfect."

Big Julie brought out five different round ideal cut diamonds. They were similar in clarity and color. Edwin chose the diamond that weighed 1.01 carats. Big Julie had the shimmering piece of ice set in a 14K white gold mounting. The center diamond, offset by several baguettes on each side, was exquisite. The ring twinkled and sparkled with each slight movement. He purchased the matching wedding band to complete the set.

Edwin paid Big Julie cash, but still asked for a receipt for insurance purposes. He put the boxed ring in his pocket and headed back to Chicago to surprise the woman of his dreams. He planned to propose to Bindi on Christmas morning.

♥♥♥

Christmas morning eventually arrived. Edwin had wrapped the smaller ring box in a larger box and then in a much larger box. No one suspected it contained jewelry, let alone an engagement ring. Edwin placed the box under the small Christmas tree.

Bindi and Edwin planned to fly that afternoon to her parent's home to celebrate the holiday. Nervous, because he had never met her parents before, he paced around the condo.

"Do you want to open presents now or after breakfast?" Bindi asked. She had a certain glow about her.

"Now, of course." He looked happy and excited. Like a kid in a candy store.

She handed him one of the presents she had purchased for him; a trip to Hawaii for both of them. After all, what do you get someone that can afford everything? Edwin, pleasantly surprised, kissed her and gave her a big hug.

"Okay, your turn." Edwin handed her the gift wrapped box. The box looked like clothing wrapped inside.

She took the package from Edwin's hand. Deep down, she hoped it would be an engagement ring. Edwin could sense a slight disappointment in Bindi's demeanor. He smiled. She thought, *Well maybe he will propose at my parents' home.*

Her hands moved lightning quick as she ripped the paper off. She opened the box to find another wrapped box. *What?* She thought as she gazed up at Edwin. He stood watching her expressions change as she unwrapped each box. At long last, she held the ring box in her hand. Before she had an opportunity to open it, Edwin grabbed it, got down on one knee and opened it.

"Bindi Maxwell, will you marry me?"

Her eyes widened. Tears streamed down her face. "Yes, yes." She held out her hand and extended her ring finger so Edwin could slip the rock on it.

She hugged him and gave him a long passionate kiss. They held each other tightly, savoring the moment. Bindi was having a very Merry Christmas.

The flight to Iowa was half-empty as most people didn't fly on Christmas Day. Bindi kept her gloves on her hand the entire car ride home. The two of them arrived at her folks' home just before three o'clock in the afternoon. She had not seen her parents since she moved to Chicago.

Bindi introduced Edwin to her entire family. As she expected, they adored him as much as she loved him. After the introductions were complete, she said, "Mom, dad . . . look what Edwin gave me for Christmas!" She held up her hand to show them the beautiful, glimmering ring that brilliantly sparkled in the light.

"Oh my God, I'm so happy for you," her mother said as she hugged her.

Bindi's father shook Edwin's hand and said, "Congratulations."

Everyone at the affair, thrilled about the couple's engagement, spent the next few hours talking about wedding plans.

Edwin sat in the living room contemplating. "Hey, what are you doing in here by yourself?" Bindi asked.

"I haven't told my parents about our engagement yet."

"Why not? Are you embarrassed about me?" she quipped mockingly.

"Of course not. I haven't spoken to them since the last time I went home. They have no idea what I've accomplished."

"Well, maybe you should call them." She handed him the telephone.

He took the phone and dialed the number to his parents' home. After a few rings, the voice on the other end said, "Hello."

"Hi dad, it's Edwin. I called to wish you and mom a Merry Christmas."

His father, stunned, retorted, "Edwin? How are you?"

"I'm fine dad. How's mom? Is she there?"

"She's fine. She's standing right here. Why are you calling on Christmas? Were Jewish?"

Margaret grabbed the phone from Sid's hand. "Edwin are you okay?"

"Yeah mom. I wanted to let you and dad know that I got engaged today."

"Oh my gosh. We didn't know you were dating anyone. When can we meet her?"

Edwin spent the rest of the conversation catching up with his parents and telling them about Bindi. She joined in the conversation excited to be a part of his family.

Afterwards, Edwin explained to Bindi about his relationship with his parents, and how he felt. As he spoke, the resentment and bitterness he felt toward them melted away. She could see the transformation in his face.

Edwin found peace within himself. He remembered the words of his mentor, Bill Beckwith, "*The best revenge is to be happy.*" He had his revenge on the world, because he was happy living the life he always imagined with the woman of his dreams.

EPILOGUE—MAY, 1992—
EIGHTEEN YEARS LATER

Tazio Accardi died of natural causes at age 86. Edwin never saw him again after their discussion about the casinos' missing money. Reading the obituary, Edwin, for a brief moment, wondered about Valerie Taylor. Her body was never found, and her disappearance remained a mystery.

Although Gwenn married a wealthy businessman, she remained Edwin's Chief Executive Officer running ERGENT. The company, under her guidance, became an international conglomerate, doing more than one hundred million dollars in revenue each year. Gwenn achieved her goal of being a CEO for a large company. She and Edwin parlayed the McDonald's franchises to purchase more than thirty other subsidiaries in numerous industries, and with diverse ventures in commercial and residential real estate, agriculture and oil exploration.

Neither Gwenn nor Edwin ever visited Las Vegas after 1974 despite several invitations from Big Julie to be his guest. The junket business faded in 1984 when big corporations took over the casinos. Junkets are still functioning today, but, for those old enough to remember, not to the extent that once made them glamorous.

Paul Bazzoli aka Joseph Carter lived in South America until his untimely demise in a freak car accident. Some people believed the Outfit caught up with him and ordered a hit. Evidence at the crash area suggested foul play.

Under current Nevada State law, markers are now legally enforced and are regulated.

Bindi and Edwin eventually outgrew the condo on LaSalle Drive. They purchased a large home in an expensive suburb of Chicago called Highland Park. Bindi became a stay-at-home-mom and raised their two children: Vivian, and Samuel.

Edwin sold his seat at The Chicago Board of Trade. Financially free to do whatever he pleased, he and Bindi traveled around the world exploring other cultures. Edwin kept a journal of his travels with the hope of someday writing a great novel. He remained fit, continuing Dick Woit's workouts on a regular basis. He feared what Woit might do to him if he ever stopped attending the classes.

ABOUT THE AUTHOR

David Medansky, born and raised in the Chicago metropolitan area, graduated from the University of Arizona School of Law in 1991. Medansky practiced family law in Phoenix, Arizona until 2004. Since then, he has become a world-class authority and trusted advisor on the game of craps. He published several books on how to play and win at craps. His teaching manual, Wholly Craps, *is considered to be the most comprehensive book on craps.*

Medansky writes with passion and purpose about Las Vegas. His first novel, Flamingo's Baby, *is an adventure thriller set in 1968 about Valentina Benjamin, age 21, a spunky, quick witted pragmatist turned protagonist, and employee at MGM Studios whose bloodline may also be her death sentence as she races to solve the mystery of her adoption upon learning that her biological parents are the mobster Benjamin "Bugsy" Siegel and his mistress, Virginia Hill.*

Medansky's book, Greatest Craps Guru in the World, *is a lively fiction thriller that could pass for non-fiction; a how to book and engaging story about making money at the craps table.*

Love's Battlefield, his next novel, soon to be released, is a romantic action thriller with intrigue about Michael Caldwell, a divorce attorney disgusted with the legal system who desperately wants to escape the business of broken hearts. Only when he meets a single mother with a ten-year-old daughter does he begin to ponder his self worth, and pursuit of happiness.

www.dmedansky.com

CPSIA information can be obtained
at www.ICGtesting.com
Printed in the USA
FFOW04n0150281217
44172939-43574FF